AMERICA'S FAVORITE COUPLE

A reality TV romance

Renee Darcy

Bright Little Light
P R E S S

Published by: Bright Little Light Press

First Print Edition: 2017

Copyright © 2017 Renee Darcy

ISBN: 1-946804-00-2
ISBN-13: 978-1-946804-00-6

To my husband.

Your faith finally got me here.

Now let's go live our love story.

CHAPTER ONE

Week Four

Casey stood in front of the open, floor-length windows, staring into the rainy afternoon as though her azure eyes could pierce the gloom and find the object of her thoughts. A long, loose sea-green gown billowed around her in the breeze, striking against her slim figure and sun-bronzed skin.

A voice spoke in her ear. "That's a great shot, Casey," praised her personal production assistant, from some remote room where he was staring at her feed. "Now, why don't you go lie on the bed and seem upset and kind of listless?"

Sighing, Casey turned away from the window and glided the few steps across the small room. She draped herself artfully across the bed, her long chestnut hair fanning onto the pillow as though each strand had been individually choreographed. She stared off into space, waiting.

A few moments passed, and then Vince was back in her ear again. "Perfect! I think we've got all the B roll we need for now, but obviously we'll keep rolling in case something interesting happens. But I think you've got some free time for the next few hours until we hear something about Nicholas."

Casey sighed and sat up. Left to her own devices, she stood and strode back to the window again. The rain was too heavy to see very far, but she stared out into the gray afternoon anyway, waiting for the next snippet of news - or the next summons from her invisible but demanding taskmaster.

"Ok, Neil, this is the stop where we need you to get off," Sandra's voice popped into his ear. He stood and moved toward the doors, balancing effortlessly against the swaying as the subway pulled into the station. He ignored the looks that came his way when the camera and sound guys got up to follow him.

After exiting the train, Sandra gave him a quick set of directions through the earpiece. He waded through the crowd, moving easily into the spaces that opened up whenever someone noticed the production crew following him.

As he left the station and the crowd thinned out, the camera and sound guys became more conspicuous. Neil stood out, too, with his perfectly styled dark hair, his chiseled features, and his "casual but smoking hot without trying too hard" shirt and jeans. He carried his leather jacket slung over his shoulder like a 50s rock icon, and he moved with the fluid grace of a runner. His face was composed and solemn, as suited his task.

When he reached his destination, he took out a photo and showed it to the woman at the admissions counter. "Have you seen this boy?"

The woman looked at the photo, then stared for a moment at Neil. Her gaze moved pointedly to take in the camera. "I'm sorry, sir, but what's this about?"

A member of the production crew stepped forward, and pulled the woman aside. He spoke to her for a few moments, while the line grew behind Neil. He glanced back to see a handful of families waiting impatiently to go inside, children in tow who were betraying various states of impatience.

After a quiet but intense dialogue, the woman came back over and motioned to Neil. "This way, please, sir. We do have a missing children's station, and I believe the young man you're looking for might be there."

His face relaxed as he followed her into the arena. She led him down a series of corridors into a small room, where the boy waited with a bored-looking security guard. "Neil!" he cried out as he dashed forward.

The woman smiled as she watched the enthusiastic greeting. "Well, I guess there's no doubt you know this young man - and that you can get him back where he belongs."

Neil nodded, wrapping an arm protectively around the child's shoulders. "I'll make sure he gets back to his mother safely. Thank you very much for your help." He reached out to shake the woman's hand, and she smiled crookedly at him in return.

"My pleasure," she crooned, her tone suggestive.

Neil pointedly failed to take the hint, and turned to lead the child back the way they had come. The camera panned to follow him, and the woman, now offscreen, found herself instead left with the production assistant and a lengthy form.

Neil headed out, unconcerned with the paperwork. Sandra spoke up in his ear. "You might want to say something to the boy. Something parental. You are a concerned adult who came all this way to look for him, after all."

Neil looked over as he walked. "So, Nicholas - care to explain how you ended up here? Your mom's worried sick, and we've all been out looking for you all afternoon."

Nicholas rolled his eyes, and tried unsuccessfully to wiggle out from under Neil's arm. "I *told* her I wanted to go to the circus for my birthday, but she said we had to wait until the show's done filming and we could celebrate my birthday *then*. That's months from now!" His voice contained all the impatience and angst of a newly-minted nine-year-old.

Neil couldn't help himself - he grinned and mussed the kid's brown hair. "So you came on your own, did you? Rode the subway all by yourself and found your way here without any help at all?"

Nicholas refused to look at him. "I'm nine now. It's time I started having real adventures of my own."

Neil smirked, but his tone was friendly. "Have you read any books about people your age having adventures? Which one is your favorite?"

"Narnia!" Nicholas shouted immediately. "Those kids got to rule an entire kingdom. Peter was 13 when they started having adventures in Narnia, and Lucy was only 8 the first time she went - and she became the most loved ruler of all of them!" He was practically dancing in his excitement.

Neil chuckled, but then his face turned serious. "All right. But do you understand that those stories are based on a magical, made-up place?"

The boy's excitement turned to a pout. "Yeah. Mom says they're just stories. None of it really happened."

Neil nodded. "I know they're fun stories, and it's exciting to think about having the kinds of adventures that the Pevensies had. But here in the real world, there isn't a magical wardrobe that will take you back to your home when you're done having adventures. You could get lost, or hurt, or a bad person could try to do something mean to you. Your mom worries about all this stuff when you take off on your own." He stopped walking, and knelt down until he was eye-to-eye with Nicholas. "You don't want to make her worry about all that stuff, do you? Or risk getting so lost that you're not able to find her again, and not able to get home?"

Nicholas's eyes turned big and round as he stared back at Neil. "No," he answered, and while there was still a hint of pout, it was clear that Neil's speech had gotten through.

"Good. So let's get you home to her, hey kiddo?" Neil roughed up his hair again, and Nicholas shrugged away, giggling, but followed Neil without complaint back into the subway station.

"Good work, champ," Sandra cheered into his earpiece. "That'll be ratings gold!"

When they were safely seated on the subway car - in a space his production team had cleared out for them - Nicholas tugged on Neil's coat. When Neil looked down, the boy stared back, his sky blue eyes soft and round. "I'm glad you're probably my daddy."

Neil's eyebrows scrunched together in confusion. "What did you just say, kid?"

Nicholas answered him matter-of-factly. "My mommy told me you were probably my daddy, but she wasn't for sure because you were gone before I was born. But I'm glad you're probably my daddy."

Neil shook his head. "I'm sorry, kid, but your mom must be confused. I've only known her for a few weeks, and you just turned nine. There's no way I could be your dad." When the boy's face fell, Neil added: "But if I did have a son, I'd want him to be as brave and adventurous - and considerate of his mom - as you are."

Nicholas snuggled into his side, contented again. The boy closed his eyes, dozing off after his adventure, and Neil's face turned stormy.

"I take it back," Sandra amended in his earpiece. "*This* is going to be ratings gold."

"Mommy!" cried the happy boy, running into the arms of a kneeling Casey. She rocked him back and forth as she squeezed him, eyes tightly closed.

"Niko," she crooned as she held him close. "I was so worried!" Tears glistened in the corners of her eyes, unshed, as she let him go and leaned back to look at him. "Are you alright?"

"Yeah," he answered nonchalantly. "I was a little worried when the police man told me I needed to come with him. But then Neil came and brought me back, so that was ok."

Casey looked up at Neil, standing awkwardly in the doorway, trying not to intrude into the intimate reunion. "Thank you so much," she said, while gently rubbing Niko's back. "I don't have words to thank you enough for bringing my boy home to me."

Neil nodded. "Sure. Anyone would have done the same," he replied dismissively. "Listen, I don't want to intrude on your family moment, but I really need to talk to you after you get him settled back in. Nicholas had some very interesting things to say while we were coming back, and I need to clear the air."

Casey's face turned serious. "Alright. Let me feed him and get him settled, and then I'll come find you." As Neil started to turn away, she added: "But I'm serious. None of this 'anyone would have done the same' stuff." She sniffed. "I am sincerely grateful to you for bringing back my son."

Neil nodded, then left the doorway.

Casey turned back to Nicholas. "So, Niko! First of all, you're in big trouble for running off like that without a word to me." His face started to screw up in complaint, but Casey plowed on before he could start whining. "But we'll deal with that later. Right now, let's get you something to eat, and you can tell me about the day you had."

She stood and took his hand, leading him toward the kitchen.

"Personally, I'm more interested in the conversation you're going to have with Neil later," Vince said in her ear. "'Lucy, you've got some 'splaining to do!'"

Casey smiled for the camera, the happy mother dutifully leading her son off to feed him, but her eyes turned steely.

Casey knocked on the open door frame, and Neil swiveled in his desk chair to face her. He stood when he saw her waiting there, and waved her into the room. His feet were bare, the top few buttons of his shirt were undone, and his jeans hung low on his waist. In short, he looked like sex on a stick.

Casey stepped into the room and sat opposite Neil on the cushioned window seat in front of his open windows. The rain had stopped, and a cool breeze fluttered into the room now and again, fluttering the curtains. His room looked onto the back of the property, with a view of the courtyard, the pool and the other wings of the mansion forming a U-shape with a view down to the ocean. Several of their housemates were out there now, enjoying the temporary elevation in lifestyle that the mansion offered.

She took a deep breath. "So. You said Niko had something interesting to say to you this afternoon?"

His eyes fixed on her face. She refused to meet his gaze, and her face was serious. "Casey, it seems like you might have something to tell me. From the way you're acting right now, I think you have a good idea of what Nicholas said to me."

She averted her gaze even more, turning her face toward the courtyard. "That depends. Did he tell you about his father?"

Neil sighed. "He told me that you said I'm probably his dad." He bent toward her, his nearness demanding she turn to face him. "Casey, what the Hell? I've known you for a matter of weeks - why would he think I'm his dad? I haven't even kissed you, for Christ's sake!"

She crossed her arms under her breasts but stood her ground, refusing to meet his gaze but not moving away from his invasion of her space. "Neil," she began calmly, her voice quiet in contrast to his anger. "Do you remember meeting a woman while you were out running in Central Park, almost ten years ago? You broke her iPod and bought her a new one, and spent the day and the night with her?"

Finally, she turned to look at him. Her eyes were pained.

Neil's mouth hung open. "How do you know that? Her name was Marie, she was blonde..."

She shook her head. "My middle name is Marie. I had just met you, you literally ran into me in the park - I didn't want to give you too much identifiable information until I knew you weren't a creep. But then you vanished."

He shook his head, echoing her gesture. "You're the one who vanished. But... Marie - Casey - I can't believe this is happening." He paused, continuing to shake his head. "I've pictured telling you this a thousand times, but not like this, and not after so many years." His blank gaze sharpened, and he stared intently into her eyes, taking her hands. "Casey, when I left your apartment that morning, I was literally hit by a bus." His hands squeezed hers. "I was in a coma for six weeks, then I was in the hospital rehabilitating from my injuries for another two months after I woke up. It was nearly four months later when I came looking for you."

As he spoke, her mouth opened into an 'o.' Her hands came up to cover her mouth as she listened to his recitation.

"My God, Neil! I had no idea." She dropped her hands to grab his again, leaning close. "I'm so sorry! All these years, I thought you just... didn't bother to call."

"No way!" He shook his head vehemently. "I was gonna call you right after I got home. I couldn't decide whether to ask you for dinner, or beg you to come have lunch with me. I was way, way into you."

Somehow, the two of them had become entwined. Her head rested against his shoulder as she leaned into him, her arms wrapped around his waist. His arms came around her shoulders and he held her close.

"I was going to call you, but everything on me that day got destroyed. No phone number, no cell phone. By the time I was able to leave the hospital and come looking for you at your apartment, you weren't there. I was asking for someone named Marie and they told me nobody by that name had ever lived there. I half wondered if I'd imagined it all in the coma."

Her eyes closed and her lips squeezed together. "By then, I would have moved out already. I figured out I was pregnant pretty quickly, but you never called, so I decided I should go home to have the baby. I needed my family's support - having a baby on my own in Manhattan wasn't even something I considered."

He held her for a moment, but then he leaned back and gently lifted her chin to face him. "Casey, are you telling me that Nicholas really is my son? Why did he say 'probably,' then?"

She grimaced. "Because I can't really say for sure." She let go of him and shifted back a few inches, putting space between them. "That day when I met you - I had just gotten out of a relationship. I'd been dating the guy for months, but we'd just broken up when I spent the night with you." Her chin dropped and she wrapped her arms around herself. "I'm not proud of it, but I wasn't expecting to meet someone when I met you. I sure as heck wasn't expecting to jump right into bed with someone."

She looked back up at him. "There was no-one after you... I kept waiting for you to call... but I had just broken up with Mike. So I can't be sure that Niko isn't his. I just always hoped he was yours - I wanted nothing to do with Mike - so I guess I've always just told Niko - and myself - that you were his dad."

Neil sighed heavily. "Wow. What a mess."

Casey nodded, then smiled tremulously. "Understatement of the century."

He gazed at her intently, his expression serious. "Casey, did it never

7

occur to you to do a paternity test? Nicholas has a right to know who his father is. If it's me, I have a right to know I have a son out there." He gestured broadly, his voice rising. "For that matter, so does the other guy if it's him. I can't speak for him, but I would definitely have wanted to be a part of his life if Nicholas was mine. I would never have wanted a son of mine to grow up without a father."

Casey stood and backed up a few steps, extending her hands to ward off his anger. "Neil, I thought you were out. Intentionally. I wasn't going to be one of those women who 'caught' a man with a baby." She shook her head dismissively. "And if it was Mike - I told you, I wanted nothing to do with him. I wouldn't have wanted him around even if he *was* Nicholas's father."

Neil stood, moving toward her. "Well, that's not just your decision to make. He, or I, have a right to be a part of Niko's life if one of us is the father. You don't get to decide for us. That's what custody hearings are for. And there's the matter of child support..."

Casey shook her head more violently, twisting around Neil and backing toward the door. "See, this is all the stuff I was trying to avoid. I never asked for child support - I've raised Niko on my own all these years - and in return, the dad, whoever he might be, has no claim on my son."

He grabbed her wrist, holding her in place. "Casey, that's bullshit. Just because the woman bears the child doesn't mean that child belongs solely to her, or that she has a right to hide its existence from the father. Every kid has two parents, and should have a right to both of them."

Casey tugged ineffectually at her wrist. Neil's grip was iron; she wasn't able to free herself, so she stood her ground, stiffening her spine and squaring her shoulders against him. "I can see that I've given you a lot to think about. And yes, you've got a valid point there - I'm sorry I never really thought about it from the father's point of view. Mostly I just assumed a guy would be happy to be let off the hook. I'm sure that's how Mike would have felt, and I thought that was how you felt since you never called me back." He started to speak, but she shook her head. "I think we both have some thinking to do. So why don't you let me go, and we'll talk again tomorrow."

He stared down to where he still held her wrist and released her, seeming almost startled to find his hand wrapped so firmly around her arm. Before she could leave the room, though, he reached toward her again, stopping short of actually grabbing her. "Just do me one favor,

Casey. We can talk about all the rest of this after we've both had time to process. But the one thing I'd ask of you - will you consent to a paternity test so I can know for sure whether Nicholas is mine?"

She looked down at the floor, refusing to meet his gaze. "I can see now how I might owe you that much, at least. I won't deny the request, if that's what you really want. But making it happen might be complicated."

He stepped toward her lightly, his expression softer. "We can ask to talk to Nathan tomorrow and see what we can figure out. I'm sure that once we explain things, he'll help us get to the bottom of this." His arms stole gently around her, and he pulled her into a tender embrace.

"It's good to finally see you again, Marie."

Her arms came around his waist, and her shoulders trembled as she sobbed softly against his chest.

In another room, with muted microphones, a group producers were giving each other high-fives, and someone had broken out a couple of bottles of champaign. "Ratings gold."

Casey glided into the large, open floorpan living space where her housemate Richard and three of the kids were hanging out around a large table. Nicholas had finished his dinner, and Richard was just clearing the plates, while the two girls, Cassidy and Natalie, played a card game. When Casey entered the room, Nicholas ran to her and threw his arms around her waist.

"Mom!" She smiled down at him and returned the hug. "Can we watch a movie now?"

She ruffled his hair and crossed the room, smiling at the girls in greeting. "I did promise, didn't I? How about something we haven't seen in a while - maybe Bolt?"

"Yeah!" Niko cheered, running across the room and jumping into the middle of the large sectional couch, feet first. "Dogs are the best! We can get a dog when we get home, right mom?"

Casey laughed as the girls ran across the room to join Nicholas on the couch. "Why don't we wait and see, ok?"

Cassidy spoke up next to him. "Cats are the best. Dogs just drool and stink and bark a lot. Cats are refined, independent pets. They're not always begging for attention, they're quiet, they clean up after themselves and you don't have to walk them outside and pick up their poo." A very mature ten, Cassidy presented her views in an affected, matter-of-fact manner. This sparked a heated debate between the three children as to which pet was the best.

Casey strolled over to where Richard was rinsing the dinner plates and leaned against the counter next to him. "Thanks for looking after him for me. I can sit with the three of them while they watch the movie. Why don't you take the rest of the evening off? Enjoy some non-dad time with the singles?"

Richard smiled in his easy way, his wide grin and white teeth positively sparkling in his handsome, tanned face. Casey admired his wide shoulders while he dried the last plate, then put it away in the cupboard. "Nah," he finally offered, turning to face her as he draped the dish towel over the front of the deep sink. "I'm old and tired and worn down. I don't feel like competing with the young bucks tonight. Some family time sounds like just the ticket." His broad grin belied the humor in his self-deprecating comments; he might not be as cut as some of the younger guys, but he had a solid, commanding physique that formed a very attractive complement to his single dad status.

Without waiting for a response, he wandered over to where the kids were now full-on bickering on the sectional. It was a few short moments from turning physical, but the three of them settled down as he stretched his full length along one side of the sectional, closest to Cassidy. Their matching blonde hair and blue eyes formed a pretty family picture as Casey crossed toward them.

"So, Natalie, what's your mom up to tonight?" she asked the third child, black-haired and brown-eyed Natalie, who was there without her parent.

"She's on a two-on-one date," Natalie answered tersely, without looking up from where she was intently examining her shoes.

"Oh, with whom?" Casey asked, trying to draw the child into conversation.

"Two of the guys," Natalie responded, oblivious in the way where it wasn't quite obvious if she was just being a child or if she was being a smartass.

Casey grinned as she stretched out on the side of the sectional opposite Richard. He grinned back. "Ok. Movie time!" She used her smartphone to wake up the massive entertainment system and navigate to Bolt, while Niko cheered and offered helpful comments in an attempt to get her to start the movie more quickly.

Soon, the three children were deeply engrossed in the movie, Niko cheering and laughing loudly whenever Bolt did something particularly entertaining, and the girls championing Mittens the cat. It was a rowdy, animated scene, with Casey or Richard occasionally interjecting to keep the peace or pose a thought-provoking comprehension question.

Drawn by the noise, Neil stood in the doorway, watching the domestic picture the five of them posed. After a few silent moments unobserved, he ambled into the room, heading toward the cabinets and rummaging around. Neither the kids nor the adults payed him any attention.

Closing the cabinets without taking anything out, Neil walked over to the sectional, stopping to stand behind the kids as they chatted and gestured to the screen. "What movie are you guys watching?" he asked no-one in particular.

"Bolt!" Niko answered enthusiastically, pointing as the dog came onto the screen. Neil nodded.

After another moment of standing awkwardly behind the sofa, he offered: "Looks like fun. I think I'll watch with you guys." He moved around the sectional to sit on one of the nearby chairs, as the only spots left on the sectional were next to Richard's or Casey's reclined feet. Casey smiled at him, but her attention quickly focused back on the kids and the movie.

A few minutes later, Cassidy interrupted the animated conversation to interject: "I need to use the restroom." Casey paused the movie and sat up, as Cassidy excused herself and headed off to the nearest bathroom.

"How about you two?" she asked Natalie and Niko. "Do either of you need to use the bathroom?" Both of them nodded, so she stood. Richard started to stand up with her, but she motioned him to stay put. "I've got it. Off to the bathroom, troops - I'm on hand duty!"

"Aww, mom!" Niko complained loudly, while Natalie got up quietly and went along without any fuss. A moment later, the three of them had vanished out the opposite door to the large main bathroom near the front entryway, leaving Neil and Richard alone in the room.

Richard smiled conspiratorially at Neil, shaking his head as he looked in the direction where Casey and the kids had vanished. "Man, what a woman."

Neil raised an eyebrow. "Oh?" he asked, his tone flat.

Richard nodded expansively. "Oh, yeah, man. The girls I usually date fall into one of two categories: either they don't have kids yet and don't have a clue what to do with them, or they're single mothers themselves, but they're desperate or messed up and just don't have their shit together." He leaned in closer, lowering his voice. "A woman like Casey is one in a million. She's a great mom, knows exactly what to do - but she's also her own person, you know?"

Neil shook his head, so Richard continued. "So many moms get lost in being a mom - they forget how to be a woman with her own interests and personality outside of 'mom mode.' And the young girls who don't have kids yet - they're fun for a while, but ultimately I want to be with someone who loves a child as much as I love my Cassidy, and understands the sacrifices I make to put her first." He shook his head slowly. "You single, childless guys have no idea how easy you've got it."

Neil's lip curled up into a snort, but Richard didn't notice. Instead, the blonde man leaned in, as if sharing a secret with Neil. "I've got my eye on Casey. She is just too amazing to miss. I've been on a couple of group dates with her, but I haven't had much time alone with her yet. When I do, though, I've gotta close the deal - I'd love for it to be her and me left at the end of the show." He smiled again, then leaned back.

"How about you?" Richard finally asked. "Have you got your eye on any of the girls in particular yet? Some of the singles are really cute, but I think the hottest ones are already starting to hook up."

Neil stared back at him, face carefully blank. After a long pause, he finally spoke up. "I'm considering my options. I'm not committed anywhere yet. I want to keep things open until after I get to know a few people better and see where things go."

Cassidy opened the door from the adjacent bathroom just then, and Neil stood. "I've changed my mind about the movie," he offered as he crossed the room toward the main entryway. "I think I'll go for a run."

"Have fun!" Richard called and waved after him.

Neil sat in front of the camera, his blue eyes flashing with anger and his dark eyebrows drawn down over them. He sighed heavily.

"I was just hanging out with Richard and Casey and three of the kids, including Nicholas."

He stopped speaking, and then shrugged his shoulders.

"What the Hell - you probably already know by now about the conversation I had earlier with Casey. So now I know she's actually this girl named Marie that I spent twenty-four hours with almost ten years ago... and I've been carrying a torch for her ever since. I've had two serious relationships since then, but I haven't been able to commit to either one - something has always been holding me back, and I think it was her."

He shook his head, and his shoulders fell as he sighed heavily. "Now here she is again - here, on America's Favorite Couple, where I've come looking for love - and I find out that not only is she here right in front of me, completely available to date and fall in love and maybe even marry at the end of all this - but we might have a son! In addition to the one woman I can't forget, she might be the mother of my child."

The camera zoomed out as he stood and began to pace in the small room. "And then, to see her hanging out with Richard and all the kids, and they're like this pretty little family." He shook his head as his pacing sped up. "And on top of that, Richard has his eye on her! Richard! Hot Father of the Year and successful business owner and all that jazz!"

Neil stopped pacing abruptly, and sat again in the room's single chair. The camera zoomed in to focus on his anguished face. "Casey had barely registered on my radar - I thought she was interesting and beautiful and nice and I thought it would be cool to get to know her better, but I don't think I was seriously considering her because she had a kid."

He shifted and stared directly into the camera lens.

"And now... the thought of her with Richard - or any of these other guys - makes me want to pound his face in."

Neil stood, and ended his confessional by tossing an "I need a run," over his shoulder as he hurriedly left the room.

"Nathan is ready for you now, Casey," Vince's voice said in her ear. She glanced at Neil, where he was standing beside her opposite the closed sitting room doors, then stepped forward to open them. Neil followed her in, and they found Nathan already sitting in a chair by the window. As they walked into the room, he looked up from the book he was reading and smiled at them.

"Come on in, guys," he waved them in, putting down his book and standing to greet them. "How are you doing?" he asked them each in turn as he hugged Casey, then shook Neil's hand. "Have a seat, have a seat," he offered, motioning to the two chairs artfully posed to his right. "So, I hear the two of you have something you need to talk to me about?"

13

he probed, as he resumed his own seat and looked at them each with a serious expression. His mouth was set in a thin line, but his blue eyes radiated concern and compassion as he gazed at them.

Casey looked at Neil, and then they both started to talk at the same moment. She grinned and ducked her head, and he smiled back at her. "Why don't you go ahead, Casey?" Neil offered.

She nodded, her smile fading. "Nathan, I'm afraid there's some information we have to share with you," Casey began. He leaned forward slightly. "Here, in the mansion, isn't the first time Neil and I have met. We actually met once nearly ten years ago, and spent a day together."

"And a night," Neil added helpfully. Casey glanced over at him, and fell silent.

Nathan sat back in his chair. "Wow, this is very serious news," he responded. "You know the whole premise of America's Favorite Couple is fifteen men and fifteen women meeting for the first time, and getting to know one another as they search for love." He looked at each of them in turn. "The two of you already knowing each other isn't exactly in keeping with the spirit of the show's premise."

Casey looked at Neil, then back at Nathan. "Nathan, I know this is serious, but if it helps - Neil didn't know I'd be here in the mansion. Or rather, there's no way he could have recognized my name in the contestant list, because he knew me by a different name the one time we met." She looked down at her hands clasped in her lap. "I know this isn't exactly what you guys intended when you put the show together, but Neil and I genuinely are people who are interested in getting to know other people - including potentially each other - as we search for love. We're both single, and we haven't met since the time we spent together almost ten years ago. I know my life is completely different than it was then, and as a mother, I'm a completely different person."

Neil nodded. "I feel the same way, Nathan. Before she told me that she was the woman I met ten years ago, I didn't have a clue it was her. I thought she was beautiful, and interesting, and I wanted to get to know her better - but I felt the same way about several of the other women here. I don't feel as though she had any sort of advantage, or I had any sort of bias toward her."

Nathan tilted his head. "And now that you know who she is?" he probed.

"Now that I know who she is, I still want to get to know her. But there are also several other women here with whom I've already started to form relationships, and I feel I owe it to myself - and to them - to see where those feelings might lead." Neil shrugged.

Nathan turned his attention to Casey. "What about you, Casey? Are you ready to call it quits now that it has come to light that you and Neil have had a prior relationship, however brief? Or have you also started to form relationships with other people in the house?"

She leaned forward, her expression earnest. "Nathan, I definitely want to stay, if you and America have it in your hearts to forgive me for keeping my prior meeting with Neil to myself. There are some great people here, and I'm starting to develop real, romantic feelings for some of them - feelings I haven't really had for a man in a long time. My goal in coming on the show was to find love - a man who could accept Nicholas and me into his life with open arms - and that's still my goal. And I feel like I'm on the right track to do that, and I'd like to stay and see it through."

Nathan pursed his lips. "Well, it's a tough question, guys. I think we're going to have to leave it up to America to decide whether you can stay. Fortunately, tonight is voting night, so we'll just put it to the vote when we go live. Your fate will be in America's hands."

Casey and Neil both nodded. "There's one more thing, though, Nathan," Casey spoke up. "Nicholas. There's a chance he might be Neil's son."

Nathan's jaw dropped open. "Let me make sure I've got this straight. The two of you only spent one day and night together, nearly ten years ago - and now you're telling me that that night might be when your son was conceived?" Casey nodded. "And you never tried to find Neil?"

She looked at Neil, then back at Nathan. "I know it's a sensitive issue, Nathan. Neil just found out that he might be a father, and he might have missed out on the first nine years of his son's life. I see now that I might have been wrong to not try to find him sooner, and to not know for sure who Niko's father is - so that's why I'd like to ask that if we do end up both staying, I want to arrange for a paternity test."

Nathan nodded. "I think that would be a good idea. If America votes for you to stay, we'll definitely arrange for a paternity test to answer this question for Neil and for you."

"Thank you, Nathan," Neil responded. "This has all been kind of a lot to take in. I really appreciate you taking the time to listen, and I hope

15

America is as curious as I am to find out whether Casey and I will find love - and if it will be with each other."

"Cut!" yelled a production assistant in the back of the room. "That was perfect, Neil. You and Casey can head back out to the mansion now - Nathan needs to go get ready for tonight's voting ceremony, and we need to cut this footage into this week's episode and make our final edits for airing."

One by one, the men and women filed into the ballroom where the show shot each week's live voting ceremony. Voting always started at nine o'clock when the show aired, and voting ran right up until they started calling names - around nine fifty-five each week. Everyone gathered for the live voting ceremony at nine fifty, leading into a tense ten minutes while they found out who would be staying and who would be going.

Voting for America's Favorite Couple could get complicated. Each contestant was allowed to vote for a certain number of people each week. This week, the show was cutting two men and two women. Each contestant was allowed to vote for seven people they'd like to get to know better.

If someone got no votes, they were up for elimination. If someone got a single vote, but they didn't vote in turn for the person who gave it to them, they might be up for elimination - it depended on how many people failed to get votes at all. If a contestant got several votes, and they also voted for those people in turn, there was a good chance they'd be safe.

So the goal was to vote for a core group of people who were also voting for you, but voting was secret - it was against the rules to talk about who you were voting for.

To complicate things even more, America voted for their favorite couples. Each week, when the show started, the contestants' voting results would scroll across the bottom of the screen. Viewers got to know who voted for whom, and could help a romance along by keeping a couple who was interested in each other - or by voting to get rid of people who they felt weren't right for a match. America's voting could save a contestant who they felt was perfect for one of their favorite participants, even if that person didn't get a vote. American voters could also vote off someone who got several votes from other participants through a special ballot format, if they felt that person had been manipulating the votes or wasn't there for the right reason.

In other words, the show runners had found a way to get - and keep - America *very* invested in the show. America's Favorite Couple audience members had a personal stake in whether or not their favorites got their dream romance - and could live the glamorous lifestyle of the participants vicariously through their votes and the show.

This week's vote was special. In addition to the normal voting to determine who would stay and who would go, America had a special ballot option to decide whether or not Neil and Casey could stay in the mansion and continue their quest for love. America could vote for just Neil to stay, or just Casey to stay, or both Neil and Casey to stay.

Nathan May stood across from the two groups of participants - the men and women lined up on risers on one side of the room. He looked resplendent in his usual hand-tailored suit, and his brown hair was perfectly coiffed. Instead of his usual geniality, though, his face was sombre this week.

"This has been an unusual week here at the mansion," he announced. "We've found out that two of our participants had a prior relationship ten years before coming on the show. After talking it out, the two of them have assured me that they're both here to find love - and that they're already developing relationships with people here in this room. Instead of making such an important decision ourselves, we've decided to let America tell us whether the two of them should stay, or whether they should leave the mansion."

He looked at the two groups in turn. "Neil. Casey. Would you step forward, please?"

Neil made his way from the second row of men to stand next to Nathan. He wore a dark gray suit with black threads running through it, and the suit had clearly been expertly tailored. The suit was paired with a red bowtie over a steel gray dress shirt. Whimsically, though, he wore a pair of leather Chuck Tailors with the suit. His expression was suitably serious as he stood in front of the crowd, and watched Casey coming to join him.

Because she had Nicholas, Casey was always in the front row. She carefully stepped down from the front riser, balancing effortlessly on her midnight blue stilettos that perfectly matched her body-hugging sheathe dress. She held Nicholas's hand as they walked toward the host, and brushed an imaginary piece of lint off the shoulder of his small grey suit as they reached the front.

"Nathan, Neil, everybody," Casey began, as she stood in front of them, awaiting the results of America's vote. "I sincerely apologize that I didn't make you all aware of the prior relationship I had with Neil ten years ago. It was such a long time ago, and lasted for so little time, that I didn't feel it was relevant to my time here. I'm sorry if you feel that I've betrayed your trust. I'm forming real, strong feelings for some of you, and I'll be extremely fortunate and grateful if I'm allowed to continue my journey here in my search to find love."

Nathan nodded. Then he looked expectantly at Neil.

"Ladies, gentlemen," Neil said, looking at each group in turn. "I didn't realize who Casey was when we arrived at the mansion - in fact, I didn't find out at all until she told me last night. I hope that speaks to the fact that I had no intent to deceive any of you. In my time here, I've begun to develop feelings for several of the women here - and I've formed some great friendships with the men - and I'd hate to leave before I have a chance to see where my journey will take me. But I'm here before you awaiting America's verdict."

Nathan nodded again. "As you see, they both claim that they're here for the right reasons. I know some of you definitely voted for them this week, and if this hadn't come up, they'd both be safe. That means they're forming real relationships with some of you. So now it's time to see if they'll be allowed to continue those relationships, or if America thinks they should go home."

Nathan looked expectantly to a production assistant standing on the side of the room, who briskly walked over to hand Nathan a platter holding a sealed envelope. Nathan picked up the envelope and held it before him, looking solemnly at the men and women assembled in the room. After a pregnant pause, he opened the envelope and looked at the card it contained. Then, he looked back at the room.

"Well, it looks like America has made its decision," Nathan began. "Both Neil and Casey will be..." he paused. Silence hung in the air, the tension growing thicker. His face was suitably serious, but his eyes sparkled as he enjoyed prolonging the moment. Finally, he continued. "Staying here at the mansion. America believes they're sincere in their quest to find love, and that they're working toward that in their time here. So this week, they won't be going home." He nodded to them, and they quickly crossed back to their respective groups, Neil getting several high fives and a few handshakes, and Casey getting hugs from a few of the women on her side.

"Instead, America has voted to say farewell to these four individuals: from the men, Chris and Danny, and from the women, Louisa and Sandy. I'm sorry. Say your goodbyes."

The four individuals named stepped forward, sharing hugs and handshakes - some tearful on the women's side - and filed out the door, shaking Nathan's hand as they passed him.

Once they were safely away, Nathan turned back to the two groups. "Alright! We've got another great week planned for you - two more awesome group dates, and several two-on-ons and one-on-ones - so get some sleep, and get ready for another busy week in the mansion!"

CHAPTER TWO

Week Five

"Did you hear about the date they sent the singles on yesterday?" Olivia asked, rolling her olive-green eyes in her heart-shaped bronze face. "They set them up with a private plane and took them to a small resort island, where they went cliff-diving and had the most amazing fresh seafood lunch catered for them. Then, they had a romantic luau on the beach - it lasted almost until dawn. And they send us here?" She shook her head, the motion jiggling her large breasts on her petite frame.

Casey looked at the dank concrete walls around them. "I don't know. I actually think it's kind of cool that they took over all of Alcatraz for a day, and set up a locked room puzzle game just for us to play with the kids. It sounds like Niko is having a blast," she added, hearing his enthusiastic voice as he worked on a puzzle with David in the next cell.

"How you doing, honey?" Olivia called to Natalie, who was in the cell on the other side of them with her date, Xander.

"Good, mom! We're working on a math puzzle."

Olivia shook her head. "I don't know where she gets her smarts. It's sure not from me - I hated school. And if her dad had half a brain, he wouldn't have walked out on us, eh, chica?" she teased.

Casey blushed. "Niko's dad didn't exactly walk out on us. More like, he didn't know about Nicholas."

Olivia 'tsked' and shook her head. "More's the pity, then. He must really have been an idiot!"

Casey frowned. "It's complicated."

The smaller woman grinned mischievously. "It always is."

Niko's victorious voice echoed from the cell next to them. "We found a key, mom! Coming to get you!" A moment later, a broadly grinning

Nicholas stood in front of the cell that Casey and Olivia shared, followed shortly after by a rather sheepish looking David. He gave Casey a shy grin, then nudged Niko's shoulder.

"Why don't you show the ladies what we found? Maybe they can help us with this puzzle."

"Yeah!" Niko exclaimed, holding up a tape recorder in front of the cell door. "We found this! David says it's some kind of really old iPod. But it's missing a battery. Do you have one of those in there?"

Casey shared a grin with Olivia. "It's not exactly like an iPod, honey. It needs a battery, yes, but it also needs a tape to play - that's kind of like a Blu-ray, it's a type of media that contains information that the tape recorder can decode and turn into sounds."

Nicholas nodded. "Ok. Do you have a tape to play?"

Casey produced a tape from behind her with a flourish, much to Nicholas's delight. "We do! But we don't have a battery. Maybe Natalie and Xander have one of those next door?"

Niko reached his hand between the bars. "Ok, we'll ask them. Gimme the tape!"

Casey handed it to him carefully, making sure the tape side was facing away from his sticky little palm. "Niko, you need to be careful with the tape. It only goes in a certain way, and the ribbon part of it can be damaged, which would mean we can't play it."

"Ok!" he responded, pulling his hand out and handing the tape to David. "Maybe you should take care of this, then, while we look for a battery." With that, Niko dashed off to the next cell still holding the tape recorder, excitedly explaining to Natalie and Xander what they'd found. David grinned at Casey through the bars, then followed, leaving her and Olivia alone again.

"Oh, chica, he's a cute one," Olivia teased her. "But so shy! I think Niko would tear through him in a day, and as for you? You need a little more substance than that, I think." Olivia winked.

Casey giggled. "Oh, my God, I can't believe you just made me giggle," she rolled her eyes and shook her head. "But yeah - David's adorable, but maybe I'm looking for a little more of a... man?" She bit her lip as Olivia laughed at her. "But, to be fair, I haven't spent much time with him, and maybe he just doesn't know how to act around kids? Or maybe just not a kid as enthusiastic as Niko?" She shook her head. "I might find he's got a lot to offer if I sat him down for a quiet dinner, just the two of us."

"Oh, honey, you're never gonna make up your mind if you're determined to give them all a chance!" Olivia chided with a broad smile. "Don't be afraid to make a choice! You don't want shy. You need passion. You want a man who lights you up inside, and makes you desperate for another moment to be near him."

Casey smiled softly at her. "Maybe that's what you need, Olivia."

The dark-haired woman shook her head, her silky hair cascading around her. "Oh, no, chica. I have enough passion for all of us! I need a man who's calm - someone who can handle things and put me in my place when I'm being overdramatic. And I'd prefer someone with large hands. Maybe someone like Richard?" she smiled.

Casey looked away, pressing her lips into a thin line. "Hmm. Richard." After a moment, she looked back at Olivia. "Do you think he feels the same?"

Olivia smiled seductively. "If he doesn't yet, he will soon." She leaned in conspiratorially, lowering her voice. "Men don't always know what's good for them," she advised. "Sometimes we have to make them see."

"Hmm." Casey replied noncommittally. "What about Xander? He's hot," Casey pointed out.

"Hah," Olivia responded. "He may be hot, but he knows it. Mark my words, chica, that one is going to be trouble before the end." Olivia nudged Casey's shoulder. "Still, he's good to look at, no?" She winked.

"Mom! Mom! We figured it out!" Niko exclaimed, popping back into view in front of their cell. "Natalie and Xander had a math puzzle that revealed a combination for a box we had in our cell, and the box had the key to their cell in it. And they had the battery for the tape recorder! Now we have to go where the tape is telling us to go to find the key to your cell," he explained. "We'll be back!"

Xander stepped into view, his short black hair still expertly coiffured. His slim black jeans hugged his body like a glove, leaving very little to the imagination. The shirt he wore had sleeves that ended at his biceps and struggled to contain them, showing off his impressive but not overblown musculature.

He gave them a cocky little half-grin. "Ladies," he offered. "We shall return shortly with your freedom." He gave a little half bow, and both he and Nicholas stepped out of view again.

Casey and Olivia looked at each other, and they both burst out laughing. "Ok, you're definitely right about him," Casey conceded. "But damn, the man can fill out a pair of jeans." She waggled her eyebrows suggestively, setting them both off into another fit of giggles.

They were still giggling when Richard stepped into view at their cell door a few minutes later. "Ladies," he greeted them with a broad smile. "I heard you were still stuck in here and thought I should come check on you, but I see you're doing just fine," he offered.

"Oh, you guys already finished your game?" Olivia returned. "You're so clever!" Her smile was honeyed, and Casey looked away.

Richard chuckled. "I wish I could take the credit, but it was all on the ladies. Lily, Violet and Cassidy had all the puzzles figured out before us poor guys could even wrap our heads around what we were looking at. We might have embarrassed ourselves a little bit with our poor performance, but those girls were on fire!"

He stuck his hand between the bars, and offered them two bottles of water. "Anyway, I heard your crew was still working on yours, so I thought I'd bring you a drink. Sitting behind bars is surprisingly thirsty work!"

Casey smiled her thanks as she grabbed the bottles, handing one to Olivia. "After hearing that door slam shut, I think the occasion calls for something a little stronger than water. But it'll have to do for now."

Olivia shuddered dramatically, wiggling her body all over - and shaking her assets in the process. "I know!" she interjected. "I might never sleep again with that sound ringing through my head! Maybe someone will be able to help tire me out." She laughed a throaty laugh, and Casey's eyes widened slightly.

Richard took it in stride with another friendly chuckle. "I'm sure Xander can help you out with that. He seems like a tiring kind of guy." He winked, and Olivia squealed.

"Oh, you bad, bad man!" She batted her eyelashes coquettishly and turned her head to the side in a caricature of girlish innocence.

Casey looked away.

"Anyway, I'd better get back to my crew," Richard took his leave. "I just wanted to make sure you ladies were doing alright and bring you a little sip to whet your whistle." He waved. "I'm sure we'll see you soon - your crew can't be far behind on getting you out of there!"

With that, he vanished.

Olivia beamed at Casey. "See, he was thinking of me! Half my work is already done."

Casey nodded, but her lips formed a thin line and she had fallen silent.

"You're falling behind," Vince teased, his voice amused in her ear. "If you're interested in that man, you'd better step up your game. That woman ain't afraid to go after what she wants."

Casey slanted a look at the camera, her eyes flashing. Vince laughed in her ear. "Save that for her, sunshine. She's your competition."

Casey sat in front of the camera with her hands crossed in her lap. Tonight she was wearing a simple sleeveless t-shirt with an interesting tribal necklace as her only ornament, and her hair was pulled back into a loose ponytail. Her expression was troubled.

"Today was a lot of fun," she began, and her expression became more animated. "Niko had a blast in Alcatraz - and I thought it was really cool, too. We were really fortunate to have that experience - a locked room game designed just for us, in a place with the history and atmosphere of Alcatraz? The whole place was shut down - there wasn't anyone there except us - and I'm sure there aren't very many people who get to see it like that, without all the tourists running around being stupid."

She paused, and laughed nervously. "And I'll admit, when we played hide and seek after lunch, and I was all alone waiting for someone to come find me - or looking for someone - that was pretty creepy! But really cool." She smiled, but then her smile faded.

"I really like Olivia. She's probably one of my best friends here. I know they encourage us single parents to hang out with the childless folks, and we really try to - but we spend more time together just because we've usually got at least some of the kids together. And really, I have so much more in common with the other parents - our lifestyles and values are so different from most of the singles. Anyway..." she trailed off.

"I didn't realize before today that Olivia liked Richard," she finally said after a long pause. "And I didn't realize before today that that would bother me," she added, giving the camera a rueful look, her half grin charmingly self-aware.

"I think I kind of thought Richard liked me. He was always a little extra friendly when we were together, and whenever I gave him a chance to run off and hang out with other people in the house, he always stayed to hang out with me and the kids. I thought he was being flirty a few times... and you know I've been voting to keep him around."

She grew silent.

The silence stretched to a minute, then two.

"When things came out with Neil, I kind of thought maybe he and I would spend some time together, see how we felt about one another - and find out if that spark we once had was still there between us. I know it was a long time ago, and it was for such a short time, but I really felt like we had a connection." She shook her head. "But now it's been days since all that came out, and we haven't been on any dates together, and we haven't really spent any time together in the house. Maybe I was silly for thinking we would."

She looked back at the camera lens. "Now after hearing Olivia talk about Richard today... I realize that I have deeper feelings for him than I had imagined. I thought he was just someone I was interested in getting to know better, but now I think he's someone I'm really developing feelings for. Strong feelings."

She looked away. "But I still feel disappointed that Neil and I haven't spent time together. And I wonder if it will change things when we finally do. And I wonder if Richard really does like Olivia."

Casey shook her head, then smiled sadly. "I guess when it comes to finding love, America, I need more time. I'm still looking."

"Beautiful," Vince's voice came in her ear. "They're gonna eat that up."

Casey stuck her tongue out at the camera, knowing they'd cut it after her heartfelt confessional. Vince's quiet chuckle was her satisfying response.

When Casey and Nicholas walked into the parlor, Neil was already there, along with Nathan May, and a third man they hadn't met before who sported glasses and a white coat. Nathan smiled, nodded, and motioned them into the room.

"Casey, Nicholas - this is Dr. Jack Teddy," Nathan introduced the newcomer. "He's a leading expert on DNA analysis, and we've asked him to come collect the samples personally for the paternity test today."

The older man nodded. "By taking the samples personally, I can validate the authenticity of the specimens, and the results of the test will be legally admissible in court."

Casey and Neil exchanged a look.

"I wasn't really thinking about court," Casey stalled.

Nathan wrapped a brotherly arm around her shoulders and led her to a nearby chair, gesturing for Nicholas to sit on the short stool next to her.

"Of course not, Casey," Nathan empathized. "But you never know what could happen. What if you do find love here - with Neil, even - and he wanted to legally adopt Nicholas? A legally valid paternity test would simplify the entire process." He glanced across to Neil. "Or what if the two of you find love with other people in the house, but Neil turns out to really be Nicholas's father? The four of you would need to figure out custody, and all the details surrounding that life change, and all of that would be so much simpler if you have a legally valid paternity test right now."

Casey took a deep breath. "I've gotta say, Nathan, I'm feeling a little railroaded right now."

Nathan's face changed to one of deep annoyance. "Cut this bit," he said aloud, swiping his hand across his throat in the universal gesture for 'cut.' Then he turned his gaze to Casey, his face twisted in rage.

"Cut the shit, Casey," he spat, his comforting, suave demeanor completely dropped. "You asked for a paternity test - this is what you get. You know why we're here. You signed up for this. So get with the program and try to act a little grateful, or we'll change the edit and you're not going to come out looking so rosy."

"Don't make eye contact with him, Case," Vince's voice came in her ear. "Look away, nod like you're afraid of him, and then give him what he wants. It'll be ok."

Casey followed Vince's instructions, looking away from Nathan and nodding timidly. She reached out and hugged Nicholas, who was looking very frightened, and composed herself. Then she looked at the collar of Nathan's shirt and nodded slightly.

"Of course, Nathan - you're completely right. I really appreciate the thoughtfulness of this gesture." Behind Nathan, out of frame, Neil's face was twisted, but he remained silent.

A moment later, everyone was in tune once again, and the shoot went forward as though there hadn't been an interruption.

"I'll be taking DNA samples from each of you," explained the doctor, as he picked up a swab. "I can do it with just the father and child, but if I also have the mother's DNA, it makes analysis much faster, because I can automatically eliminate DNA consistent with the mother's sample." He carefully swabbed Casey's cheek, then tucked the swab into a tube and labeled it clearly.

"How long will it take to get the results back?" Casey asked, as the doctor swabbed Nicholas. He carefully tucked the sample away, then looked at Nathan.

"We'll have the result for you in several weeks," the doctor answered, not meeting Casey's gaze.

Casey glanced back and forth between the doctor and Nathan, then bit her lip.

"So long?" Neil interjected, when the doctor had finished swabbing him.

The doctor began packing up his materials, then looked up and smiled at them. "This is what we have agreed. We'll get the result to you in a few weeks." Then he nodded to Nathan, got up, and left, carrying his bag.

"All right!" Nathan said with a bright smile. "In just a few short weeks, you'll know if Neil is really the father of your child. In the meantime, let's continue this journey and see where the next few weeks take you, emotionally!"

Both Casey and Neil smiled in return, but Casey's smile had a strained quality to it. Nicholas, picking up on the tension in the room, looked confused. The pause went on a few beats longer, and then Nathan yelled out "Ok, cut, we're done!" Without looking at them, he got up and left the room.

"That... could have gone better," Vince said into Casey's ear. She looked at Neil, the smiles gone, and he returned her serious gaze.

Casey sat on her bed, legs bent at the knees, and gazed intently at the book resting against her legs. She was dressed down, which still meant a nice pair of shorts - that showed off her long, tanned, runner's legs - and a turquoise sleeveless blouse. She wore a set of gold earrings that matched a rope bracelet on her wrist. Her hair was down, and loose around her shoulders.

"So they're changing things up a bit next week," Casey heard in her ear - an unexpected heads-up from Vince. "Keep reading - don't react - but they're adding someone to the show. A few people, to mask the reality, but one of them is your other ex - the guy you were dating when you met Neil. The other guy who might be Nicholas's father."

Casey's nostrils flared, and her eyes widened. To cover, she muttered a quiet "Wow, I can't believe she did that," as if reacting to her book.

"Nice," Vince praised her. "So yeah. They're bringing Mike onto the show. They're really going to play up the angle of which guy is Nicholas's real father. Incidentally, that's why the results are going to take so long from the paternity test. They can actually get them in three to five business days - or twenty-four hours in some rush cases - so it's just the show asking them to take so long so they can play out this story arc."

Casey shook her head, rubbing her eyes, careful to stare at the book as though she were reacting to what she read.

"I'm sorry, Case," Vince added. "I know you guys signed up for this and they think they can do whatever because you consented to be on the show... but this feels like too far to me. Maybe you should just hook up with Richard and stroll off into the sunset."

"If I ever met the person who wrote this book," Casey said quietly, closing the book in her lap. "I'd have to thank them for giving me so much to think about."

"You're welcome," Vince replied. "But look, I shouldn't have to tell you that they can't know I gave you this information. You've gotta figure out a way to do whatever you want to do without making it look like you knew about this stuff in advance. And for Crikey's sake, don't get caught telling Neil or anyone else about it!"

Casey sat down at the small desk in the room and took out a blank piece of paper. She started writing, then scratched out the line and started again. For nearly two hours, she worked intently, throwing out page after page. Eventually, she folded up a well-covered page, stuck it in the back pocket of her shorts, and headed out into the mansion.

The Vote was surprising only in how surprising it wasn't. Neither Casey nor Neil were in any danger of being eliminated; they both had enough votes from enough people that they weren't up. Richard and Olivia were also safe. Xander, Olivia's date from the group date, and Lily, Richard's date, were both called for a final vote. It turned out that Xander and Lily had hooked up after the date, and had been sneaking into each other's rooms every night since then. America apparently decided that the two of them didn't need any more time to find love, as they were voted off.

One minor upset was the voting off of one of the single parents - Derek. He hadn't really formed any strong relationships with any of the people remaining, and his son, Avery, had been rather quiet and reserved. In short, they weren't a part of anyone's story, so they were too boring to keep around.

With their elimination, it was down to seven people in the mansion.

Three of the four single parents - Richard, Olivia, and Casey - and four of the singles - Neil, Violet, Connor and Anastasia.

"The next week is going to be really interesting here in the mansion," Nathan announced at the end of the Vote. "We've only got one group date this week, but then we've got several two-on-one and one-on-one dates planned. And we're working on a surprise that we hope to have ready for you by the end of the week. So get ready for things to change, as we're relying on you to really start building on the relationships you've begun in your time here. The next few weeks are going to be crucial to determine if you can see a future with someone here, or if it's time to excuse yourself and let the others vie for the coveted title of America's Favorite Couple."

CHAPTER THREE

Week Six

Casey and Nicholas spent a quiet day in the mansion, as most of her housemates were out on the group date. She was the only single parent excluded from this date, which had taken Richard, Olivia, Neil, Violet, Anastasia, and David away at first light. Connor was still around the mansion somewhere, but he hadn't made much effort to spend time with Casey and Nicholas, and she left him alone in return.

"You and Niko should hang out in the main living space for the next twenty minutes," Vince said in her ear. "Official production request."

Casey smiled at her son, who was playing with action figures near the edge of the pool. "Hey, Niko," Casey interrupted his play. "I want you to take a break from that for a little while - it's time to do something educational! We're going to go read a chapter of your book inside for a little bit. Maybe we can come back out when we're done."

"Aww, ma," Niko complained halfheartedly, but he picked up his action figures, put them in his backpack, and followed her into the house. She sat them down in a grouping of chairs that had a good view of the stairs and the front door, and had him start to read aloud from the book they were working through: Alice's Adventures in Wonderland. They had just gotten to the part where Alice has grown huge in the White Rabbit's house, when Connor came storming down the front stairs, hauling his heavy suitcase.

When he reached the bottom of the stairs, he stopped to look at them. His heavy brows were pulled down low over his broad nose, and his green eyes were angry. "Well, then. Just you lot here to see me off?"

"See you off?" Casey asked, her tone carefully neutral.

"I'm leaving the mansion," Connor growled. "Me and this place, we're not getting along."

"What do you mean?" Casey asked. "Are you having a problem with someone here?"

"Good girl," Vince said in her ear. "Keep him talking. Get him to explain why he's leaving, then you can let him go."

"Am I having a problem with someone here?" he parroted, his tone sardonic. Then, he shook his head. "No, no problem." His tone changed. "But I've got a girlfriend back home - or I did, but we broke up before I came here. Now I realize that I want to give it another go."

"Oh," Casey stood, and walked over to give him a quick hug. "Well, best of luck to both of you!" She stepped away.

"Right," he growled. "You, too. Good luck with... everything here," he finally said, then picked up his suitcase in a huff and stormed out.

"That was weird, mom!" Nicholas blurted.

"From the mouths of babes," Vince teased in her ear.

"Did you hear he left because he had some mysterious girlfriend and he wanted to work it out?" Anastasia said, flicking her long, blonde hair over her shoulder.

Casey nodded. "That's what he told me when he left," she confirmed. "But he seemed awfully angry for someone who was going home to work things out with his girlfriend."

Olivia leaned forward, lowering her voice. "Maybe he just didn't want one of the girls here to find out he's got a small..." she held her hands out parallel to one another, a few inches apart.

Anastasia giggled, her laugh sounding like chimes. Violet laughed out loud, deep and throaty. "Pity, I was working on that," Violet bragged. "We made out a few times, and damn, the man could kiss! And those arms. Those big strong arms around you just made you feel like *ALL* woman." She waggled her eyebrows suggestively, and Olivia giggled back at her.

"Well, now it's just the four of us, but only three guys," Anastasia pouted.

Olivia grinned. "I claim Richard. Casey's got Neil, on account of they probably have a son together. I guess that just leaves the two of you to fight over shy David."

Casey shook her head. "Now, now, 'Liv, Neil and I haven't even been on a one-on-one date. And I like Richard, too! I'm not giving up the fight so easily." Her voice was light and flirty, and she was grinning, but her eyes glinted. Then she turned back to the other two women. "But the two of you can definitely fight over David," she teased.

"Did I hear my name?" David asked, strolling into the room.

"Maybe," Olivia teased, and he grinned back sheepishly, blushing a little.

"Well, I hope you're only saying good things."

Anastasia smiled politely, but Violet gave him a very pointed once-over, and then licked her lips. "I know what to do with the shy ones," she said to the group of women in a low voice. Olivia looked delighted, Anastasia scandalized. Casey glanced at David, raised an eyebrow, and grinned.

He cleared his throat nervously. "So, uh, I've got date assignments for today!" he announced. "Violet, I'm with you, Anastasia, you've got a one-on-one with Neil, and Olivia, you've got a one-on-one with Richard." All of the women in the group looked various states of satisfied, except Casey. "Casey," he added, "these are intended to be romantic dates, so you've got kid duty for Olivia and Richard."

"Awesome!" she responded. "I'll have a nice night in with Niko, Natalie and Cassidy. It'll be his own little two-on-one, and I'll chaperone." She winked at the group.

"Aww, chica," Olivia commiserated. "It's not fair. You didn't get to go on the group date, and now you don't get to go on a one-on-one. We're all having time to form these relationships, and it feels like you're getting left behind."

Casey winked again. "Now I know why they've kept me on - someone has to be babysitter."

"No, Derek would have been better suited for that role," Olivia chided. "You're here to fight for the affections of these eligible men." She narrowed her eyes at Anastasia. "Don't get too cozy with Neil - he's probably the baby daddy, and you know when they get a one-on-one they're gonna be fast at work making baby number two!"

Anastasia narrowed her eyes and pinched her lips together in annoyance. Before she could respond, though, Casey jumped in. "Don't get too comfortable, yourself, 'Liv," she leaned in and winked. "Maybe Richard is the guy I've got my eye on."

"Ooo, chica, don't be greedy," Olivia giggled. "Leave some of the mens for the rest of us."

With that, the group broke up, heading off to their various dates and leaving Casey to her babysitting duties for the night.

The four of them were arranged on the sectional again, watching another movie. It was Niko's turn to choose again, and he had picked Star Wars: Return of the Jedi. "All these years later, kids still love their Ewoks," Casey shook her head, as the three children cheered the appearance of the first Ewok.

"They're like big teddy bears!" Natalie explained, an adorable grin on her face.

Niko pumped his fist in the air. "Yeah, badass teddy bears that can kill you!" he exclaimed.

Cassidy turned to look at him primly. "You shouldn't say badass," she corrected him. "It's uncouth, and anyway, part of it's a naughty word."

"Aww, there's nothing wrong with a little naughty word now and again," came a voice behind them. Casey turned to look, and found a man in a cream-colored suit standing behind them. "It's Mike," he said to Casey by way of greeting.

Glancing over at the kids, Casey quickly jumped up and scurried around the couch. "Guys, hang out and watch the movie, will you? I need to talk with Mike, here, out by the pool. Come get me if you need anything." Without waiting for a reply, she grabbed him by the wrist and dragged him out the nearby double glass doors, closing them behind him. Releasing his wrist, she motioned for him to follow.

"The years have been good to you, Casey," he observed, walking behind her to a small seating area near the pool. "You look amazing. And motherhood clearly agrees with you."

She spun to face him, pausing to look him up and down. "You seem to be doing well for yourself, Mike," she answered. "Nice suit."

"After all these years - and this unexpected news - can you blame a guy for trying to make a good impression?"

"Have a seat," she invited, breathing out a broad sigh and sitting down heavily. He followed her lead, then smiled at her nervously.

"So," she began, then paused before speaking again. "I never expected to see you again. How is it that you're here?"

His smile grew. "Well, I got a phone call a week or two ago with some unexpected news. It turns out, the one that got away was making some waves with some sort of dramatic TV show moment." His face turned serious. "One of my buddies from way back - do you remember Rick?

His girlfriend watches this show called America's Favorite Couple, and they've got a deal that he'll watch it with her if she watches football with him. The Sunday ticket." He grinned briefly, then grew serious again. "Well... Rick recognized you. He remembered you, and you had a son, and the age of your son, and some sort of debate over whether or not some other guy was really his dad..."

He scooted closer to her on the small sofa. "Casey, how could you have a child and not tell me? I watched the episode later - you said on TV that you were only with that other guy for one night. You and me were together for months. You know he's probably my son." He looked down at her hands in her lap, then took them in his. "I don't understand why you never reached out to me. I know we were over, but everything would have been different if you'd told me you were having our baby. I would have been there for you. We could have tried to make things work."

Casey shook her head, but didn't pull her hands away. "But that's just it, Mike. That's exactly why I didn't reach out to you. We were over. I didn't want to be with someone who only wanted to be with me because I was having a baby." Then she did gently remove her hands. "And I'm not saying this to be hurtful, but I kept hoping I'd hear from Neil. I really wanted to see how things could be with him. You were really the last thing on my mind."

Mike laid a hand over his heart and grinned disarmingly. "Ouch! You really know where to hit a man."

"Sorry," Casey responded, but she was able to smile because his joke had broken the tension.

"Look, all of that is ancient history," Mike waved it off. "I'm only bringing it up because I want you to know that I would have wanted to be there for you. For him. And that's why I'm here now." Casey raised an eyebrow, inquiring. "I also gave a sample for the paternity test. There's a chance - and I believe it's a good chance - that he's my son. I want to know, and I think he deserves to know, too."

"What?" Casey asked, incredulous.

"Yeah." He scooted closer, taking her face in his hand. "But there's another reason I'm here, Casey. You." He leaned in and gently kissed her, the kiss stretching for a moment, two. "I always wondered what might have been. And now I'm here to find out if there's a chance for us."

She sat in front of the camera in the small room, silent. She began to speak once, twice, but then lapsed into silence again. Finally, she began, her gaze unfocused.

"My mind is reeling right now," Casey shook her head. "I haven't thought of Mike in so long. And all of a sudden, here he is." She focused on the camera lens. "And he is hot. I'll admit it - he's aged well. And it's nice to hear he has become a successful businessman. It's flattering that he wants to provide for Niko, and I guess it's understandable since he believes he missed out on so many years of his son's life."

She shook her head again, and gazed off into the distance. "Still, I believe that Neil is Nicholas's father. I always have, and I still do. I guess the paternity test will tell us all, but until then, the three of us are going to spend the next several weeks wondering..."

She looked back at the camera. "I have a feeling that the others are not going to be very happy about another guy being dropped into the mix at this late date."

Nathan stood before the informally-gathered group where they sat and stood around in the main living space. "I hope you all have had great dates this evening," he began, smiling and making eye contact with a few of them. "I know you're probably wondering why you've been called here, but I have an announcement to make."

Olivia looked to Casey, but she wouldn't meet the other woman's gaze. Violet and David were holding hands, and Anastasia stood possessively near Neil, but wasn't actually touching him. Richard sat off to one side with Cassidy.

"Things are a little uneven here in the house since Connor took himself out of the competition. That's why we've done something unprecedented here in the house - we've invited a new guy here to stay and see if he might be a good match for one of the remaining women."

Casey looked at the floor. Olivia and Anastasia met each other's gaze. Neil looked toward Richard. Violet and David glanced at each other, and David blushed, but neither seemed terribly concerned.

"Let me introduce Mike," Nathan said without further fanfare, holding out a hand to summon the newest member of the house. Neil's head shot around, and his eyes locked onto the newcomer. Richard noted his focus, and glanced over to Casey, who had gone pale and was holding her hands tightly clenched together in her lap.

"Mike, as it happens, is an old friend of Casey's," Nathan continued, clapping his hand on the other man's wide shoulder as he came to stand next to him. "And in the interest of full disclosure, I should tell you all - he's the other man who might be Nicholas's father."

"And the reason for Niko's absence suddenly becomes conspicuously clear," Anastasia shot in clipped tones. She reached out to grab Neil's shoulder, but he shook her off. "So what, now this becomes the Casey show? These two maybe baby-daddies compete for her affection, while the rest of us are just set dressing?"

"Look, I don't want to upset anyone," Mike offered, speaking for the first time in front of the group. "But Casey is here looking for love, on a journey that could very well result in her becoming engaged. This is an experience that could shape the rest of her life - and potentially my son's, too. And I couldn't live with myself if I didn't at least try to throw my hat in the ring. I couldn't watch the mother of my child - and a woman I once loved - fall in love with someone else without at least trying to see if she and I might be able to build a life together."

"This is bullshit," the word fell unnaturally from the normally proper Anastasia's lips. "I am here to find love, but how am I supposed to do that if two of the guys are competing for one woman's hand? And what man in his right mind is going to turn his back on the mother of his child on national television? Neither of these guys is going to seriously give the rest of us a chance. This is bullshit."

The normally quiet Richard spoke up. "Who said it's just two of them? I'm not ready to give up on a chance to build a relationship with Casey just because these two guys spent some time with her ten years ago." Olivia's gaze darted to Richard, her mouth dropping open, but he didn't seem to notice. "I get that at least one of these guys is going to be around as the father of her son - and as a father myself, I respect that - after all, my ex is gonna be around as the mother of my daughter. But the fact that one of them may have some sort of ongoing relationship with her in the future doesn't mean that relationship has to be romantic. Maybe she'll find that with someone else."

Casey turned to look at him, color rushing into her cheeks. He smiled slightly when he met her gaze.

"Alright, then. Game on!" Mike responded, fixing Richard with a hard stare.

"This is unbelievable!" Anastasia threw her hands up in the air and stormed out of the room, her stiletto heels clicking madly against the marble floor.

"I, too, cannot believe this," Olivia added, slowly rising and following Anastasia out of the room.

"Welcome to the house," Violet grinned wickedly. David blushed, but then he smiled crookedly and squeezed her hand.

"Ok, this week's vote will go a little differently," Nathan said. "First of all, because Mike just arrived and hasn't been on any dates, he's not eligible for voting. That means you can't vote for him, and he can't be voted off. Casey, Neil, Richard and Olivia are safe due to this week's house voting results. That means the only people who are at risk of going home this week are David, Violet and Anastasia."

Nathan looked at them each in turn.

"I know things have changed here in the house in the past few weeks, but the object of the show is still for you to find love, and for one lucky couple to be voted America's Favorite Couple. So Casey, Richard, Olivia and Neil - congratulations on your progress toward this goal. It's clear that you are each forming relationships within the house that warrant further exploration, and I hope things become clearer for you in the next few weeks."

Nathan turned his attention back to the groups at large. "This is the last week we'll be voting off two people. From here on out, we'll be voting off people one by one, as relationships get more serious and we see where things are developing."

"David, Violet and Anastasia - please step forward." The three of them walked to the front, standing next to Nathan and facing the remaining members of the house. David grabbed Violet's hand, and she smiled at him. He smiled back, showing no sign of blushing.

"All right, let's find out who it's going to be." Nathan held out his hand, and a producer delivered the envelope to him. He opened it, looked over the top of the envelope and then smiled.

"I don't think this will come as a surprise to anyone, but David, Violet, the two of you are going home this week." He smiled at each of them in turn. "I think it's safe to say you don't need more time to find love, so I'm happy to consider you another success story. But, unfortunately, you will not be America's Favorite Couple. Please say your farewells." He turned to Anastasia. "Anastasia, you're safe for another week. I advise you to use this time wisely to explore whether you might be able to find love with one of the remaining people in the house." She strode back to stand next to Olivia, but refused to meet anyone's gaze.

Violet came over to hug each of the remaining women, and she stopped to whisper something to Casey when they embraced. Casey smiled broadly and chuckled, her eyes glistening with tears unshed tears. Olivia hugged her warmly, but Anastasia was stiff and perfunctory in her goodbye.

David, meanwhile, shook hands with the other men, and shared a quick hug with Neil. Then he came over to the women, smiling and shaking each of their hands in turn. When he came to Casey, he clasped her hand in both of his, and gave her a sparkling, genuine smile. "It may not make you popular with the other ladies," he said to her, loudly enough that everyone could hear. "But do what you need to do. You're here to find love, and you owe it to yourself, and your son, to leave no stone unturned. You might be surprised where you find it."

He glanced at Violet and his eyes softened, while his smile widened. She smiled back affectionately, for once no trace of vulgarity, bawdiness or slyness in her gaze. She stepped over and wrapped an arm around him. "That's right - you listen to my man." Then she pinched his ass. "Come on, sweet cheeks." He blushed, the three of them laughed, and Violet and David walked out, arms wrapped around one another.

Nathan watched them go, smiling, and then turned back to the group. His face turned serious. "Ok. Now that there are so few of you, the stakes are higher than ever. So this next week is when things really start to change. There will be no more group dates - only two-on-ones and one-on-ones. This will also be our last week in the mansion. After this week, we'll be visiting hometowns to meet your families and see what day-to-day life will be like, and the following week will start our exotic fantasy dates. So head back to your rooms, get some rest, and prepare for an intense few weeks."

CHAPTER FOUR

Week Seven

"Today there will be two two-one-one dates, and then the rest of the week we've got one-on-one dates planned." Nathan looked around at them. "I'll give you today's date announcement, but for the rest of the week, you'll find a card slid under your door in the mornings that will tell you your date plans." His face was stern. "This is when things get serious, people, so I urge you to use your time wisely and really explore your feelings. Make every moment count, and try not to worry too much about whether you might be hurting someone's feelings. You don't want to miss out on a relationship that could be the one that lasts for the rest of your life because you're worried about someone getting their feelings hurt by rejection."

He held up a sealed envelope. "So here's today's date."

Nathan made a show of opening the envelope and looking at the card it contained for a long moment.

"Alright. The first two-on-one date will be Richard, Olivia and Casey. You three will be taking your kids to an amusement park that we've rented for the day, where you can enjoy all the rides and games without any waiting in line. It should be a fun day." He smiled.

Casey and Olivia conspicuously avoided looking at one another. Richard grinned, but he looked mildly uncomfortable. Nathan turned his attention to the other three.

"The other two-on-one date will be Neil, Mike and Anastasia. You three will enjoy the morning and afternoon at an ice rink. You'll be figure skating - and playing ice hockey - so there's something for everyone. And we've invited a few people to come be spectators, and maybe make life a little interesting for you."

Neil looked annoyed, but Anastasia smiled. Mike looked over at Casey, a wistful expression on his face.

"Alright, everyone - have a great day!"

As the three parents headed back toward their rooms to pack last-minute bags and collect their kids, Casey put out her hands to stop them. She gently grabbed their arms. Richard stopped, turned and looked at her, but Olivia shrugged her off, making an annoyed face.

"Look, before we spend the day with our kids, I think the three of us need to address the elephant in the room," Casey began. When Olivia started to move off again, Casey called out after her. "Olivia, please, stop and talk for a moment."

Olivia whirled to face her. "You want me to talk? Ok. I talk. I tell you that I'm interested in Richard - that he's the one man here who interests me - and you can't just let me have him? Instead, you have to go and stab me in the back, even when the rest of the show has become about you with your two baby daddies?"

"That's not fair," Casey responded, her voice calm but her expression hurt. "You never bothered to ask me if I liked Richard at all - just announced that you were going to 'make him like you' - or however you put it."

"Ladies, please, calm down," Richard interjected. "I'm flattered that you're both interested in me, I really am, but honestly, I think I'm part of the problem here."

Olivia spun to face him. "Oh, you think you're part of the problem? Yes, you are! Why couldn't you leave this crazy chica alone to deal with her two baby daddies - you had to go and put your nose in. But I am right here, and I am falling for you, and you don't even see me."

"Now, Olivia, I'm sorry you feel that way," he stepped toward her, his voice softening. "And I never said that I don't see you, or don't have feelings for you -"

"Just stop," Olivia shook her head at him, but the ferocity had gone out of her tone. "I can see the writing is on the wall. Let us not fight, and just have a good day with our kids, no?"

"That's all I want," Casey said. Olivia turned her head to look at her, and her eyes narrowed, but she had no quick rejoinder.

Finally, Olivia sighed. "Then let us go have a good day."

Predictably, the day at the amusement park was heartily approved by the kids. Cassidy was a little fussy at first about mussing her hair, but after a little good-natured ribbing from her dad, she loosened up enough to ride every ride. Niko wasn't quite tall enough for the biggest roller coasters, so Casey kept him and Natalie company while Richard, Olivia and Cassidy rode some of the larger rides.

"Don't worry, kiddo," Casey said to him at one point, when he was watching the others ride a roller coaster that went upside down seven times. "Your turn will come. I promise I'll bring you back here when you're a little older, and we'll ride every last one of these things."

"Will dad come with us?" Niko asked.

Casey frowned. "I don't know yet what our life is going to look like down the road, Niko," she tried to explain. "I don't know whether your dad will be a big part of your life, or whether he'll only see you sometimes, like on some weekends or special occasions." She knelt down in front of him. "But I know, however often you'll see him, your dad will be proud of you, and he'd want to be there for fun stuff like riding all the big roller coasters.

She pulled Niko to sit down beside her, then glanced over to where Natalie was playing a game on her mom's phone. "How would you feel if Richard was around all the time, and if he came with us when we come back to ride the big roller coasters?" she asked Niko more quietly.

Niko scuffed his shoes on the ground. "I guess he's ok," he finally conceded. "Does that mean Cassidy would be there, too?"

Casey nodded. "She might not be there all the time, but yeah, if Richard was around a lot, Cassidy would be, too."

"I guess that would be ok," Niko allowed, still not looking up at her. "She's kinda prissy, but it's nice to have another kid around all the time. And she's smart and knows lots of stuff, so I might be able to learn some things from her."

Casey smiled broadly, relieved. "I'm glad to hear it. And you're wise to recognize a smart woman when you meet her, and to not be intimidated by her."

"What's intimidated?" Niko asked, stumbling a little over the word.

"Ahh," Casey frowned. "It's kinda like being afraid of her, but in this case it's not exactly her you're afraid of. More like being afraid of what she can do." She gave him a lopsided smile. "Never be afraid of smart women, Niko," she advised. "They can teach you a lot, and sometimes they need a friend more than you realize."

"Ok, mom," he said, his tone clearly placating. "Can we find something I can ride next?"

They were pouring over the park map together when the others returned from the ride. Cassidy skipped ahead, a broad grin on her face. "That was awesome!"

Niko smiled back. "Cool! I can't wait to ride it when I'm tall enough."

Olivia and Richard strolled after her, Olivia laughing expansively and clinging onto Richard's arm. He smiled indulgently, but made a beeline to where Casey and Nicholas were still holding the map.

"Niko wanted to find something he can ride next, so I told him we'd try this roller coaster," she pointed at the map.

"Sounds good, champ!" Richard mussed his hair. "Let's get to it!" As the group strolled in the direction of the next roller coaster, Richard casually threw his arm around Casey's shoulders. Olivia huffed, stormed a few steps ahead and took Natalie's hand. Casey ignored them, sliding an arm around Richard's waist and smiling up at him.

"Are you having a good day?" he asked softly, so as not to upset Olivia further.

"I am now," Casey answered, her grin turning shy. Then she glanced to the kids ahead, Niko talking animatedly with Cassidy, and Natalie and her mother walking quietly hand-in-hand. "Niko's having a lot of fun, too, but he's a little disappointed that he isn't tall enough to ride the really big rollercoasters. I promised I'd bring him back after he grows a little so he can ride everything in the park."

"That sounds like a lot of fun," Richard said. Then he leaned toward her ear and whispered, his breath tickling the side of her face. "I'm really looking forward to coming back here with you, just the four of us."

Casey shivered as goosebumps sprang up on her bare arms. She stopped walking for a moment, and Richard paused with her as she stared up into his eyes. "I really wish I could kiss you right now," she confessed, her voice low.

He smiled broadly, wrapping his strong arms around her and leaning in. "Good," he answered softly, his breath brushing across her cheek.

"Come on, mom, hurry up!" Niko shouted, breaking the moment. Casey grinned ruefully and started walking again, grabbing Richard's hand. Neither of them noticed Olivia watching them, her lips compressed into a thin line.

"Look out for that one," Vince's voice piped into her ear. "Hell hath no fury, and all that."

As the sun started its final descent and the shadows began to grow long, the producers gathered them to the main gate and handed Richard a sealed envelope. Looking around at the gathered group, he opened the envelope and read aloud.

"We hope you've enjoyed a magical day here at Six Flags Magic Mountain." Niko cheered, and Richard smiled indulgently at him before resuming his reading. "It's time for the kids to go home and get some rest, but we've got a romantic evening planned for the grown-ups. You'll enjoy a gourmet picnic at the top of Sky Tower, and then we've arranged for you to dance under the stars at a a very special private concert. But there's one catch, Richard - you'll have to pick which of the ladies is staying with you for a romantic evening, and which one is going home with the kids."

Olivia's face fell when she heard the last line of the card. Casey, on the other hand, was trying not to look too excited, forcing her face to stillness although she was unable to mute the sparkle in her eyes. Richard took a long look at each of them before speaking. "Right about now, I'm put in mind of what Nathan said about taking things seriously this week. I really hate to hurt anyone's feelings, but I need to make a decision that will help me really see where my feelings are for one of these ladies, so I'm going to have to ask Casey to spend the evening. I'm really sorry, Olivia."

She held her hand up to his face in the old 'talk to the hand' gesture, and turned away. "Come along, Natalie," she said to her daughter, grabbing her hand and walking her toward the main gates of the park, where a van waited to take them back to the mansion.

Casey stared after her, biting her lower lip, but she made no move to follow. Instead, she stepped over and hugged Nicholas, bending down to face him eye-to-eye. "Niko, I'm going to stay here with Richard, now, while you and the others head back to the house. You know who to ask if you need anything, but I need you to keep Cassidy company, because she'll be going back, too, while her dad stays here." She tucked her hair behind her ear, dragging it out of his face as he sputtered at her. She ignored his dramatics and continued. "After dinner, I want you to brush your teeth, and you know when bedtime is. Don't stay up too late, or I'll know! And only one hour of screen time. You've had a busy day, and you need to get some rest."

"Ok, mom," Nicholas answered, looking away, refusing to meet her eyes. "I'm not a little kid. I know the rules."

She smiled at him. "You're right. And I know I can rely on you to follow them, right, kiddo?" She winked, and he grinned back, finally turning to face her again. "I doubt I'll make it home before your bedtime, so goodnight, Niko. We'll read two chapters tomorrow before bed to make it up to you."

"It's fine, mom," he complained, making a shooing motion at her. "I'm not a baby. Go have fun. I'll be fine."

Richard was having a similar conversation with Cassidy, but he seemed a lot more laid back about it. She hugged him, and then she and Niko walked off toward where Olivia and Natalie had vanished. A couple of production staffers met them at the front gates and walked toward the car with them.

Richard turned to look at her. "Milady?" he asked, holding out his arm for her.

"Why, thank you," she grinned, grabbing his arm and heading toward the main park.

She glanced over her shoulder where the kids had vanished. "I know he's only just turned nine, but I can already start to see the teenager in him. I'll admit, I'm a little terrified. Where is my baby going? Is he going to turn into one of those surly, stinky gangly things that can't be bothered to spend time with mom?" Richard laughed, and she grinned ruefully. "Well, don't you worry about Cassidy growing up?"

His smile turned wistful. "What parent doesn't? You just have to trust that you've raised them right, and hope your relationship is good enough that they'll come to you if something goes wrong. But honestly, I got lucky with Cassidy - that girl practically raises herself. Although I wish she wasn't quite so sophisticated - her mom's doing, unfortunately."

Casey smiled. "She is more like a small adult than a kid, really. Sometimes I think she'd dress better than I do, if she were a little older. Don't you worry about boys?"

He wrinkled his nose in a charming smile. "Every day of my life. I remember what it was like to be a boy. But Cassidy's too busy and too proper to worry much about boys. I think she'll be a late bloomer in the romance department - and maybe by then she'll have her law degree and a wonderful job, and I won't have to worry about getting a knocked-up daughter through high school."

Casey burst out laughing. "If you think she'll wait until she graduates law school to start thinking about a relationship, you're delusional. Those hormones are almost as bad for girls as they are for boys. Your proper little girl is going to be just as bad as the rest of us, when her time comes. Better start getting real, daddy, and think of a way to talk to her about the hard stuff before it gets too late."

His face turned sober. "Now why do you have to go making me think about that? Here I was busy congratulating myself for having such a good girl. The last thing I want is to have to think about her with some boy panting after her - and her not keeping him at arm's bay!"

Casey grinned apologetically. "Sorry. You've probably got a little time yet, if it's any consolation. Enjoy it while she's still your little girl, and worry about the rest later."

Vince's voice broke into their shared moment. "Alright, enough parent-to-parent bonding, you two - it's time to turn on the romance. Casey, you're going to the left, and Richard will be going to the right - we've got dressing rooms set up where you can change into something more appropriate for an adult dinner date. Get ready for things to get steamy!"

Casey blushed, even though Richard couldn't hear Vince's teasing. He had a distant look on his face, and a small smile - she could only assume he was getting his own instructions from his handler. She gave him a little wave, and he reached out to grab her hand before she could step away. Without speaking, he brought the back of her hand gently to his lips, his warm breath lingering over it as he gave it a soft kiss. His gaze burned into hers, and the slight smile on his face promised a more serious evening ahead. He gave a slight bow over her hand, and then released it, turning away toward his distant dressing room.

Casey took a deep breath as she gazed after him. "Yikes," she said under her breath.

"I know, right?" Vince said in her ear. "The man has game. The fans *love* him. If you don't end up with him at the end of all this, I'll bet money he'll be back next year. He's too good to let go without a match."

When the two of them met up again at the top of the Sky Tower, they had both changed to evening clothes. Casey was wearing a dark blue, sleeveless blouse with a silver necklace, and a black asymmetrical skirt that ended mid-thigh. She had a matching black wrap slung around her shoulders, and her hair was styled into an elaborate updo, complete with silver ornaments woven into her long locks.

Richard was wearing a pair of dark slacks, shiny black dress shoes and a beautifully tailored dark gray dress shirt. It had black threads running through it, and it seemed to shimmer when he moved. The top four buttons were open, giving him a laid-back, sexy vibe.

"Just in time for sunset," he observed, holding his hand out for hers. She smiled and took his hand, and they walked together toward the wall of windows. "You look amazing, by the way."

Her smiled broadened. "Thank you. I figured it's my first chance to really enjoy one of these amazing romantic evenings, the least I can do is look the part."

He chuckled. "You haven't been missing much. But I think, tonight, things are about to change." He twirled her into his embrace and leaned his face toward hers. "Now if I recall correctly," he said softly, his breath mingling with hers and smelling sweetly of spearmint. "You were saying something earlier about kissing?"

His lips closed in, warm and soft against hers, in a kiss that started slowly but promised more. Her arms slipped around his neck as the kiss deepened. The two of them drew closer, Richard pressing the length of his body against her. One of her hands crept into his hair, her fingers closing into a fist as the kiss grew more intense. A long moment later, they broke apart, Casey retreating a few inches to gaze into Richard's face. "You're really good at that," she observed breathlessly.

"It's about time you figured that out," he murmured, smiling slightly, before bridging the gap between them once more.

Eventually, Casey freed herself, taking a few deep breaths. "As much as I'm enjoying this, we have all night. Let's not miss the sunset entirely."

He grinned ruefully. "Sorry about that," he apologized, turning toward the glorious reds, pinks, oranges and yellows blazing across the sky. He loosened the embrace, but didn't let her go, holding her as they looked toward the sunset. "I've just been waiting a while to do that, and once you got me started, I didn't want to stop again."

She smiled as she nestled her head against his chest. "I can relate."

They fell silent as the sunset burned brighter, the colors changing and deepening - and then slowly fading. Minutes passed as they held each other into the deepening gloom.

"That was a really beautiful moment," Casey finally broke the silence.

"And I feel really fortunate to have been here and shared it with you."

It had grown too dark to see Richard's face, but his voice was light. "That's one of the things I love about you. How you're so good at being in the moment, recognizing when it's good, and being grateful for it. Living a life of mindful gratitude is a great way to be happy - and to show your son how he should approach life, too."

"Listen to you," she teased. "'Living a life of mindful gratitude.' You sound like my old shrink."

He drew away slightly. "I can't wait to spend the night learning more about you, but maybe we should find a little more light?" He took her hand, and led her toward the romantic candlelit picnic waiting for them on the other side of the Sky Tower. The whole scene was illuminated by low ambient lighting, to make it possible for the cameras to film the date, but the candles were everywhere and the scene was very romantic. Through the windows, lights twinkled throughout the park and beyond as twilight gave way to darkness.

Casey settled onto the thick nest of blankets, snuggling into a massive pile of pillows, and kicked off her heels, tucking her bare feet under her. Richard grinned and did the same, sliding off his shiny dress shoes and reclining into the pile of pillows, gazing at her. "Are you hungry?" he asked, motioning to the impressive array of nibbles spread across the blanket in front of them.

"Not yet," she answered, her smile turning shy again. "A little nervous. This is the first time we've been together without the kids. Or the housemates. And you looking at me like that is giving me butterflies."

His smile was slow, easy, but intense. He reached out and laid his hand over hers, and she clasped his fingers. "Good," he said, his voice deep and husky.

"Wow," Casey babbled. "I've always sort of thought of you as solid and comfortable, kind of like a favorite old t-shirt. I had no idea you could be so..." her voice trailed off as he leaned in. "Sexy," she whispered, as his lips captured hers. Their eyes drifted shut and the kiss deepened, Richard's hand sliding over Casey's hip, his other snaking into her hair as he held her face. Her hands moved of their own volition, one sliding up to caress his neck, the other slipping around his hip and under the waistband of his slacks, her thumb coming to rest in a belt loop.

Slowly, automatically, their bodies adjusted as they moved closer together. When they finally broke the kiss, Casey panting slightly, she was lying on her back in the mass of pillows, Richard's solid chest on top of her trapping her in place. "I'm glad you find me sexy," Richard whispered to her. "Because you are about the most gorgeous woman I've ever met, and I'd love to get you in bed for a week and make sure you never want to leave again."

Casey shuddered, drawing in a deep breath. With a lazy grin, Richard released her, sliding back a few inches to recline once again in the nest of pillows, facing her. His left hand never left her waist, though, and her right hand slid along his shoulder and down his arm to rest on his bicep as she rolled toward him.

"Make no mistake, I'll get you back for that," Casey promised, her voice throaty and a mischievous grin on her face. "You've just caught me a little off guard is all. It's just taken me a minute to go from thinking of you as 'Cassidy's dad and nice guy Richard' to 'sexy ladykiller Richard.'" Her hand squeezed his bicep. "But two can play at that game, and I'll get you when you're not expecting it."

He grinned, lowering his face to hers and nibbling her earlobe. "I'm counting on it," he whispered into her ear, making her shiver.

Casey's head fell back, and Richard traced along the line of her neck with his fingertips before taking a deep breath and visibly pulling himself together.

"I really don't mean to get ahead of myself," he told her, drawing away slightly, but his voice was still several octaves lower than usual. "But you do things to me, woman," he growled, grinning ruefully.

She took a deep breath and situated herself a little more vertically, then turned to face him.

"So," he began, after she'd settled again. "Have you given much thought to having more kids?"

Casey snorted, raising an eyebrow. "Dive right in, why don't you?"

"I'm asking this," Richard continued, his hand on her waist sliding a little further and giving a squeeze. "Because I think I'd love to have a kid or three with you."

Her jaw dropped. "You do know we each have a child already, right?"

"Mhmm," he confirmed, leaning close to breathe in the scent of her hair, but then drawing back again. "I've always been partial to a handful of kids, but things didn't work out that way with my ex. But the idea of making some babies with you sounds really good to me." He grinned again, his eyes hooded.

"Hold on there, cowboy," Casey cautioned, her tone wry but her expression a little less relaxed. "Getting a little ahead of yourself again, aren't you?"

He leaned back and slid his hand to a more family-friendly spot on her waist. "I don't mean right this minute," he teased her, toning the sexy down a few notches. "But in general. What do you think of the idea of having more kids?"

She looked down for a moment, then looked back up at him. "I'm not really sure. Niko came as a bit of a surprise. We've made the best of it, and I wouldn't undo any of it for a moment - he's been such a blessing in my life - but I haven't really been in a serious enough relationship to contemplate the idea of more children."

"Well, I'd like you to contemplate it," Richard said gently. "I'm not saying it's a deal-breaker - if you never wanted to have another child again, I'm sure you, me, Nicholas and Cassidy would make a wonderful little family." Casey's face grew more serious. "I know," he continued before she could speak. "You haven't said you want to be with me, and we don't know if it would work - all that is still ahead of us. But I'd like you to think about what life would be like, if it was the four of us. What would that look like to you? What would you want for us?"

She smiled a little sadly. "What would Cassidy think of the idea, do you think?" she asked. "Would she tolerate having me around?"

Richard grinned a little sheepishly. "Well, as a matter of fact, I think we'd have some friction for a while." He shook his head. "She's a good girl, but I know in her heart of hearts, she's always secretly hoped that me and her momma would get back together. I've dated some, but I think if she saw me in a serious relationship with another woman, it would make her unhappy at first."

Casey tilted her head. "Have you talked about it? Getting back together with her mother?"

"No, ma'am," Richard answered immediately. "I forget that you don't know this already. Her momma up and left us when Cassidy was only two years old. She just went out one day and never came back." His accent got folksier for a moment as he slipped into what was clearly an often-told story. His expression was so sad, though, that Casey couldn't help but run a hand gently down his face.

"I'm so sorry."

"Naw, don't be," he smiled sadly. "I'm not sad for me. I got over that a long time ago. But to this day, I don't understand how she could just walk out on her little baby daughter like that. Cassidy was the sweetest little thing, and she had nothing but love for her momma."

"I didn't know if I would ever hear from her again, and I didn't - not for years. By then, me and Cassidy had learned to get along without her. But when Cassidy was six, I finally heard from her momma again, asking for a divorce. She was ready to get married to some other man, you see." His sad smile had turned wry. "I told her no deal unless she'd come see one of Cassidy's ballet recitals. She showed up, saw her little girl again, and realized what she'd been missing. I agreed to the divorce, and she agreed to be a regular part of Cassidy's life."

He shook his head. "Things haven't always been easy. But now we've got a nice little routine figured out. She takes Cassidy one weekend a month, and one night a week. Then, one other night per week, she comes to us and spends the evening with Cassidy at our house. So the girls spend a few hours together twice a week, and then they have their one weekend a month. Lavinia hasn't asked for more than that, and I haven't offered." His voice had grown fierce.

"Lavinia, eh?" Casey teased. "With a name like that, you should have known better!"

He chuckled. "Lavinia is a proper Southern Belle, that's for sure. She's won beauty pageants and runs some sort of local women's society. But she was always so concerned at keeping up appearances, instead of actually living. She's an event planner, now," he added. "And husband number two did stick, but I half think that's just because she couldn't bear the scandal of another separation. She hasn't had any more kids, and I don't see any on the horizon. I think Cassidy's going to be the only chance she has at motherhood." He shook his head. "Hell, maybe that's what drove her away - maybe motherhood didn't agree with her. I never did ask. I figured all of that was in the past, and I was more concerned about giving my daughter her mother back than making accusations or dragging up ancient history."

Casey nodded. "That's very wise - and very brave - of you. Neil didn't know about Nicholas, and we only spent a very short time together, but even so, I couldn't resist asking him what happened. It should have all been about Niko, I know, but I just had to have an explanation."

"Did it make you feel better?"

"Yes, and no. Yes, I felt validated that I hadn't imagined our connection, and hadn't been crazy thinking he would have called me again. But I also felt a deep regret for what might have been, knowing he was just as interested as I was in seeing where things might go."

"And now?" Richard asked quietly, his voice low. His eyes were sad, as though he was afraid of the answer.

Casey shook her head. "I wish I could tell you what you want to hear, but the truth is I don't know. I haven't had a chance to spend any time with him. I have no idea if the connection we once had is still there, or if it was bad timing and just never meant to be."

Richard's face had fallen, and Casey reached out to caress it. "But that doesn't mean that what you and I have isn't special. What I feel for you is very real, and it may very well be that once I spend some time with him, I can let it go, and you and I can be free to move forward together with no shadow hanging over us."

"Well," Richard said briskly, not meeting her gaze. "I suppose I shouldn't have expected anything else. You need to do what you need to do, and I need to give you the space to do it." He distanced himself from her, then sat up and reached out to the food spread before them. "Let's not let this delicious-looking spread go to waste."

Casey sat up and scooted close to him, resting her hand on his knee. "Richard," she said softly, waiting until he turned to look at her. "We were having an amazing evening. Let's not let this conversation ruin it."

He smiled. "Don't you worry, sweet thing," his smile turned to a grin. "I have no intention of wasting any time I get to spend with you. If this is all we get, I intend to make the most of it." He held out a cracker with cheese that he'd assembled, and waited for her to take a bite. Then, he leaned in and licked the crumbs off her lips, his eyes dancing.

The rest of the night passed in a blur; or more accurately, a montage of carefully cut scenes. They nibbled at the picnic, feeding each other, giggling and kissing a lot. They shared a bottle of champaign. When they'd had enough of the food, they took their glasses and wandered down to the park, strolling hand-in-hand under the twinkling lights until they found themselves in front of a small stage. While they stood nearby, sipping champagne and wondering who they'd see, Thomas Rhett strolled onto the stage with his guitar. Sparing them a grin for their loud cheers, he launched into some of his most popular tunes, and Casey and Richard passed off their champagne glasses to a nearby production assistant and started dancing.

His concert ended with the very apt "Die a Happy Man." Richard held Casey close, his head tilted down to her hair, as they swayed in time with the music. He sang along with the last chorus, quietly, his lips near her ear: "Oh if all I got is your hand in my hand... baby I could die a happy man."

The two kissed as Rhett smiled on the stage and the lights dimmed, leaving their silhouettes lost in the dusk.

The sun shined brightly down on them as Casey double-checked Nicholas's lifejacket for the third time, then patted his chest and said "Ok, my man - you're all set!"

He cheered and ran toward the staging area, where Mike was waiting in a pair of swim trunks, holding three giant river rafting tubes in the water.

"Are you sure it's safe for a kid his age?" Casey asked the rafting consultant.

"This time of year is usually peak for whitewater tubing on the Kern, but this year, flow rates are very low due to low snowfall this past winter. So it'll be more of a lazy float than an action-packed tubing adventure, but I wouldn't hesitate to send a kid down even as young as six." He smiled reassuringly. "So yeah - it's safe. Just keep an eye on him and make sure you guys don't get separated."

Casey nodded. "Ok. Let's do this!" She strode over to where the guys waited, all business. Her rich magenta bikini showed off her tanned skin to good advantage, and her chestnut hair was pulled back into a tidy bun.

She smiled as she walked up to the two of them, as Mike's well cared-for physique made itself very apparent. His arms bulged with muscles, and his chest, abs and back were equally ripped. His musculature was surprisingly pleasing; he wasn't so muscle-bound that it seemed he used steroids or was some kind of mindless gym-monkey, but he was clearly a weightlifter - not a cardio kind of guy. His tan showed that either he spent a lot of time in the sun, or was vain enough to visit tanning beds regularly.

"Ready?" he asked as she walked up. Niko jumped up and down, unable to contain his excitement.

"Let's go!" she exclaimed as she ran the last few steps, grabbed a tube and jumped into the river, landing across the tube on her stomach. Grinning, she flipped over, settling in and waving.

Niko tried to imitate her, but he tripped along the way. Fortunately, he fell into the large tube as it slipped into the water.

"Easy, there, little man," Mike cautioned, grabbing Nicholas and settling him properly into the tube. Niko laughed and sputtered, but it was clear he wasn't distressed - he was already having a great time. Once Niko was situated, Mike gave him a little shove to send him cruising down the river, catching up to where Casey slowly paddled in place to wait for the two of them. Then, Mike launched himself onto the last tube with a shove, paddling to catch up with them. When he was more-or-less even with them, he flipped over until the three were lazily floating down the river together.

Niko squealed and splashed water everywhere, flopping around and breaking the stillness with his happy chaos. Casey smiled indulgently, keeping a close eye on him and lazily dipping her hands and feet in the water now and again. She tipped back her face to feel the sun on it, and her smile grew wider.

Suddenly, Mike splashed them with a powerful kick, spraying water everywhere and breaking Casey's moment of Zen. Niko yelled delightedly, flipping around so he could kick a great volume of water at Mike, and then he began to splash at Casey with his flailing hand.

"Oh, you asked for it, boyos," Casey warned, first sending a few big bow waves at Niko, then slipping down through her tube and vanishing.

"Where did she go?" Niko wondered aloud, his kicking slowing as he looked for his mom.

Mike figured it out a moment too late, starting to turn as Casey popped up from the water next to him, using her momentum to flip his tube over and dump him unceremoniously into the river. "I'm Queen of the Tube!" she announced, crawling onto Mike's captured tube as Niko cheered her on. Before Mike could retaliate, she paddled quickly away, catching Niko and giving him a high five as they watched Mike warily swam toward Casey's abandoned tube.

"I see how it is," he griped, as he reached the tube and crawled out of the river onto it. "Two against one!"

Casey grinned. "Well, we've been two peas in a pod long enough, it's just second nature by now." As he turned a grumpy expression on her, the smile faded. "Sorry - I guess two against one isn't very nice."

"Especially when the third person would rather have been working with you than against you - or maybe the poor bugger was floating along all alone without even knowing you were out there," he shot pointedly.

Casey nodded contritely. "You're right." She turned to Niko. "When someone tells you they feel left out, it's important to listen to them and try to find a way to include them. You might not always be able to do that, but if you can, you should try. Otherwise, that person might not want to hang out with you anymore, or might have their feelings hurt - or might even think you're being a bully if you're having fun at their expense."

She twisted back around to face Mike again. "I'm sorry, Mike. I know I might end up owing you a much bigger apology, depending on how things turn out, but I really am sorry."

The irritation smoothed out of his face. "Aww, I know. I didn't mean to come down so hard. I guess I'm still upset about..." He looked at Niko. "Coming into everything so late. I wish I could have been here from the start, and I'm unhappy because I feel that option was taken out of my hands without even realizing there *was* an option..." He chuckled. "Ok, enough with all this vague coded talk. Let's just have fun!" He splashed Niko without warning, who squealed and started splashing back.

They spent the rest of the morning tubing down the river, and then they stopped to have lunch in a broad meadow. The producers had provided them with an ample picnic lunch, along with a frisbee, so they ate and played and napped until late afternoon. Then they took to the river for another short paddle, and all too soon they had arrived at the landing site and it was time for Niko to go home. Casey would be staying for the evening portion of the date with Mike.

When Mike and Casey met up again, they were both dressed in comfortable clothes for a cool evening outside. Mike wore a pair of black workout pants, a gym shirt and a hoodie, with a pair of sneakers. It was the most casual Casey had seen him - aside from the swim trunks. Casey was similarly dressed, in a pair of jeans, hiking boots, a long-sleeved top and a light jacket. Her hair was pulled back into two braids.

"Hey," Mike greeted her, his hands in his pockets.

"Hey," she answered, giving him a quick peck on the cheek.

"Oh, so that's how it is, hey?" he teased, smirking at her. "Polite strangers or occasional acquaintances?"

"You started it by greeting me with your hands in your pockets!" she shot back, sticking her tongue out at him.

He burst out laughing. "I won't make that mistake again," he retorted, but his laughter didn't stop.

"What?" she finally asked.

"You, with your hair in pigtails, sticking your tongue out at me," Mike answered, his eyes sparkling. "You look like a twelve-year-old girl."

"Oho." She sat down on a log by the fire, pouting playfully, foregoing the cozy nest of blankets and pillows just a few feet away.

"Aww, come on, don't be like that," Mike wheedled, sitting on a log a few feet away. "It was just funny and cute. I didn't mean anything by it."

She turned to look at him, tilting her head, her expression growing serious. "Why did you come here, Mike? Really?"

He sighed, his shoulders slumping. "I told you already."

She shook her head. "No. I mean why are you here? Why aren't you at home, with a wife, tending to your business? Some sort of perfect life? How did you get here?"

He stared into the fire for a long time before answering. "I know we said it was mutual, and maybe I even believed it at the time, but when you and me broke up, it hit me hard. I wasn't really sure why we were doing it. I guess I just assumed we wanted different things, and maybe I wanted to sow some more wild oats before I settled down. But afterward, whenever I thought about what I wanted in my life, your face kept popping up."

She exhaled softly, scooting to face him. "I had no idea, Mike. You seemed pretty willing to end things when it all went down. I just assumed you weren't that serious about us, or you had wanted out for a while but just hadn't gotten around to ending it yourself."

He shrugged. "I don't know, really. I bounced around a lot after that. Went through a bunch of women. I ended up working at three different companies in under a year. Nothing really seemed to stick; I was always looking for something else. Something I didn't have." He looked up at her. "When I met Elena, two years after we split up, I thought she might have been what I was waiting for. She was everything; a breath of fresh air, reason to get up in the morning, something to look forward to at the end of the day. It was because I wanted to be a better man for her that I finally straightened out my life. Did a real, proper job search. Found someplace I could stick; a place where I could make a contribution, and somewhere that had a good career track that appealed to me. We rented an apartment together; my first time living with a woman. Two years later, we got married and bought a condo together. Everything seemed to be on track."

He grew silent. The pause stretched between them. Casey leaned toward him, willing him to go on. The fire crackled noisily nearby as she waited to hear what came next.

"And then. I don't know - I just woke up one morning and realized that something was still missing. I couldn't say what it was. I kept thinking if only I could figure it out, I could buy it or learn it or... something. And then my life would be perfect. I wouldn't have to mess with the good thing we had going."

He sighed, and shook his head. "But... I never could figure it out. It just started eating away at me. I didn't even realize it, but it was poisoning my relationship. Elena told me later that I started to grow distant, started to spend more time at work, going in earlier and coming home later. And that when I was home, I was silent and looming. Every now and again, I would seem to 'wake up and come alive,' giving her a glimpse of the man she married, but it always vanished again as I continued to obsess over what I was missing."

"She was a good woman. She put up with that for years. She tried to engage me; tried to figure out what was happening, but I couldn't articulate it. At least, not in a way she could understand. We tried counseling, but she thought I was chasing something that wasn't real. That I was obsessed with something that didn't exist. Whatever I was looking for was all in my head; I could just make a conscious decision to stop looking and everything would go back to normal. But it never did."

"It wasn't until she served me with the divorce papers that I realized how serious things had gotten. Or how long it had been going on. I seemed to wake up, but it was too late for my marriage. I had damaged our relationship beyond repair. I started going to counseling on my own, to try to figure out what had happened. My therapist believed that maybe I had sabotaged things on purpose, because they were too perfect. Or maybe I was just bored. But I still believe I was looking for something I didn't have. I just don't know what that was."

He fixed her with his gaze. "Once I found out about you and Nicholas... I thought maybe what I'd been looking for was you."

She sighed, and her face fell as she looked at him. "Mike, I don't believe that. Not for a moment. I genuinely believe that Neil is Nicholas's father, but even if he isn't - there isn't some mystical tie between you and him, or you and me. It's all just..." She shrugged. "Relationships. Being there. Getting to know each other. Learning to love each other. There's no mystical, spiritual connection that transcends all that."

He tilted his head at her. "What if I disagree?"

She shrugged again. "Then... you're wrong?"

He grinned at her. "If it comforts you to believe that, go ahead. I learned through years of marriage that sometimes the wife is right. Or at least, has to believe she's right for the sake of marital happiness."

"Hey, now," she complained, reaching over to smack his knee playfully. He grabbed her wrist and tugged, sending her sprawling toward him, but before she could trip, he caught her, balancing her on his knee. Their mirth faded as they stared at one another across the inches separating them. Carefully, as though she were a timid bird that might take wing if she were startled, he slipped his hand behind her head and gently caressed her neck, sending shivers down her spine. Before she could recover, he leaned in and captured her lips in his, the kiss firm and passionate. Casey gave in to it, her hands sliding up to rest against his chest as his other arm wrapped around her, pulling her closer.

When he finally released her, she drew back as far as he would let her, taking a deep breath.

"Tell me that didn't mean anything to you," he probed.

She sighed. "That was never our problem, Mike. We were always good at that part."

"Well, then, where do you think we went wrong?" he asked her gently. Before she could answer, he stood, shifting one arm under her knees and tightening his grip on the arm around her back, and carried her lightly to the nest of pillows and blankets a few feet from the flickering flames. He laid her down gently, reclining next to her and pulling a blanket up over them. "You looked cold," he explained to the unasked question lingering in her eyes.

She snorted. "Yeah. Right. This was just an excuse to get me on my back, wasn't it, Connolly?" She grinned after she said it, though, and didn't pull away.

He grinned back. "I'm gonna plead the fifth here." His gaze grew serious again. "Anyway, you were saying? Where do you think we went wrong?"

She sighed. "We wanted different things?" she finally answered, her tone uncertain.

He shook his head at her. "Try again."

"I don't really know, Mike. It seemed the thing to do. You and I were... different. Maybe I could tell you weren't ready to settle down. Maybe I wasn't ready to settle down. Maybe we were just too young. Maybe the timing was off. I don't know."

"Exactly," he said. "Neither of us knows." He ran a finger down the bridge of her nose, then lightly traced her face. "People should be able to tell what goes wrong when they decide to break up. Everyone has a reason." He cupped her jaw in his hand. "But not us."

Without waiting for an answer, he kissed her again.

The cameras lingered on them for a moment as their kiss grew more passionate, and then faded to black.

Casey's eyes were wide as she watched the guides fit Nicholas with a harness for their zip line outing. Neil noticed her concern, leaned in, and asked quietly: "Are you ok with this? We can figure out something else to do if you don't think this is safe enough for Nicholas."

She gave him a quick smile. "No, I'm sure it'll be ok. I just can't not double check everything, even though they're the professionals." She shrugged. "As an only parent, I've just been used to taking care of everything myself over the years, and I guess it may have made me a little overprotective."

Neil glanced over at Nicholas, who was listening to the guide's instructions with wide eyes, paying close attention. "Clearly you've done a good job," he observed. "He's a great kid."

Her smile grew bittersweet. "He is. And I'm sorry you haven't been a part of things up 'til now. In the past few weeks, I've really come to see how hurtful it's been for me to have kept him to myself. I should have come looking for you a long time ago."

"I wish you had." His blue eyes were intense as he gazed at her.

She ducked her head, breaking eye contact, and then focused on her own harness. The guides proclaimed them ready to go, so they piled into a safari truck for a ride up toward the course. Niko, predictably, was enjoying himself, bouncing around in the truck and watching the scenery go by. Whenever they passed one of the zipline setups, Niko pointed them out. "Will we be going on that one?" The guides answered him cheerfully, and Neil watched the exchange, smiling indulgently. Casey watched Neil, noting the interest he was taking in Niko.

At the end of the truck ride, they had a short hike to the start of the zipline course. Niko followed eagerly behind the guides, taking in the desert scenery and chatting away to the guides. Neil followed a little further behind, a few feet ahead of Casey. After a few minutes of hiking, he slowed down so she could draw even with him, and then quietly took her hand. They didn't speak as they ascended to the start of the course - just held hands and watched Niko frolicking along ahead of them.

When they got to first zipline, they had the inevitable question of who would go first.

"I think one of us should go first, and then Niko, and then the other one of us." she said to Neil. "That way, one of us is there when Niko gets to the next spot, and one of us is here with him to help him get going."

"Ok," Neil nodded. "So would you like to go first, or should I?"

Casey looked at the zipline, then back at Neil. A wide grin crept over her face. "Would you mind terribly if I go first? It looks like a lot of fun!"

He laughed at her. "Go for it! I guess you're not gonna be one of those girls who has to be 'talked into' doing something 'scary?'"

She laughed back. "Never!" She skipped over to where the guide was ready to clip her harness in, and smiled at Niko. "Let Super Mom show you how it's done!" When the guide gave her the 'all set,' she didn't hesitate - she launched herself with a gleeful "Yippee!" Nicholas and Neil cheered her as she whooped and hollered to the end of the first zipline.

When it was Niko's turn, he followed the brave example set by his mom and took off with a loud cheer, launching himself and bouncing around on the line as he zoomed toward the next station. When Casey saw him coming, she cheered him on, shouting "Go Niko, go Niko, go!" over and over again, dancing and fist-pumping until he reached the end of the line and the guide unhooked him. When he got off the line, she grabbed him and hugged him, spinning him around. Then she sat him down carefully, with a "Whoo! You're getting too big for that, my friend."

Next, it was Neil's turn, and he came flying toward them with his arms out, a massive grin on his face as he was clearly having a great time. Casey and Niko cheered him on, and when he had stopped and gotten unhooked, Casey gave him a high five. "Good job!"

Neil laughed at her. "You know I'm not a nine-year-old, right?"

Casey put a hand on her hip and raised an eyebrow. "What would you prefer?"

He stepped close, grabbing her harness at her hips and pulling her against him. "I had something a little more like this in mind," he grinned as he leaned down and kissed her. Niko and the guides cheered, so he smiled against her mouth and ended the kiss with a flourish, spinning her around.

"And that, my friends, is how you do that." He smirked and walked over to the next station, hooking into the line. "May I go first this time?"

Casey, caught off guard by the sudden kiss and his surprising, bold, playfulness, sputtered.

"I'll take that as a yes," he grinned, then nodded to the guide. "Good to go?" he asked. The guide came over, checked his line and harness, and gave him a big smile and a thumbs up. With that, Neil took off with an exuberant "Whoop!"

Niko smiled up at his mom. "I like him."

She grinned back, her eyes sparkling. "Me, too, kiddo. Me, too."

The rest of the day passed in a whirlwind. The three of them worked their way down the zipline course, then had a picnic lunch that the production staff assembled for them not far from the entrance to Skull Canyon Zipline. They laughed easily, Neil and Niko seemed to get along splendidly, and it all seemed very casual and familiar.

"The family people are going to eat this up," Vince said in her ear at one point. "You guys make such a happy little crew - it's like you've been doing this for years. It'll be a shame if Mike turns out to be the dad. I'm not sure he's as much into Niko as he is into the idea of being a good dad and looking good in front of America."

Casey laughed at a joke Niko had made, but her smile was troubled.

"I've never been to a hot spring before," Casey said to Neil, as she pulled her robe tighter against the cool evening air and padded toward the hot pool.

"Well, there's hot springs, and there's hot springs," he answered conversationally, walking easily beside her. His thick robe hung open, revealing his sculpted abs and swim trunks. "I've been to some awesome hot springs in Costa Rica. They weren't nearly as developed as this place, although they did make it into a pretty significant tourist attraction. And there's this great little hot springs place in Mexico. There are a bunch of cabins and pools scattered around a mountain, and the pools pour into one another, cascading down the mountainside. You can get to pools right outside your cabin door, or you can hike to more remote pools along the cliffside that feel like your own private discovery, and each one is a little different. And there are these amazing caves that form the source for several of the pools... anyway, it's a magical, relaxing place. I'll bet you'd love it. And Niko would have a blast running and playing there."

"So you've done a lot of traveling, then?" Casey asked, her voice wistful.

Neil nodded. "After I gave up on finding you in Manhattan, I traveled a lot. I'd work hard, and then save up my money and my vacation time and take these wonderful trips. Just wander around places, experiencing the people and the culture, soak it all up. It became my outlet."

They reached a series of pools, and Neil smiled, pointing toward one in particular. "Try that one," he advised. "It's the Saline Pool - the water is warm and contains Epsom salt, and you'll find it's a really interesting experience." Following his own advice, he shrugged off his robe, draped it across a nearby chair and stepped onto the top step of the pool. He stopped and held his hand out for her. Casey bit her lip as she watched him standing there, his chiseled body on display. His slim physique was nicely balanced by his toned muscles, giving him the look of an Adonis rather than a muscle-bound gym rat. Under her pause and prolonged gaze, his grin widened, and he raised an eyebrow at her. "Like what you see?" His dimple winked at her.

She giggled nervously, averting her gaze. "Sorry. It's just been a long time since I've seen you like this. You've improved with age," she added, then bit her lip again as she stepped over to the chair where he'd draped his robe. In a quick motion, she dropped her robe, ran past him and submerged herself in the pool, flailing and splashing around as her body tried to float of its own accord and she struggled to remain upright.

He laughed at her. "It's neutrally buoyant. That's one of the benefits of the epsom salts. Although there's not quite enough salt in a pool this size to be a true float pool, but that's one of the things it's going for."

He stepped toward her, submerging himself in the warm pool as he came. Once the water was chest deep, he smoothly launched himself, skimming the top of the water to float beside her. "Come on, now," he chided gently. "What have you got to be so concerned about?"

She frowned at him. "I'm a mother, Neil. My body has... changed, a bit, since you've last seen it."

He turned to look at her seriously, treading water and grabbing onto the ledge at the side of the pool to try to remain upright. "You're not going to hear any complaints from me," he told her, sliding his free hand down her arm in a soothing caress. "Motherhood is a beautiful gift. It just means you're using your body the way it was intended. And if it turns out you are the mother of my child... I would worship every inch of you, changes or no, for bearing and raising my boy." He took her hand and kissed it, his eyes never leaving her face.

She sighed and closed her own eyes, pushing away from the wall and allowing her body to float naturally. Neil was right; it wasn't truly neutrally buoyant, as her body hovered a few inches below the surface. Today's bikini was a deep, sapphire blue, and her hair was loose, floating in a hazy cloud around her head.

Neil splashed slightly in the water beside her, but she didn't open her eyes. He reached out and took her hand, and the two of them floated side-by-side in companionable silence.

Some time later, he interrupted the quiet. "Casey, I'm sorry to cut this short, but I'm afraid if we continue to float here, we might fall asleep and miss out on our entire night together."

She opened her eyes with a start, then attempted to stand up. "You're right," she confirmed. "I might have been asleep already, just then. Either that, or really, really relaxed."

He nodded. "Alright. I have a plan. Follow my lead." He swam over to the stairs, and climbed out of the pool. Casey watched his wet swim trunks cling to his well-built form for a moment before following him to the stairs and climbing out. He waited for her, then grabbed her hand and took off running for one of the nearby pools. She followed, running along beside him, grinning hugely. At the last moment, he let go of her hand and took a mighty leap into the small pool. She let her momentum carry her along behind, leaping in next to him just as he came up sputtering. She surfaced with a loud shriek.

"Now we're awake!" Without waiting for a reply, he swam toward the side of the pool and climbed out.

"Why, you little..." she sputtered, scraping her wet hair out of her face. "You didn't warn me it was a cold pool!" She waded toward the side of the pool, then climbed out.

"Don't worry," he told her, grinning unrepentantly. "This will make up for it." Without waiting for her, he jumped into the next pool, then glided out of the way to make room for her.

A moment after she followed him in, she surfaced again, her face looking much more relaxed. "Ohh, that's nice," she agreed. "The heat *almost* makes up for the cold pool." She sent a small splash in his direction, her face contorted into an approximation of annoyance, but she couldn't quite hide her smile.

"Come here." His expression serious, he waded over to her and gathered her in his arms, tucking her against him. "I've been waiting for this for ten years." Casey relaxed, smiling against his chest. "And for what it's worth, you have absolutely nothing to feel self-conscious about," he continued, stroking her wet hair, gathering it and tucking it behind her ear as she rested the side of her face against his chest. He gently captured her chin, turning her face toward his. "You are a beautiful woman, Casey. Motherhood agrees with you. Your curves have grown lush and sensuous; you are womanly, in all your glory, compared to the girl I knew all those years ago."

She blushed and looked away. "I don't know how you can say that with a straight face," she teased, deflecting.

"Because it's true," he answered simply.

She turned to look back at him, her voice barely more than a whisper. "I think you might be too good to be true, Neil Seaton."

"I've been thinking the same thing about you for ten years, Casey Marie Kelly." His voice was low as he caressed her face. "There have been times when I worried that I had imagined you. Conjured you up out of some fantasy while I was in the coma. You were like a fairy sent to bewitch me, only I never quite woke up from the spell."

He kissed her, gently, at first, but the kiss turned fierce and possessive. She wrapped her arms around him, her fingernails dragging against his bare back as the kiss grew more passionate. Their bodies pressed together as his fingers fisted in her hair.

Finally, he broke away, gazing at her with an intense look. "But here you are. You're real."

The mood was tense for the Week 7 vote. Everyone filed in, dressed to the nines, but there was no smiling and no feeling of amiability among the participants. Nathan May stood at the front of the room, ready and waiting for them, and his expression was serious.

"As you know," he began right away. "The stakes are getting more serious than ever. We're down to three men and three women, and tonight, someone will be going home. Who will it be?"

He looked at each of the participants in turn, building the sense of dramatic tension. Instead of asking for an envelope, Nathan announced: "This week's vote was unanimous, and America did not vote to save this individual. So while I am sorry to see her go, the time has come to say farewell to Olivia, and her daughter Natalie." He met her gaze. "I'm sorry, Olivia - you will not be a part of America's Favorite Couple. Please say your farewells."

Olivia stepped forward, holding Natalie's hand. She turned to face the other participants. Instead of addressing them, though, she leaned down and spoke to her daughter. "Natalie, go say goodbye to your friends." Natalie ran to Cassidy and Nicholas in turn, hugging them, her face sad and pale but composed.

As Natalie turned back to Olivia, Casey stepped forward, moving toward her one-time friend. Olivia saw her coming and held out her hand, palm out, stopping her in her tracks. "No," she said firmly, her voice controlled but angry. "You do not get to speak to me. You do not get to say farewell. You have subverted the entire purpose of this experience with your baby mama drama." She stamped her foot, her sturdy heel clicking loudly in the silent room. "But I advise you to remember one thing, chica: you cannot have all three, no matter what you try. And if you are not careful, you will lose the one you want in the meantime. So I look forward to watching the rest of this on tv, and watching it all blow up in your face."

With that, Olivia spun and stomped out of the room, pulling Natalie along beside her.

Casey's jaw was slack, her features contorted in shock and pain. Wrapping her arms around herself, she closed her mouth and stepped back into line, standing next to Anastasia. Her eyes glistened with unshed tears, but she maintained her composure and waited quietly for Nathan to finish the live voting ceremony.

"Well, Olivia sure knows how to make an exit, doesn't she?" he observed, turning back to the group. "Ok, everyone - now that we're down to five, things are more serious than ever. There will be two two-on-one dates this week - one for each of the ladies - and the rest of the dates will be the one-on-one hometown dates. We'll be filming this season's hometown dates in the guys' towns, so ladies, be ready for the guys to plan the dates, and for them to show you what life would be like if you choose to be with one of them. At the end of this week, we'll send one more person home. Then, next week, we'll be down to four, and it will be our exotic fantasy date weeks. And then you know what happens after that - another person goes home, and we enter the final week, where we find out who's going to be America's Favorite Couple - and what the future will be for that couple."

"I told you this last week, and I'll remind you again this week: now that things are really getting down to the wire, it's more important than ever that you make the most of your time together. Depending on how things work out, you may only have two or three more dates to decide how you really feel about one another, and what you want your future to be. Now is the time to ask the hard questions, think about what life would look like for you going forward, and be clear and honest with each other about what you want and how you're feeling."

"One more thing: in a little twist, I'm going to tell you tonight who's going to be on the two-on-one dates. Anastasia, your two on one date will be tomorrow, and you'll be going out with Mike and Richard." He turned to look at Casey. "Casey, your two-on-one will be on Tuesday, and you'll be going out with Mike and Neil." Anastasia's expression was tight, and Casey sighed quietly when she heard the arrangement.

"Anastasia, your hometown with Richard will be on Tuesday, Mike will be Wednesday and Neil will be Thursday. Casey, your hometown dates will be in the same order, one day later." He looked around the group. "Saturday, we'll travel back here, and we'll have a cocktail party on Saturday night so you can resolve any questions that come up or have any conversations you need to have. The vote is on Sunday, and then we'll head out to our first exotic date destination."

"Oh, I almost forgot: Casey and Neil, neither of you has a date scheduled on Monday. Because we've reached such a critical point in this experience, we're asking that you keep to yourselves in different parts of the house. As you know, normally you'd be allowed to socialize and spend time with one another when you're not on a date. But because time is now so important, we ask that you not do that in order to avoid any unfair advantage, and to keep the relationship from getting ahead of where you are with others, so you can give each participant fair consideration."

"I think that's it for this week. Best of luck to all of you, and I wish you well as you prepare for the critical coming week here on America's Favorite Couple."

* * *

Casey was startled awake by a hand on her shoulder and a finger on her lips. When her eyes flew open, she saw Richard standing over her, motioning her to silence. He took her hand and gestured for her to follow. She threw back her covers and stepped out of the room with him, quietly closing the door behind her without waking Nicholas.

"What do you need?" she asked, her eyes heavy with sleep.

"I'm sorry to wake you," Richard told her, stepping close and speaking low to avoid waking up the housemates. "But I wanted a few minutes, if that's ok. Can we go talk by the pool?"

Casey nodded and padded sleepily behind him, rubbing her hands up and down her arms to fight the chill in her sleeveless night dress. They quietly crept out the back, and sat on a padded bench together. When Richard saw her rubbing her arms again, he took off his robe and draped it over her like a blanket, then wrapped his arm around her, pulling her against his side.

The sleep faded from her eyes as they roved over his nearly-naked form. He was wearing only a pair of boxers, and his body was solid, firm. He didn't have the chiseled physique of a Neil or the massive weightlifting muscles that Mike sported, but looked more like a man who spent his days in the real world, without endless hours to spend in the gym. Casey couldn't resist running her fingers through his chest hair, then sliding her hand over his shoulder to wrap around his neck.

"What did you need?" she finally asked, smiling at him.

"Just you," he replied, gathering her close and resting his head on top of hers. "It's been days since I've gotten to spend any time with you, and it'll be days again until our next date. I didn't want to wait that long, so I had to steal a few minutes with you."

"Aww, you're sweet," she said into his neck. As her lips brushed against his skin, she began to nuzzle him, then kissed his neck. Richard groaned and swung her around toward him, bringing her astride his hips as he wrapped both arms around her. She wrapped her arms around his neck, tilting his head back as she kissed the hollow of his throat, then the base of his ear, before finally nibbling his earlobe. She exhaled a small breath across his ear, and then whispered: "I told you I'd get you back." He groaned again as she gyrated her hips on his and captured his lips in hers, the kiss fierce and passionate. When she finally released his mouth, leaning back a few inches to catch her breath, her eyes were dark with desire.

"Have I mentioned that you do things to me, woman?" he whispered, his voice husky and barely audible. "Because damn, do you do things to me. And you make me really want to do things to you." He pulled her head down to his, kissing her deeply, as his other hand firmly gripped her ass and pulled her against him. He writhed his hips under her, probing at her core with his hardness. Her breathing grew more labored as she ground against him, fisting her fingers in his hair.

Finally, she drew away again, panting heavily. "Maybe we should leave things at that, or I'm going to need a lot more than a few minutes with you." She looked around at the courtyard around them, the bench where they were positioned visible to anyone who looked out toward the pool area. "And as much as I could get carried away, right here, right now - I'd rather a more intimate setting for what I have in mind."

He sighed heavily, drawing a deep breath and continuing to work his hips slightly against her. "I hear you, pretty lady - but damn, do you make it hard for a man to leave well enough alone. If I had any idea what you meant when you said you'd get me back, I might not have been so cavalier about it."

She laughed, a throaty sound loaded with seduction and desire. Slowly, she swung herself off his lap, moving to sit on the bench next to him. Instead of sitting back, though, she leapt up and ran to the pool, dropping the robe Richard had covered her with and jumping into the pool with a splash. When she surfaced again, the nightgown that she still wore had turned translucent, and was clinging wetly against her skin.

Richard growled low in his chest. "Are you trying to make things harder for me, woman?" he asked, grumpy, as he held one of the couch pillows over his lap.

She laughed again. "Not exactly. More like I thought I could use a cool dip to return me to my senses," she explained, treading water. "I figured the lesser of two evils was to leave the nightgown on, but..." she shrugged as she looked down at herself. "I didn't quite anticipate this outcome." She submerged herself more deeply in the water, down to her neck.

Richard stood and walked over to the edge of the pool, still holding the couch cushion over his lower half. Before he could jump in, Casey held out a hand to stop him. "Please don't do that," she asked, her voice husky. "If you come in after me, we might find ourselves in an even more difficult position."

He grinned. "Actually, it's not that difficult. I just hold you against the side of the pool. Or we go sit on the steps..."

She smirked. "I guess I'll keep that in mind. But what I mean is, if you come in here, I'll have gotten all wet for nothing. I don't think I'd be able to restrain myself."

His grin widened as he sat down on the side of the pool, dangling his legs and feet into the water. "Actually, I think you got all wet to very good effect. And I'd show you if I came in there with you. But I get your point," he held up a placating hand and laughed as she sent a splash of water at him. "I submit! I'll sit tamely on the side of the pool here like a trained puppy if you come closer and talk with me a bit." As Casey glided closer, he lowered his voice. "I really didn't bring you down here for this. I just wanted to spend some time with you. Have a conversation. But then you..." he sighed mightily and shook his head.

She smiled. "I didn't intend to get quite so carried away, either. But obviously we have good chemistry. I'm kinda happy to discover that in addition to all the other things I admire about you, I don't wanna keep my hands off of you. Bodes well if our relationship continues."

His smile faded. "That's kind of what I wanted to talk to you about. Our relationship. I wanted to see if I could find out a little more about how you're feeling right now. And I'm a mite sad to hear you say 'if our relationship continues.'"

She reached out and put her hand on his knee, her smile fading in response. "I didn't mean anything by it, truly. Just that we're all here to discover if we're going to find love, and the next few weeks are critical to figuring out which relationships are going to continue and which ones just aren't meant to be. I was talking in the overall context of the show."

He covered her hand with his, intertwining their fingers. "That's the thing. I'm not here to figure out which relationship is going to continue anymore. As far as I'm concerned, you're it. I've felt that way for a while. That's why I couldn't go on another date with Olivia - I didn't want to lead the poor woman on." He shook his head. "And Anastasia is a nice girl, and all, but she's... not you. Fortunately, I think she's more into Neil, so I don't think my dates with her this week are going to be too awkward. But I have zero expectation of finding that she's a person I want to continue a relationship with. That's just you." He looked deep into her eyes, his face serious. "I was kinda hoping you felt the same way."

She took a deep breath. "I definitely want to spend more time with you, Richard," she agreed. "I'm not ready for our relationship to end, and I'm still discovering whole new aspects to my feelings for you. Like how physically compatible we are, for example," she joked, but her grin was weak and Richard didn't return her smile. She looked down, not meeting his gaze as she continued.

"But Neil and Mike are both still here, and one of those men is the father of my child. I can't just ignore that. However things go here, I hope to leave in a lasting relationship. But if I do that with you, right now - commit to a future together with you - I'll never again have the chance to explore whether or not I could form a lasting relationship with the father of my child."

She looked up at him, squeezing his hand. "I'm not saying this to be hurtful, but you already had a chance to see whether you could have a relationship with the mother of your child - and it didn't work out. Now you can move on with a clear conscience and an open heart, knowing that your future is ahead of you. But I haven't had that chance. If I tried to move forward without seeing where things could take me with the father of my child, I'll always wonder 'what if' - like I have for the past ten years. I don't want that hanging over my future, casting a shadow on my happiness and potentially poisoning my future relationships. Especially if it's a future with you, because you don't deserve to go through all that."

He sighed. "That makes sense, I know it. And you gave me the short version of this talk at our date earlier this week. I was just hoping that now that you'd had a chance to spend time with them, you had satisfied your curiosity. I guess that's not the case."

He set the couch cushion aside and leaned forward, taking her hand in both of his and staring intently into her eyes. "I just want to be very clear about one thing: I'm falling in love with you, Casey Kelly, and I know I want you to be a part of my life for all my days to come. If I'm still standing at the end, I'll get down on bended knee and do things properly, but for now, I want you to know that I'm ready to make that commitment, and I'm hoping every day that I'll get that chance." He bent forward and laid a kiss on her forehead. Then, he let go of her hands and drew his legs out of the pool, standing up.

"I'm going to go now, because I don't want to make things more awkward. But I'll leave you my robe so you can get back to your room with dignity intact." He took up his robe and walked it over to the stairs out of the pool, draping it across the rail so it would be easily accessible when Casey came out.

"Goodnight, you sweet, wonderful, seductive, vexing, amazing woman." Before she could respond, Richard stepped through the doors of the house and closed them behind him. Casey stood staring after him for a long moment before she made her way out of the pool, grabbing the robe off the rail and draping it around herself.

If she had looked up, she would have seen Neil staring out his window, where he'd been watching the entire scene. He continued staring out his window until she vanished into the house, his face stony and unreadable.

CHAPTER FIVE

Week Eight

"Ready to go, bud?" Casey asked, glancing over at Niko strapped into the ROV beside her. He nodded, grinning gleefully. "Let's do it!" she shouted, accelerating up the side of the sand dune and piloting them expertly over the crest. They half sped, half slid down the other side of the dune, as another ROV crested the dune behind them - only to get stuck at the top. Once Casey reached the bottom, she turned to check on the guys behind her, and saw that they were stuck. She laughed out loud and turned perpendicular to the dune, driving out of their path if they should manage to free themselves. Once she was safely out of the way, she picked up the radio and spoke into the microphone.

"Little trouble, boys?" she asked, her voice full of amusement.

"Neil was driving," Mike shot back over the radio, right away. Casey laughed again.

"And I suppose you can do better, Mike?" she teased.

"Well, maybe you'll find out, if we manage to get free up here."

Casey watched as the two of them used their sand ladders to dig sand away from the center of their Polaris ROV, where it was holding them in place and preventing them from getting enough traction to crest the dune. "Well, I guess we'll make another run at that dune while you guys play around up there," she finally replied. "Over and out." With that, Casey put the microphone back on its perch and glanced over at Niko. "Hold on, kiddo, we're going to cross the dune again and then come back. It'll take them a little while to get free." He grinned back and held a thumb up, having the time of his life.

Casey rolled away from the dune to give them a good running start, and then faced the dune head-on, accelerating gently but steadily. They sped up the dune with plenty of power to spare, and she slowed down as she approached the crest a few car lengths away from the other trapped ROV. "Wave to the guys!" she said to Niko, and they waved and grinned at the sweaty men as they crested the dune again and drove down the other side.

By the time they reached the bottom and lined up for another run, the ROV ahead of them was just rolling off the peak of the dune. Casey eased off the throttle as they crested the dune again themselves, making sure the path ahead was clear, and but not slowing down enough to get bogged down. They topped the dune and made their way down the other side, whooping and hollering as they sped down the tall dune. When they reached the bottom, they turned over to where the guys were waiting for them.

"Ok, I have to ask, where did you learn to drive dunes like that?" Mike shouted over to them.

Casey laughed aloud. "What, do you think I've been sitting in my house for the past ten years, or that I didn't have a life before that? I'm just full of surprises!"

"More!" Niko shouted, impatient with their banter. Casey smiled over at him.

"So you know how to drive dunes, do you, Mike?" she shouted across to them.

"Well, I'm no expert, but I can usually get the job done," he answered.

"Why don't we trade passengers, then? I'll give Neil some pointers and he can drive my ROV, and you can take Niko," she offered.

"Sounds good!" Mike shouted back. "Come on, little man!"

Casey unfastened her restraints, then walked around the Polaris to help Niko undo his seatbelts. He jumped down and ran over to the other ROV, and Neil fastened him in next to Mike before heading over to sit next to Casey. He was silent as he fastened himself in, then glanced over to see if she was ready. She gave him a thumbs up, and watched as Mike rolled off ahead of them to tackle the next dune. Finally, she looked over to Neil.

"You don't have to be embarrassed about getting stuck. Driving in sand can be kind of counterintuitive if you've never done it before, and cresting a dune is an art all on its own."

"I'm not," he answered tersely. Then he lined up to tackle the next dune, hitting the accelerator hard.

"Whoa, there, cowboy, take it easy," she cautioned. "When you accelerate fast like that, you risk digging us in. Slow and steady is the way to go on sand."

"Fine," he responded, and eased off the accelerator some. Slowly but surely, they lost momentum as they rolled up the next dune.

"Little more throttle," Casey advised. "You don't have enough revs to crest the dune, and if we don't have enough momentum to get up there, our back wheels can lose it and we could end up sliding backwards, getting stuck - or worse."

He followed her instructions silently, his jaw tense. He slowly applied more throttle, and they gained the momentum they needed to reach and crest the dune. Just before they hit the top, Casey advised: "Usually it's a good idea to slow down when you're about to crest the dune, but you're going the right speed. You want to be slow enough to try to get a look at what's on the other side, but if you're too slow, you won't make it over. This part can be very dangerous - sometimes the dune's a knife edge at the top, and you can fly over the crest to nothing but thin air. And if you hit the other side sideways, you could roll. But you're doing a great job," she finished.

He nodded. They rolled down the other side in silence, gaining speed. Casey smiled automatically, but her smile faded when she looked over and noticed Neil's stony expression.

When they reached the bottom, Mike had paused to wait for them to draw alongside. "You must be a good teacher," he yelled over, "because that was way better! Good job, man," he added to Neil.

Neil nodded, and Casey shouted "Thanks!"

"Wanna keep going, or want to switch back?"

She looked over at Neil, who didn't bother to answer. "Let's do a few more," she finally replied, after the pause had grown long enough to become awkward. "Then Niko can ride with Neil," she added. They both nodded, and Mike took off again, Nicholas cheering him on. Casey smile as they rolled off, but her smile faded as she looked back at Neil's expressionless face.

The next few dunes were brutal. Casey gave Neil occasional advice, but he seemed to have gotten the hang of the techniques involved, so she was mostly silent. He didn't bother to say anything else; just nodded in response to her instructions from time to time. The mood was thoroughly tense when they stopped again, and Mike suggested they switch passengers.

Casey unbuckled herself, and helped Nicholas get situated when he ran over to Neil's Polaris. "All set?" she asked. Niko nodded. She addressed Neil directly. "Do you feel comfortable enough to drive him?"

He looked at her, his face softening for the first time. "You're a good teacher. We'll be fine. I wouldn't let anything happen to him - I'd tell you if I didn't think I could handle it."

She nodded, her eyes sparkling with sudden unshed tears. "Awesome. Have fun, guys!" she waved as she trudged through the soft sand to Mike's ROV. She buckled herself in, then glanced over to Mike's smiling face.

"Ready to have some fun?" he asked, his eyes sparkling with mischief. His grin was contagious, and Casey smiled back, her mood lightening after the silent, tense ride she'd just had with Neil.

"Let's see what you've got!" she challenged.

Mike took off, pushing her back into her seat with the sudden acceleration, but otherwise handling the Polaris competently. They flew over the dunes, stopping occasionally to check on Neil and Niko's progress, and chatting amiably all the while. Casey smiled to see Niko and Neil grinning like kids, Niko cheering Neil on as he gained confidence in the ROV. Whatever had been bugging him when Casey was in the Polaris with him didn't seem to be bothering him now, as he drove Niko over dune after dune.

When they reached Patton Vally they stopped for lunch under a large tent the producers had erected for them. The shade was welcome, and walls on two sides helped cut down the wind that had been kicking up. They lounged on pillows strewn around a large rug, and enjoyed a hearty picnic. Afterward, Neil and Niko moved over to the sand and began to build an elaborate sand castle, while Mike and Casey lounged together under the tent.

"So, Mike," Casey probed casually. "Where did you learn to drive sand like that?"

He grinned, his expression giving him the look of the boyish college guy that Casey had known ten years ago. "A few buddies and I used to go down to Baja once or twice a year. We'd party and play in the dunes, and generally get up to no good. I stopped when I met the wife, but I actually really miss it. I've thought about getting it started again since we've split up, but the guys are mostly married now and have families, and their getting into trouble days are behind them. This brings back a lot of memories."

She smiled. "Maybe you could do a slightly less trouble-filled version of the trip?"

"Ahh, but where would be the fun in that?" He smirked. "But nah, I've tried. They come up with all kinds of excuses. Like they have to save money, or they only get a limited amount of vacation time a year and they like to spend it with their families, stuff like that. Can't say I really blame them. I felt the same way when I was with Elena." He sighed.

"Well, maybe you could start a tradition of doing this with your next significant other." She winked. "Just make sure you pick someone who thinks this kinda thing is fun."

He grinned, wrapping an arm around her and pulling her against his side. "I'm game. When do we start?"

Casey shrugged him off, scooting away and looking over at Neil. He didn't seem to notice; he was deep in sand castle construction with Nicholas. "Umm, I'll admit, Mike, I find this whole two-on-one thing pretty awkward. I think we've all done a good job so far, but I'd rather not engage in any PDA because I don't want to hurt anyone's feelings."

He nodded. "I get it. Sorry, Casey - I didn't mean to put you in an awkward position. But I do mean it - I'm game to see where a relationship with you could go. I think we'd have a lot of fun together. And if the kid turns out to be mine, we'd be fools not to give it a shot."

"I hear you," she said, still looking at Neil. Finally, she turned her attention back to Mike. "But a lot of things are still up in the air." She reached out and took his hand, smiling at him. "But it's nice to hear you say that - I'm looking forward to seeing what happens."

He grinned back. "Good. Now how about you? Where'd you learn to drive dunes like that? I was surprised to find you're so damn good at it."

"Hah!" she shot back. "Girls can't be good at driving in sand, eh?"

He shook his head. "No. I just meant, with the mom thing, finding out you're so good at something adventurous like that caught me a little off guard."

She frowned at him, her eyes drawing down in anger. "Just because I'm a mom doesn't mean I'm not also a person who enjoys doing stuff. I love my son, and I make a lot of sacrifices for our life together, but I'm still my own person - my entire identity doesn't boil down to just being 'mom.'" She sighed heavily, visibly restraining herself. "I'm going to chalk your ignorant statement up to the fact that maybe you don't know a lot of mothers. When kids are young, yeah, they take a lot of time and are a lot of work - but even then you can still find ways to be independent. But when they get older, there's no reason not to have a life outside of them. I was never going to be the kind of woman who was only a mom, and who had a major identity crisis when her kid grew up and moved out on his own. I was always going to be me, too, alongside of being a mom."

"Man, I'm sorry," he said, holding his hands out in a pacifying gesture. "I can see that I've hit a nerve. I didn't mean to offend you. Maybe I've got the wrong idea of what motherhood entails, but I've never really been a parent. From watching my buddies, I've always just assumed that life outside of the kids pretty much ends when the kids come along. Everything changes and you go to some limited-admission parent land, where you stop having interests of your own, and everything is cartoons and Disney movies and dirty diapers and driving the kids to sports and family vacations to magical wonderlands."

She sighed. "You're right and you're wrong at the same time." She leaned back, propping her elbows on the ground to hold herself up. "I guess I can't really blame you since you've never raised a kid. But when you've got that kind of idea of parenthood, it kinda surprises me at all that you want to be involved in Nicholas's life, if he turns out to be your son."

He shrugged. "I think I'm ready. I told you I felt like I was looking for something; maybe what I need is the grounding influence of being a father. The idea that people need me, rely on me. I've had my fun; maybe now it's time for me to settle down and get serious for a change."

She stared over at Neil and Niko, where they were putting finishing touches on the expansive sand castle they'd been building. "Well, back to what you asked - it's a family connection. We had family in Arizona, and when I was growing up, we'd visit them sometimes on vacation. For a couple of years, I even spent the summer with them. My cousins were boys, so we spent a lot of time playing outdoors - and they taught me to ride pretty much anything on pretty much any surface. I can ride dirt bikes, motorcycles, ATVs and ROVs. I've logged miles on pavement, dirt, some mud, and a lot of sand. We played in the dunes a lot." She looked back at Mike. "I haven't done it so much since Niko was born, but once he was a few years old, we started visiting them again." She smiled. "He has a small dirt bike and a mini quad he rides out there, now, and all of us go out together now and again." Her smile faded, and she gazed at him, her expression serious. "Maybe I don't push quite as hard as I would have before he was born - I'm his only parent, after all, and it's always in the back of my mind that he needs me to stay safe so I can take care of him. But that doesn't mean I can't have fun at all. We just make it a family activity, and take it a little easier."

"Mom! Mom! Come check out the awesome sand castle that Neil and I built!" Niko ran over and tugged at her arm, dragging her up.

She grinned indulgently at Mike, then made her way over to where Neil waited next to their creation, smiling. "Wow, that's really impressive, you guys!" she exclaimed, giving Niko's shoulders a squeeze. "Tell me all about it!"

He raved about what they'd built together, pointing out the doors, the towers they'd built, and the moat they had dug around it. "It's a castle," he finished, smiling happily. "It's where the royal family lives - the king and queen and prince - and they're happy and safe, because nothing can get to them there. It's even dragon proof!"

Casey looked over at Neil, and he met her gaze, his face turned serious once again.

Nicholas grinned mischievously at Neil, not noticing the tension between the adults. "But it's not earthquake-proof!" he exclaimed, yelling "Boom! Boom!" and bashing away at the carefully constructed sand castle. Neil watched for a moment, then joined in, helping Niko destroy the structure they'd spent so much time building.

"It's just sand," he said to Casey, shrugging.

One of the production assistants chose that moment to wander over, handing Casey a sealed envelope. She shared a glance at Neil before opening it. After she had read it, she yelled over to Mike "Hey, Mike, would you come here? We've got a task."

Mike stood and joined them, and Casey read the card aloud. "The sun will be setting soon, so it's time to think about the evening portion of your date. Only one guy will be going with Casey, but we're not going to make her choose. Instead, we're going to have a competition. Mike and Neil, you will each take a Polaris and race into the dunes to the north until you see a flag. You must drive out to the flag, make the turn around it, and then drive back here to the finish line. Whoever finishes first will get to spend the evening with Casey."

She looked up, glancing at each of them in turn. "Good luck, guys. Be careful," she cautioned, her gaze resting on Neil.

They nodded, shaking hands, and then they each climbed into a Polaris that had been lined up to start. The production assistant handed Casey a starting pistol, so she counted them down and fired the gun.

They took off. Mike accelerated aggressively, and got off to an early start. But then he started to bog down, losing speed and digging in as his wheels spun. He recovered quickly, but by the time he had freed himself, Neil had drawn alongside, accelerating smoothly and steadily. As they climbed the dune, Mike pulled ahead again, speeding up the loose sand. She lost sight of them as they both crested the dune, and could only wait until they returned.

She gathered Niko close in a hug. "Did you have fun today?" she asked, smiling down at him.

"Yeah!" he replied enthusiastically. He looked in the direction where the guys had sped off. "Mike drives good, so I think he'll be fast, but I really want Neil to win."

"Mike drives well," Casey corrected automatically, following Niko's gaze. "Well is an adverb that modifies the action verb drives. Good doesn't work in that sentence."

Niko nodded without replying as they both watched into the distance, waiting to see who would return first. A few minutes later, one of the ROVs came into view, but they couldn't tell who it was from so far away. The Polaris paused on the crest, and after a moment, it was clear it was stuck. Casey sighed. "I guess that's Neil," she said, as the other Polaris crested the dune smoothly and came speeding back toward them. The driver of the first ROV got out and started digging.

As the second Polaris came closer, the driver became more distinct. "It's Neil!" Niko shouted, jumping up and down and cheering. "He's gonna win!" He waved his arms happily, cheering Neil to the finish line. As the ROV passed the flagged line, Neil slowed and stopped it, unfastening his restraints and climbing out with a huge grin. Nicholas ran to him and jumped at him, and Neil caught the boy, picking him up and spinning him around in a big hug.

"Well done," Casey congratulated him, stepping close as he slowed his twirling and lowered Niko back to the ground. She smiled broadly at him, but as he looked at her, his smile faded and his gaze became serious again.

Instead of replying, he turned back to the Polaris and picked up the radio mic, speaking into it. "Doing ok?" he asked Mike, and they turned to watch him pause his digging on the distant dune. A moment later, his voice came back.

"Yeah, I'll be fine - just got a little excited and drove a little recklessly, I guess. Digging out now - I should be back in a few minutes. Congrats on the win, man," he offered.

"Thanks," Neil answered, still not looking at Casey. "Let us know if you need any help."

"Roger that," Mike replied, then went radio silent as he resumed his digging.

"Ok. I guess it's just us tonight," Neil finally said, turning back to Casey with a grim expression.

Niko, oblivious, smiled up at them. "Yay!"

The production staff began dismantling the site as they prepared to move to the evening shoot.

When Casey and Neil met for dinner outside of the Main Squeeze winery in downtown Yuma, she wasted no time on polite greetings. "Can we please address the elephant in the room?" she asked. "Before we go inside?"

He refused to meet her gaze, but the corners of his lips were turned down and his jaw was clenched. "What are you talking about?"

She sighed. "Neil, you've been acting pissed off at me all day. Or maybe pissed off at the world, I'm not sure. Did I do something?" She reached out to lightly touch his arm, and he shrugged her off. "Ok, I guess that answers that question... are you upset about Mike, or something?"

He laughed a short, mirthless laugh. "Mike. Yeah. I'm really concerned about Mike right now."

She tilted her head and let out a frustrated sigh, then stepped around into his field of vision. "Ok. So what then? Please don't just shut down on me - if this is going to work, I need you to communicate."

"Oh, really?" he answered, his voice rising and his eyes flashing in anger. "There's a chance for this to work? Because last night - or should I say early this morning - it looked pretty clearly like you had chosen Richard and all that's left is some meaningless formalities."

She paled. "This morning?" she asked, her voice weak.

"Yeah. By the pool. It looked like things were working with him pretty damn well."

She sighed and looked at the ground. "I'm so sorry. I would never have wanted to cause you pain by having you see that."

"So what then?" he probed, his shoulders slumped and a tone of defeat in his voice. "Is there even any point in us going inside and having dinner? You've made up your mind and the rest of us are just set dressing for the next few weeks?"

She laid her hand alongside his face and tilted it to look at her. "Not at all, Neil. Not in the slightest. If you'd actually been able to hear the conversation, instead of just seeing some things that probably looked very hurtful out of context, you would have heard me telling him that I have to explore whether a relationship between you and I can work. I told him that the 'what if' has been hanging over my life for ten years, and before I can begin to move forward with anyone else, I'd have to know whether you and I could have something."

His hand came up to clasp her hand against the side of his face, and he leaned into it. "Really?" he asked, his eyes wide and his voice full of longing.

"Yes," she whispered, stepping up on her tiptoes to reach up and kiss him softy. When she broke away again, she added: "Neil, I haven't been able to stop thinking about you for ten years. And that's even after I thought you had just abandoned me after one amazing day and night together. Now that I know you looked for me, that you didn't just disappear - there's no way I could just walk away from us until we've had a real chance, you know?"

His face broke into a brilliant smile, like the sun coming out from the clouds behind a storm. "Oh, thank God. I thought for sure, after seeing you... and him..." the smile faded into a frown again. "So if you really want to give us a chance, then why the Hell were you sitting on his lap, making out with him? Astride him? And then jumping into the pool and your nightgown turning completely see-through? How is that giving us a chance?" His voice ended on a growl.

She frowned in return. "How do I even answer that?"

"Try," he growled at her.

She yanked her hand away, her voice growing heated in return. "First of all, you were never intended to see that. What I do when I'm with other men here on this journey has nothing to do with what's happening with me and you." She put a hand on her hip, wagging a finger at him.

"I'm sure you've made out with other women while you're here, and I haven't asked you word one about that, nor have I made you feel like an asshole for it."

She sighed, her posture softening. "If I'm in the moment with someone, and it feels romantic or I want to kiss him, how could I possibly be exploring relationships and giving things an honest chance if I'm thinking to myself 'I want to see how things are going to be with Neil, so I can't kiss this other person, even though that's part of a normal relationship and I also want to see if there could be one of those here.' I can't be worrying about what other people would be thinking, because that would shape how I interact with everyone here, and that wouldn't give me a chance to explore any relationships honestly."

"But yes, things this morning with Richard got a little more carried away than I would have expected at this point. I'm not going to lie to you - I did not expect to feel those things or do those things at this point in the journey. But that was what came from the moment, and I won't apologize for it, because I'm here to find a relationship that will last for the rest of my life - and that means I need to explore possible relationships."

He sighed. "So you view your relationship with Richard as a possible relationship, even though you say you want to give us a real chance."

"What do you want me to say?" She tilted her head, stepping away from him, then back. "If we were out in the real world, and I could date you first, and see how things go, and then date Richard if things didn't work out with you... maybe that would be ideal. But maybe I would already have begun dating Richard and wouldn't be willing to explore a relationship with you, because I tend to be a committed, monogamous relationship kind of girl." She stepped closer, leaning in, her voice low. "But we're not in the real world. We're all living in a house together, and we only have ten weeks to explore all the possible relationships in an attempt to figure out which one is going to be the one we walk away with at the end. And I hope to God that the one I walk away with is the one that's going to last the rest of my life, so I want to get it right. But I don't have the time or the option to date you all separately for a while and see which one of you is the best fit for the man I hope to marry. So yes, I am forming multiple relationships at the same time in an attempt to see which one is the one I want to say 'yes' to at the end. And no, this isn't how I'd do things in the outside world. But we're here, and things are different here, and that's just the way it is. And you should have understood that when you signed up, because I should not be made to apologize or feel bad for doing what's best and right for me in the end."

He sighed. "I get it. I do. And clearly I owe you an apology. It just made me feel like shit to see you and him together like that. I know, in the back of my mind, things like that might be going on with the other people in the house - and you're right, you're not the only person I've made out with in my time here - but I never thought I'd have to see it. I have real feelings for you, Casey. I'm developing strong feelings for you. To see you in the arms of another man, on the verge of giving yourself to him right in front of me... God, I can't explain to you how difficult that was."

They both sighed. "How are things going with Anastasia?" Casey finally asked.

"What?" Neil responded, caught off guard.

"Anastasia. I know she has a thing for you. Have you given her reason to think she has a chance at a future with you?"

He sighed and looked away. "How am I supposed to answer that?"

She smirked at him. "Now you know how I feel."

There was a long pause. "You don't really want me to answer that, then, do you?"

"Actually, yes, I would like to hear your answer," Casey replied, but her voice was gentle.

"Well. Yeah, I like Anastasia. We've had some good times together. We do have some stuff in common, and she's a beautiful woman - so I don't think it's unreasonable for a guy to want to explore a relationship with her." He bent toward her. "But truthfully, Casey, it's been some time since I seriously thought there might be a relationship with her. I think I checked out the night you told me that Nicholas might be my son, and that you were the Marie I knew all those years ago. But I couldn't admit that to myself at the time - let alone anyone else - so things might have gone further with Anastasia than they needed to go if I could have admitted the truth."

"So," Casey probed. "Are you leading her on?"

He wouldn't meet her gaze. "Not leading her on, exactly. I am still trying to see if there could be anything there with her. But in my heart of hearts, if I'm honest with you - and I do want to be honest with you - I don't see that as a real possibility."

"So. Do you feel bad about that? Dating her and potentially leading her to develop deeper feelings for you, even though you don't think you'll have them for her? Even though you've 'checked out' and are invested in building a relationship with me, and no-one else?"

"Yeah?" He seemed confused. "It's not my normal style, that's true. But I think she knows she signed up for an uncertain thing here. I don't think she'll be too hurt when she finds out that things with me and her aren't going to work out."

Casey sighed. "Well, I do think people are going to be hurt when things with me and them don't work out. And at least one person is going to get hurt, because there's only one of me and there are multiple relationships I'm building. So it's hard for me to be honest and authentic and truly in the moment with these people knowing I'm likely to hurt one of them. But when you give me crap for it, it makes things that much harder."

He nodded. "So, don't."

She nodded back. "Yes, please."

He pulled her to him, gently, taking her in a light embrace. "Alright. I get it. And I'm sorry. Thank you for taking the time to really talk things through with me. I'd hate for this to have been hanging over the rest of our date. We have so little time together, and I wouldn't want to lose some of it to some sort of stupid resentful nothing."

She hugged him back, squeezing him tightly. "Ok. So now let's go inside and have a fantastic evening." She smiled, and he smiled in return, his face and posture relaxed for the first time all day. With her arm still wrapped around his waist, and his arm around her shoulders, they went inside.

The staff ushered them to the patio, which had been transformed into a magical fairy land through liberal application of twinkle lights, rose petals and candles. One side of the patio had been turned into a lounge, with a wide, cushioned area boasting a pile of pillows and a couple of blankets in case they got chilled. Burning sconces sat on either side of the lounge, providing heat and a romantic ambiance. The closer end of the patio sported a small seating area, consisting of two chairs and a small table between them. The table contained a tray of nibbles, artfully arranged, including fruits, cheeses, crackers and almonds. A second platter of various meats and cheeses sat on another small table nearby.

"We've prepared a customized wine tasting for you, and our chef has created unique small plates to go with each course just for you. We'll be pouring three reds and three whites for you this evening, and if you have any questions, our owners, Fred and Mary, will be happy to answer them for you." She motioned them to the seating area, and they sat opposite one another. "Would you like to get started?" Casey smiled and nodded, and the woman vanished inside and returned a moment later with a bottle of red wine.

The staff proceeded to take them through the flight of six wines, describing each as they poured and presenting a special dish designed to match with each wine. The pours were small, so when the flight was complete, the woman presented them with a final bottle of wine. This one had a customized wine label that included a picture of the two of them, and the words 'America's Favorite Couple Pinot Noir.' "We'll leave you with this and let you have some privacy to enjoy yourselves, but if you need any more wine, any water or anything else, just pop your head inside and we'll be happy to fix you up." They smiled and thanked her, and then looked at each other for a moment after she went inside.

"Shall we take this over there?" Neil asked, picking up the bottle of wine and motioning to the cushy lounge area the producers had created for them. Casey nodded, smiling, and grabbed their glasses, following him across the patio.

"That's quite the mural, don't you think?" Casey observed, waving a glass at the large mural splashed across the outside of the restaurant. It featured the owners in front of a large vineyard, and various other people scattered around appearing to enjoy themselves with glasses of wine.

Neil took the glasses from her, setting them on the shelf arrayed on the side of the lounge area and holding her hand to help her climb in and get settled. Then, he climbed in after her, wrapping an arm around her and kissing her thoroughly. Eventually, he broke free and gazed into her eyes for a long moment, a slight smile playing across his lips. Then, he turned to the glasses and wine bottle and poured for them, handing her a glass and taking his own as he stared at the mural. "So, you wish to discuss the relative merits of a mediocre painting?" he teased.

She laughed. "Now, don't be mean. I'm sure the owners are very proud of it, and undoubtably the artist was grateful to get a chance to create such a sizable, permanent piece."

"Ahh," he replied, swirling the wine around in his glass as he continued to stare seriously at the painting. "So the size of the mural is a point in its favor?" he asked. "And do you think the pride of the owners is directly proportional to the size of the painting?"

She gave him a playful shove. "Now you're making fun of me," she complained, grinning at him.

"Not at all," he replied, still looking at the mural. "I just want to understand what you see in this piece."

She grabbed his face and turned it toward her. "Shut up," she commanded, before capturing his lips with hers to ensure his compliance. The kiss lingered as she leaned into him, pressing the length of her body against his. Eventually, she released him, and set her glass of wine off to the side.

"Could you hand me one of those blankets, please?" she requested, pointing.

He moved with alacrity, setting his glass aside and taking up the pile of blankets. "Lean forward," he told her, then wrapped a blanket around her top half when she complied. She clasped it around her like a cape. When she leaned back again, he spread another blanket over both of them, covering them from the waist down. He moved the remaining blankets close at hand, where either of them could reach them. Then he wrapped an arm around her, pulling her against him.

She smiled. "Thank you."

He gently kissed her forehead. "You're welcome." Then, he rested his head alongside hers, and they sat together in companionable silence, occasionally sipping their glasses of wine, the flames flickering on either side of them.

Eventually, she spoke. "So. I can't think of a way to say this that doesn't sound awkward, but I'm curious what your dating life has been like in the past ten years. Both Richard and Mike have been married, although that hasn't worked out for either of them. Have you been in a serious relationship? Engaged? Married?"

He grinned, and turned to look at her. "Curious, eh? Jealous, maybe?"

She smiled. "No. Probably not. But curious, yes."

His grin faded. "Well, the long and the short of it is: no. I haven't really had a serious relationship in the past ten years. Certainly nothing that would have led to an engagement or marriage. I've definitely dated. I've had a number of relationships that lasted a few months. And while we'd inevitably end up spending most nights together, I've never formally lived with a woman. We've always kept our separate places, and I've never asked anyone to move in, nor have I ever really contemplated moving in. It was never quite serious enough to convince me that was a good idea."

She tilted her head. "Ten years is a long time to go without a serious relationship. Do you have some sort of commitment issues?"

He rolled his eyes. "Commitment issues. That's always a woman's go-to when a guy doesn't want to get serious." Her eyes narrowed. "No, Casey, I don't have commitment issues. I'd be happy to move in with the right person. I actually aspire to be married someday - even someday soon. I just need to find the right person."

"Women always say it's commitment issues?" she probed, her voice carrying an edge.

The corners of his mouth turned up in a slight grin. "I've been told that by more than one woman after ending a relationship. They always seem to want some sort of reason it didn't work out, and they never want to hear that it just wasn't the relationship I was looking for. So they throw 'commitment issues' at me. Or 'self-destructive tendencies.'" He lowered his voice and leaned in toward her, fixing her with his intense gaze. "But make no mistake, Casey - I'm very ready to commit to the right relationship, for the rest of our lives." His gaze dropped to her lips, but he didn't lean in the remaining few inches for a kiss; instead, he returned his stare to meet her eyes. "It's very important to me that you understand that."

She shivered under the intensity of his gaze. Before she could think of a response, though, he leaned back, smirking slightly. "What about you? Any serious relationships? Engaged? Married?" He raised an eyebrow as he waited for a response.

"Oh, that's how it's going to be," she smirked back at him. "Ok. Fair enough. Yes, one serious relationship; no, never engaged or married. We didn't move in together." She looked away and took a sip of her wine. "I met him when Nicholas was three, and things got serious when he was four. I held him off for a long time; I had dated a bit, here and there, but it's difficult with a small child, so I made him wait a long time for the first date, and then I wouldn't go out with him very often; maybe twice a month for a few months." She looked back at Neil, whose face had grown still as he watched her.

"Basically, he wore me down. I have no idea why he wasted so much time on me, but eventually we started going out more often. I kept him away from Niko for months while we got to know each other better and dated more often, but eventually, I decided it was getting serious enough that I should see how they were together." She shook her head.

"Even now, when I think about it, it was a really confusing situation. I was lonely, I'll admit it." Neil took her hand and squeezed. "But I was also reluctant for him to spend too much time with Niko until I could decide how I felt about him. After I saw him with Niko, that first time, I realized that Nicholas was going to get confused if the guy was around too often. He might start to look at him as a father figure, and then if things didn't work out, Niko would be devastated not to have him in our life anymore. It's so hard at that age." She shook her head. "So we sort of dated, for a long while, but I only included Niko a handful of times in all those months. It got the point where I almost felt like I was having an affair; I was carrying on this secret life with this guy, where we'd meet when Niko was in daycare, or I'd have him over after Niko was asleep for the night, or I'd hire a sitter and go out. But eventually I realized it couldn't keep going on like that; I'd either have to let him in, or he was out."

She sighed. "Well, ok, truthfully, he gave me an ultimatum. He got tired of only being able to see me when I could keep him away from Niko; I guess the novelty of 'sneaking around' wore off for him. So when I realized I either had to let him in all the way, or get rid of him..." she looked at Neil, smiling wanly. "Well, I told him to take a hike. Nicholas was five by then. It dragged out far longer than it should have, I guess."

"I just liked being held. I liked being made to feel like I was a woman - not just someone's mom. And frankly, I was direly in need of a good orgasm or three," she grinned. "I saw so much more clearly - and felt so much more relaxed - once I was getting laid regularly again."

He sputtered on the wine he'd been sipping, but then grinned back. "I guess that makes sense. I always feel a bit... blocked up... when I haven't been in a relationship in a while. So what happened after that guy? Any more serious relationships?"

She shook her head. "Nope. I've dated. Now that Nicholas is older, it's a little easier. I'm still careful about bringing guys around - he's only met a few of the guys I've dated, and it's always been in a very casual way, and I make sure they're not around often - but I can explain things a bit more to him, and he understands that just because I bring a guy around doesn't mean he's getting a new dad. That I'm just trying out a new friendship to see if things might turn into more."

She grinned, taking a big swig of her wine and holding out the glass for a refill. "It helps that I've found a fuck buddy. When it hasn't been months since I've had sex, it's a lot easier to think clearly and not be so desperate for a relationship."

Neil glanced into her eyes, then looked carefully back to her glass as he filled it again. "Fuck buddy, eh? How long has that been going on?"

She grinned wider, amused at his careful avoidance of her gaze. "A few years. It's very casual. If one of us is dating someone, we stop. But if we're both single, we get together a few times a week when Niko isn't around for a little stress relief."

Neil filled his own glass, then carefully put the bottle back on the shelf, still avoiding her gaze. "So do you have feelings for this guy?"

Casey chuckled. "Oh, yeah, loads of feelings." Neil's eyes darted to her face, and she laughed aloud. "Neil, chill out. We live in the twenty-first century. Women have sexual urges, too. But just because I have a friend who is good enough to help me out when I'm feeling like a little romp doesn't mean I'm secretly in love with him, or I'm just waiting for one day when he'll realize we've been meant for a relationship all along. We're just two friends who aren't interested in being together, but who enjoy a good roll around in bed now and again when neither of us is dating someone."

Her face grew more serious, and she clasped his hand in hers, squeezing it. "And he knows why I'm here. He knows that if this all works out, I'll be coming back in a committed relationship, and there will be no more friends with benefits. He fully supports this whole experience, by the way - he's always saying that I deserve someone to love me and really appreciate me, and I think he'll be happy for me if I find someone in all this."

She leaned closer. "Especially if it's you."

Neil's eyes widened. "Why me?"

She smiled. "Because he's heard all about you. I told you I haven't stopped thinking about you in ten years; apparently I talk about you to anyone who gets to know me well enough. If I end up with you at the end of this, he's going to be thrilled."

He took a deep breath. "So this guy really isn't interested in a relationship with you?"

She laughed. "No, silly. Honestly, I think he's in love with his best friend's wife. He's never admitted it to me, but the way he talks about her... I just have a feeling. He dates sometimes, but nothing ever seems to stick, and I think it's because his heart is given elsewhere. I feel a little sorry for the poor guy, really." She sighed, and Neil pulled her close.

"Ok, I find it really unnerving with how casually you talk about sex. And how casually you have it, apparently."

"Hey!" she complained, lightly whacking his arm. "I don't have sex casually. I generally only have sex in a committed relationship, which is pretty damn rare since I'm so careful about Niko - or with my friend. I don't go around sleeping with any man who will hop into the sack."

He closed his arms more tightly around her. "Ok, that came out wrong. That's not what I meant. But you didn't let me finish. I was going to say that as much as I find it unsettling to hear about you talking with your encounters with other men, I also really admire you for being so rational and clearheaded about it. I'm not trying to stereotype, but for a lot of women I know, sex gets mixed up with all kinds of other emotions, and it leads to them getting hurt, or making poor decisions about relationships. By making sure you can get sexual gratification outside of a relationship, you're freeing yourself up to make smart decisions about relationships. And as the the mother of a boy who might be my son, I appreciate that you put so much effort into not hurting him, and to making sure that he doesn't have any unrealistic expectations about men who may be in and out of his life. And in keeping that number low."

He tilted her head up to look at him. "But I sincerely hope I don't ever have to think about you in a sexual encounter with any other man, ever again. And I'd really like to be the man who helps you take care of those needs from now on."

He kissed her deeply, sensuously, with intent. She responded by wrapping her arms around him and pressing her body against his.

When Casey stepped out of the van, she saw Richard standing outside the front door of the restaurant and broke into a run. He wrapped his arms around her in a huge bear hug, lifting her off the ground as he held her tight. "My God, it is good to see you," he said into her ear, his voice low. She smiled.

Richard put her down, and she turned around to wave Nicholas forward. Richard leaned down and shook his hand. "Good to see you, buddy. Welcome to my hometown! Cassidy's around the side here on the porch, waiting for you guys to arrive. Along with a few people who want to meet you."

Casey glanced nervously to Richard, but he took her hand firmly in his and led them around to the porch on the side of the restaurant. It seemed full of people, several of whom stood to greet them when they strolled up. "Casey, Nicholas - this is my family," Richard introduced them. "Those lovely people there are my mom and dad, Carolina and Boone."

They came forward and hugged her, Carolina offering an "I'm so glad to meet you," with a genuine smile. "Richard has been telling us all about the two of you." They leaned down to Nicholas's height and shook his hand, Boone offering a few comforting words. "And you, young man! It's nice for Cassidy to have someone close to her own age to spend time with, and if you end up spending much time here, I've got a whole lot of things I've been hankering to teach a boy." Nicholas smiled shyly.

Richard turned to the next couple. "This is my sister, Charlotte, and her husband Wade, and their two daughters Penny and Betsey." They stepped forward and embraced Casey in turn, offering a few kind words of greeting. Penny and Betsey were very young; three and five, respectively; and they hid behind their mother's legs and gave her a shy smile.

He waved the next couple forward. "And this is my other sister, Lucinda, and her partner Rose." The two stepped forward and Casey greeted them warmly. "They've got a new baby at home, but Avalie is a little too young for this type of thing, so she's with Rose's mom right now."

Richard motioned for the last couple to come forward. They seemed more reserved, the woman looking Casey over with an appraising eye. "And this is Cassidy's mom, Lavinia, and her husband, Hank," Richard introduced them.

Lavinia came forward and took Casey's hand, but didn't quite shake it. "Charmed, I'm sure," she said by way of greeting. Her smile was proper and polite, but didn't quite meet her eyes. Her husband, Hank, followed her lead, but seemed a little bored by the whole thing. He kept glancing toward the door of the restaurant as if wondering when the food would be served.

"Lavinia wanted to meet you and Nicholas," Richard explained to Casey's unspoken question. "If you were to wind up spending a lot of time with me and Cassidy, she'd like to get to know you a little."

"Well, of course," Casey smiled at her. "I'd want the same thing if

Nicholas was going to be spending a lot of time with people I'd never met before." She looked down at Niko, who was hovering shyly at her side. "Hey, bud - I see Cassidy sitting back there with Betsey and Penny. Why don't you go greet her, and you guys can hang out while I get to know Richard's family a bit?"

Nicholas followed her suggestion, slipping through the crowd and hugging a reserved Cassidy. He sat down at the table with the girls, and soon they were in animated conversation as they showed him a game they were playing.

"Why don't we have a seat?" Richard suggested, guiding Casey to a nearby picnic table with a hand at the small of her back. She smiled over at him, and when his parents noticed, they glanced at one another and smiled knowingly. Soon, they were all seated around two picnic tables that had been shoved together. Casey and Richard were in the middle, seated across from his parents. On Casey's left sat his sister, Lucinda, and her partner, Rose. Across from them were Charlotte and Wade, sitting closest to the table where the kids were occupied. On Richard's right sat Lavinia and Hank, Lavinia positioned across the table next to his parents so she had a clear view of the two of them.

"So," said Lavinia, breaking in before any small talk had time to start. "What is it you do again?"

Casey glanced at Richard. "I work in marketing," she replied, her smile forced.

Richard put an arm around her and squeezed her shoulders. "She's being modest. She's the Executive Creative Director at a large public relations firm in Philadelphia. Personally, I think she's being groomed for Chief Creative Officer when their current lead retires in a few years."

Casey smiled broadly at him, squeezing his knee. "I had no idea you were paying that much attention when I rambled on about my job."

He grinned back, his eyes smoldering. "I always pay attention," he responded, his voice hinting at so much more.

His sisters looked at each other and whooped, grinning. His parents smiled at each other, then at Casey, whose cheeks were flaming bright red while she sported a helpless grin. Lavinia's expression had turned sour, as though she'd bit into a lemon.

"Down boy," his brother-in-law teased with a friendly grin. "You're gonna embarrass the poor girl in front of mom and dad."

Richard chuckled, but didn't apologize. His arm around Casey's shoulder slid down to her waist, and he slid her closer, squeezing her against him. She fanned herself with her hand, her eyes roving all over the patio as she avoided meeting anyone's gaze. "Ok, so maybe it's time to bring on the barbecue!" she tried changing the subject.

Richard's mother reached across the table, resting her hand over Casey's wrist and giving her a gentle smile. "No need to feel embarrassed, my dear. The Nathan men are very passionate when they meet the right woman."

Casey's eyebrows shot up and her smile grew rueful as she blushed a deeper shade of red.

"Come on, now, Mama, you're really embarrassing her," Lucinda chided. She reached over and squeezed Casey's hand. "It's not our habit to tease newcomers mercilessly - unless it's clear that one of us is head-over-heels, and then all bets are off. Everyone's just glad to see Richard so happy. He hasn't looked at anyone like that in a long time."

Casey's smile grew more genuine at the gentle reassurance, and she stole a glance at Richard, who beamed at her. "Well, I haven't felt the way I feel about him in a long time, either," she responded, squeezing his knee again.

"So," Lavinia cut in again. "If you're such a big-shot-executive in training, why are you wasting your time with a landscaper?"

The smile vanished from Casey's face, and her jaw dropped open. Richard's grin faded, too, and his jaw tightened as he looked at his ex wife. "Well, I don't really think of him as just a landscaper," Casey finally answered, rallying. "I think of him as a successful business owner; someone who's organized, competent, good with his customers and good at what he does. Someone who's capable of managing a staff as efficiently as he runs his household. And someone who does all that while making time to take care of his wonderful daughter as a single dad." She looked to him and smiled. "And besides, I've looked at some of his designs and I think they're really impressive. Even if he was 'just a landscaper,' he's talented and creative and he spends his days bringing beauty into the world. I think that's pretty good, as professions go."

Richard smiled, leaning over to kiss her in front of everyone. The kiss lingered, and eventually Casey was the one who broke away, glancing down at her hands crossed in her lap and grinning shyly.

"Here, here!" shouted his mother, smiling across at them. Richard dropped another kiss on Casey's temple, and she leaned her head into his shoulder.

"Very nice little speech," Lavinia said, her smile twisted. "But what are you going to do about work, then? You can't very well become a big shot executive if you move to Asheville to be with Richard. And he's sure not abandoning his business and taking our daughter somewhere else - I won't have it."

"Lavinia, you are out of line," Richard shot. "And you are setting a bad example for our daughter." He leaned across the table toward her, lowering his voice. "I invited you here as a goodwill gesture so you could get to know two people who I hope are going to become a big part of our lives. But I will not tolerate your jabs, implications and outright and attacking the woman I love. I need you to leave. We'll talk later about trying this another time."

Lavinia's eyes narrowed, and she let her breath out in a huff. "Fine. I'll take Cassidy and-"

"No, you will not," Richard commanded quietly. "It's not your day, and I have plans after lunch for the four of us. Then, Cassidy and Nicholas will stay with my parents while Casey and I enjoy a special date I've planned for our evening. So you and your husband will leave quietly, and I'll talk with you later."

Hank stood, glaring down at Richard. "Now look here," he began. "I will not have you speaking to my wife like that."

Richard rose from his spot at the picnic table and turned to face Hank, the family looking on in various states of shock and disbelief. "With respect, Hank, you need to let this one go." His voice was quiet and serious, full of implied threat.

"Or what?" he shot back, shoving his sleeves up his forearms one by one.

Richard turned to look at everyone staring at the two of them, and took a deep breath. Then he turned back to other man. "Hank, I have always made it a point to never speak ill of the mother of my child in front of our daughter. But the two of you need to leave, right now, or I fear this conversation is going to become unsuitable for little ears. If you feel like we still have something to talk about, you call me later and we'll make an appointment to hash this out face to face. But right now, I'm asking you to let my family go on with our day, and take your wife home."

"So, what, you get to impress your little tv girlfriend, but I'm not allowed to defend my wife's honor? Bullshit, Nathan." Hank spat onto the ground near Richard's feet.

"This woman," Richard shot back. "Is the woman I love, and I hope to God she's going to consent to be a part of the rest of my life." He grabbed the other man's shoulder roughly, half shoving, half dragging him out of the patio and toward Hank and Lavinia's car. "I have not impugned your wife's character or her honor - all I've said is that she's behaving badly, because I do not want Cassidy to think it's ok to carry on like that unchecked." Lavinia jumped up from the table, grabbed her purse and followed after the two men. "Now you've made a scene in front of my daughter, and several other children I care deeply about, and you've done a fine job of making your wife's behavior look like child's play. So I'm asking, as a personal favor, to get in your car and drive away from here before this goes any further."

Hank glanced over to the patio, where Wade and Boone had stood and begun walking toward them. Lavinia scurried ahead of them, looking harrowed. The kids stared at them, mouths agape. Cassidy looked like she was about to cry.

"Fine," Hank said at last, looking back at Richard and leaning into his face. "But this isn't over," he added, clenching his jaw.

Richard nodded. "So be it. But if you feel the need to continue this discussion, do me the courtesy of calling so we can arrange a time and place where my daughter won't have to see two grown men behaving like a couple of stupid boys."

Lavinia opened the passenger door and called across the car to her husband. "Let's go, Hank," she requested, and he slowly opened his door and climbed into the car, glaring at Richard the entire time. Richard stepped back as Wade and Boone flanked him, and the three of them stared after the retreating couple until the car had left the parking lot.

"What a jerk," Boone observed as they turned back to the group.

Meanwhile, Richard's mother had sat down next to Cassidy, holding the girl against her side and stroking her hair. Cassidy looked sad and deflated, but the threat of imminent tears had passed. Richard shared a glance with Casey, but moved past her to squat down in front of his daughter. "Cassidy, honey, I'm real sorry you had to see that," he said softly, reaching out to stroke her face with a gentle finger.

"Why was mother acting so mean?" she asked, her voice thin and wavering.

"It's hard to say for sure, honey, but I think maybe she was feeling sad, or maybe a little bit threatened, and didn't know how to deal with it," he tried to explain.

"Why would she feel threatened?" Cassidy probed.

Richard looked over to where Casey sat. "Well, honey, you know how we talked about the possibility that Casey and Nicholas might come to live with us, if we're lucky," he began. "Maybe your mother is afraid that Casey is going to try to take her place as your mom. But you and I have talked about that, and we know that nobody will ever be your mom but your mom. Casey would never try to take her place. But your mom might not realize that."

Cassidy sat up, sniffing and running her fingers through her hair to straighten it. "But why wouldn't mother just talk to you about that, then? Then she wouldn't have to feel sad or threatened, and she wouldn't have to be mean. Because it's not nice to be mean," Cassidy added, nodding decisively.

"That's true, honey," Richard answered. "And I'm glad you remember that. But sometimes people forget to be nice, or they're afraid to talk about things because the conversation might not go the way they want it to. But I think it's always better to talk things through, because then you're not guessing at what the other person is thinking, and you're not putting yourself in a position to behave inappropriately because you don't know what's going on."

She nodded. "Ok. Thanks, dad. Now you and grandma can go and sit back with the grown ups, and we'll go back to our game." Richard chuckled and shared a glance with his mother, but they took their places at the table. Boone and Wade were back where the'd been seated before, and the food had come out while they were occupied.

"I'm sorry she spoke to you like that, Casey," he said to her, his tone serious. "If I'd had any idea she would behave so poorly, I would never have invited her." He wrapped his arms around her and held her against him.

"But you handled her like a champion," Carolina offered wryly, and Casey chuckled against Richard's chest. "If she was hoping to show you up, she was sorely disappointed."

Richard released her, and Casey leaned back, staring up at him. "Well, I might have surprised myself a little, too. I could understand her sniping at me, somewhat, but she was being so disrespectful to you!" She shook her head, and Richard's lips turned up in a grin.

"Well, I don't think anyone has ever described what I do in such grandiose terms," he teased.

Lucinda, on her other side, grabbed her arm. "Well, I, for one, like you. I know we may be jumping the gun, here, but welcome to the family." Her sister, Charlotte, echoed her from the other side of the table. And Richard's parents smiled across at her, adding their own "Welcome to the family."

Casey blushed, but smiled broadly, and tucked into the tasty barbecue that had been placed in front of her.

After lunch, the four of them broke away to move on to Richard's next planned activity: horseback riding. Cassidy, an experienced equestrian, quickly took over Nicholas's instruction, seeming to take great delight in bossing him around and showing him how to hold his feet and where to put his hands and to 'mind your posture!'

Casey and Richard took it easy; she riding slowly around the expansive ranch on a polite but beautiful Chestnut, and he riding easily on a large dappled gray named Greatheart. "So the two of you ride often?" she asked, watching the easy way Richard handled his horse.

He nodded. "Ballet and horses - I've just been trying to keep up with her. Thankfully, I didn't have to learn ballet - all I had to do was show up at her recitals. But horses; she wouldn't be satisfied if I didn't have one of my own to ride alongside her, although I don't do any of the fancy equestrian stuff that she does."

Casey's jaw dropped. "You own that horse?"

He chuckled. "Yeah, I own Greatheart, here - Cassidy named him when she was six - and her Princess," he nodded at the small, honey-colored mare Cassidy was riding. "The horses you and Nicholas are riding belong to a friend. We stable here because I don't have time to take care of horses on top of everything else, but Cassidy is here most days anyway - I couldn't keep her away if I tried. She really missed them while we were at the mansion."

Casey shook her head. "I know I said that I understood you were successful, but I didn't realize you had horse money. I hear these things are not cheap."

Richard laughed at her. "Well, yeah, it's an expensive hobby. Stabling, the cost of the horses, vet bills, Cassidy's riding gear and all the fees for her lessons and events add up. It's a bit more costly than ballet. But she's such a good girl, and she's been through so much with her momma leaving us the way she did - I just have a hard time denying that girl anything she really wants." He lowered his voice conspiratorially and waggled his eyebrows. "And her horse friends are a lot more responsible and well-behaved than some of the kids her age. Don't get me started on cheerleading. God up in Heaven let her not take up cheerleading."

Casey laughed aloud. "What have you got against cheerleading?"

His face was grim. "I dated cheerleaders. I know what they get up to. I do not want some guy thinking and trying the stuff with her that I did with those cheerleaders." He shook his head.

Casey laughed again. "Had a rethink since we last talked about this? She's just starting to get to that age, too. Another couple of years, and you've got your hands full." She leaned toward him, shooting a glance at the kids to make sure they were too far away to hear her. "When I found out I was having a boy, a dear friend told me: 'Oh, girl, you're getting off easy. With a boy, you only have to worry about one penis. If you had a girl, you'd have to worry about ALL of the penises.'"

Richard's face paled, and his jaw clenched. "I never thought of it quite that way. Oh, man."

Casey chuckled, and reached across to pat his leg. "Don't worry. I know you're raising her right." She leaned toward him again. "But maybe don't wait too long to have the sex talk," she added, her voice low and her eyes sparkling with mischief.

"Dear God, woman, why are you putting these thoughts in my head again?" he groaned as she laughed at him.

"I have an idea how I can make it up to you," she told him, smirking and biting her lower lip. "Maybe you can practice on me." As Richard sputtered, she spurred her horse into a canter, catching up to the kids who were pulling away ahead and leaving him in a cloud of dust.

"So what are we doing this evening?" Casey asked with a smile as she greeted Richard.

"Mmm, you look good enough to eat," he ignored her question, admiring her slacks, sparkly sleeveless top and sexy jacket. He pulled her in close and kissed her thoroughly, wrapping one arm around her waist and the other in her hair. His tongue snaked into her mouth as she kissed him back, her arms coming to wrap around his waist, pulling him more firmly against her. A moment later, they broke apart, both of them panting slightly.

"I figured I'd better take you somewhere public," Richard finally responded to her earlier question. "Or else something like that is going to lead a little too far." He grinned as he turned her to face the building they were standing in front of. "It's an art gallery opening. A friend of mine is a photographer, and he's debuting an exhibit this evening." He gazed at her seriously. "I wanted you to know that just because we're down South doesn't mean we don't have culture and intellectual passtimes."

She frowned at him. "Richard, I don't think that."

He looked at the ground. "Well, you've lived in Manhattan and Philadelphia; you've probably had a ton of dates take you to lectures and museums and all kinds of intellectual stuff. I wanted to make sure you know we have that too; in fact, our River Arts District is full of painters, illustrators, sculptors and a host of other creative types. Asheville isn't just about the outdoors and mountain living; we've got great food and art and..."

Casey silenced him with a finger across his lips. "Richard. You don't need to work to make me fall in love with Asheville. From what I've seen - and read, I made a stop at the visitor's bureau - it's a pretty amazing place. I don't have any hesitation about moving here if things get that serious between us."

He tilted his head at her. "So you would move here? We haven't really talked about it - Lavinia's barbs this afternoon made me realize it's a pretty important conversation we haven't had."

She nodded. "Sure I would. You've got your business here, and Lavinia's not wrong about you not taking Cassidy away from the place she knows and loves, with her family - including her mom - left behind. Me and Nicholas appreciate having my family close by, but since his dad hasn't been in the picture, we're a lot more flexible about where we live than you are. I always kinda assumed that if you and I ended up together, I'd be moving here. I never even considered you coming to Philadelphia. Especially now that I know about Cassidy's horses," she teased.

He pulled her in for tight embrace. "You are such an amazing woman, Casey Kelly." After a moment, he leaned back, gazing into her eyes. "I would, though. If it was a deal breaker, I'd move to Philadelphia for you. I'd find some way to make it work with Cassidy and her mom. And I can always get another job."

She clucked at him. "That's sweet, but don't be silly, Richard. You belong here. And I can definitely see it's charms." She smiled. "So shall we go in and admire your friend's work?"

He grinned, his gaze turning mischievous again. "Yeah, we'd better. Otherwise, I'm going to start getting ideas again, and then the only place we'll wind up is looking for a bed." He winked, and she giggled, leading him into the gallery.

After a delightful evening with Richard's friends, they ended up back on the sidewalk again, the warm lights spilling out of the large industrial windows of the studio to soften the harsh glow of the streetlights. Richard pulled her into a shadow in the parking lot across the street, enfolding her in a solid embrace.

"I hate to let you go," he told her, his voice quiet. "I won't get to see you again until the cocktail party, and then you'll have to be wearing a public face. Maybe I can steal you away for a little while, but even that won't be enough. I just want you to be here, now, for real - not leaving me at the end of the night, but coming home with me."

She sighed against his chest. "That sounds wonderful. It's getting so hard to leave at the end of the night. It would be nice to be free to do whatever I want."

He tilted her face gently up to look into his eyes. "Then do it. Quit the show. Stay with me. Maybe you won't become a part of America's Favorite Couple, but we can start our future together right now."

She gazed into his eyes for a long moment, a smile playing softly around her lips. "I wish I could say yes, Richard, but I can't do that. I committed to this process from start to end, and I intend to see it through. It's only a few more weeks, anyway."

He shook his head. "You're here, now. Nicholas is here with my parents. Come home with me. We can spend a glorious night together, and then go collect the kids in the morning. Why waste more time playing at finding love when it's right here in front of you?" Without waiting for a reply, he captured her lips in his, kissing her passionately and leaving her breathless.

"Damn it, Richard, why do you have to make this so hard?" she complained.

"You're the one making it hard," he grinned, but his eyes were sad and there was more to his words than the obvious intimation.

Eventually, Casey tugged herself free from his grip. "I have to go, Richard, while I still can. But I want you to know how difficult this is. I'm not immune to the charms of your suggestion." She gave his hand a quick squeeze. "But everything will be clean and clear if we just see things through. Hang in there. Not too much longer to go."

He groaned, but let her lead him across the street to the van that would take her to pick up Nicholas, and then to the airport to travel to her next hometown date. Before she climbed into the van, it was Casey who wrapped her arms around him and pulled him close, giving him a passionate kiss that held the promise of so much more. When she pulled away, he stared after her helplessly. "Good night," she said, blowing him a kiss before closing the van door and driving off into the darkness.

"You did the right thing, you know," Vince said in her ear. Casey startled, as she'd been so wrapped up in the evening with Richard that she had half forgotten he was there. "They would never let you quit this close to the end. For better or worse, the show is really about you and Niko now. People are dying to know - who's his father? Will you pick his father? Will his father pick you? Or will you and Richard end up together? They'd never tolerate you ending that early and running off into the sunset with Richard. You're entertainment now, dollface." His voice was sad for her.

When Casey and Nicholas climbed out of the van, they stepped onto the bustling streets of New York City's Times Square. They were standing outside of a gigantic Toys R' Us, and Mike walked forward to greet them, hugging Casey and ruffling Niko's hair.

"Wow!" Nicholas gushed, looking up at the massive Toys R' Us storefront. Casey looked around them.

"Do you know where we are, Niko?"

"Yeah, we're at a giant toy store!"

She laughed. "Yes, but this giant toy store is in the middle of Times Square." He looked at her blankly. "Times Square is where the New Years Eve celebration we watch happens. They drop the ball just over there!" She pointed.

"Ok," he answered, unimpressed.

"Alright," she squatted down, turning him to face the bustling streets. "Let's play the Imagine game real quick."

"Look at all this space, and all these people walking by. Now picture this: the streets are closed. There are no cars driving through here. Instead, Times Square is full of people - hundreds of thousands of people. See all these people - imagine twice that many. And twice that again. Keep imagining more people until the entire space is one big crowd, people standing shoulder to shoulder, no-one able to move because there are so many of them. And it's cold. It's winter, and it's dark, but there are lots of lights. People are wearing hats and scarfs and winter coats, and they're standing out here for hours to celebrate the change to the new year."

She turned him. "Now look up there. See that spire? That's where the big, glowing New Years ball sits. After standing in the cold and the dark for hours, all those people start counting down at once when the giant, glowing ball begins to drop. Hundreds of thousands of voices all chanting at the same time - Ten, Nine, Eight..."

Niko, growing excited, pointed and started counting with her. "Seven, six, five..."

Mike, getting caught up in the moment, joined them. "Four, three, two, one! Happy New Year!" They shouted and hugged one another, Niko cheering.

"You're right, mom, this is super cool. All of my friends are going to die when I tell them I was here." His grin was huge and contagious. "Now can we go inside?"

Mike laughed. "Sure, kid, let's go." Casey grinned ruefully and followed after them, as Niko turned and dashed into the store.

"That was pretty awesome," Mike said to Casey as they headed through the doors.

"We work on it. I don't want him to get too bogged down in reality. Being a kid is awesome - it's the time of peak imagination - and I want him to enjoy it." She smirked and squeezed Mike's bicep. "After all, imagination is like a muscle. You have to exercise it often if you want it to grow big and strong."

He laughed. "Ok, fair enough."

Niko came running up to them and grabbed Casey's hand, tugging on it. "Mom! Mom! Can we ride the ferris wheel?" She looked at the giant structure filling the space. Before she could answer, Mike, laughing, replied "Sure," grabbed Casey's other hand and walked them over to the entrance. The guy running the ride waved them past the line, and they got into the next car - the Monopoly car, plastered with fake money and topped off with a giant Rich Uncle Pennybags figure. Niko's grin was huge as they went around and around, his eyes wide as he took in various things he wanted to see when they got off. When their turn was over, they climbed out of the car and Mike pulled them off to the side, kneeling in front of Nicholas.

"So here's the deal, little man. I feel bad that I've missed all these years of birthdays and Christmas presents, so I'm going to buy you something today. It can be anything you want - price doesn't matter."

Niko's face lit up, but Casey shook her head. "Oh, no, we're not doing that."

"But mom!"

"No. You know how this works. First of all," she chided, looking at Mike. "We never give gifts out of obligation."

He laughed. "But what about Christmas? Birthdays?"

She shook her head with a stern expression. "Christmas is about love, celebrating family, and if you have abundance, helping those who don't. At Christmas, we're lucky enough to be able to give to Niko's favorite animal shelter, a local soup kitchen, and we always give a few Toys for Tots, so people who are having a hard time still get to enjoy something special. We mostly make the gifts that we give friends and family."

"If other people are feeling generous toward us, Niko picks one thing he really wants and gets to keep it. The rest gets donated."

Mike's jaw hung open. "So then how do you get the latest video game system? Games? Electronics?"

Casey frowned at him. "Well, we don't *need* any of that stuff. But if Niko really wants something, he gets a chance to work for it. When his pop pop got him a Playstation 4 last year, Niko had to get straight As for a year - *and* he had to do a new extracurricular activity. He chose drawing class, which he liked so much that I've promised him a comic book class when we get home."

Mike shook his head. "Man, you are one strict mama."

Niko frowned at him. "Working for the things I really want instills a solid work ethic and teaches me to value the things I get."

Mike raised his eyebrows. "Dude, way to tow the party line."

Nicholas tilted his head. "What's 'tow the party line?'"

Casey hugged Niko. "Let's make a deal. If Mike is feeling generous, and wants to get you something to commemorate the day we're spending together today, that's ok. But you only get one thing. And let's not take advantage of his generosity and ask for the most expensive thing, ok?"

He looked serious, considering. "Anything?"

She frowned at him. "You know the rules. No violence, no gore.

Preferably age appropriate, although that's negotiable if it's educational or if I feel the age restriction is arbitrary."

Nicholas nodded. "Ok. That's fair. Let's go find something cool!" Without waiting, he grabbed Casey's hand and tugged her off into the store. She glanced at Mike helplessly, and followed after the determined boy.

They spent hours browsing the store, checking out all the toys that Niko might want - and the impressive store displays. Mike was a little uncomfortable when Niko wanted to go check out the Barbie house, but Casey followed him through and admired various toys with him while Mike stood around lamely outside. Mike was all about the giant T-rex though, practically dragging Niko over to check it out, and spending a lot of time inside the Jurassic Park area. The biggest hit with all three of them, though, was the Lego area. They all spent a while wandering around, admiring the giant Lego sculptures and checking out the various kits.

In the end, the toy that Niko chose was the result of a major negotiation. He asked for a Meccano personal robot building kit that cost nearly three hundred dollars. Casey was against such an extravagant expense, but Mike pointed out that it was extremely educational, with a kit that could build a wide variety of robotic creatures, and a programmable brain that could learn a variety of commands. Casey conceded, but by the time they left the store, the light was already fading.

"Ok, kiddo - time for you to go hang with Abbey while Mike and I go do whatever he has planned for us tonight. You'll probably be asleep by the time I get back to our room, so have a good night, and sweet dreams!" She hugged him. "Oh, and don't take that toy out yet. We've got a flight and a drive ahead of us in the morning, so you don't have much time to play with it and you might lose pieces if it's open when we travel."

Nicholas rolled his eyes at her. "Fine, mom. Goodnight." He jumped into the van with Abbey, the production assistant who looked after Nicholas when Casey was busy, and she was left alone with Mike.

"So where are we off to now?"

He smiled. "Our next stop is on fifth ave, around a mile away. Care for a walk?" he invited, holding out his arm.

She took it and smiled back at him, walking down the busy sidewalk arm-in-arm. "So will we be meeting your family at this next stop?"

He laughed aloud. "Umm, no," he responded, blushing. "You'll see why that's so funny when we get there," he grinned.

She nodded. "Ok. So when do we meet your family? After?"

He shook his head. "No, the family's not here for this visit, actually."

"Oh," she said, her voice carefully neutral. "They weren't able to make it?"

He shrugged. "Well. I don't know. They're in Salt Lake City. It seemed like an awfully long hike just to spend a few hours with you."

She nodded, staring straight ahead. "And they didn't want to meet Nicholas?"

"Well," he hedged. "I haven't really told them about Nicholas," he confided eventually.

She nodded again. "Planning to surprise them, then? Show up in Salt Lake and 'Hey, guys, meet your grandson!'"

Mike looked over at her, but she was still staring straight ahead, not meeting his gaze. "Well, we haven't gotten the paternity test results, you know? I didn't want to get them all bent out of shape about something that might not even matter, in the end."

Casey stopped walking, waiting for him to turn and face her before speaking. "I thought you were convinced that Nicholas was your son? That you were somehow missing us on some mystical, spiritual level and that's why your marriage didn't work out?"

"Well, sure," he answered, looking down at the sidewalk. "But I don't *know*, you know?"

Casey nodded, walking on without him. "And you wanted to keep your options open. Because you're not interested in Nicholas in general - only if it turns out that he's your son. And, by extension, you're not interested in me in general - only if it turns out I'm the mother of your child."

He grabbed her arm, forcing her to turn and face him. "Casey, that's not how it is."

She put her hands on her hips, staring him down, nostrils flaring. "Then how is it, Mike?"

He shrugged. "Well, I don't know - I haven't seen you in ten years! And when you pop up on my radar again, you've got a son - who might be mine. I'm doing the best I can. I'm just trying to figure it out, you know?"

She shook her head. "No, I don't know. You're going to have to enlighten me."

"Look, this whole thing is all about getting to know one another again and seeing if we might be able to have a relationship. So what are we fighting about? Why don't we just spend some time together, get to know one another, and see what there might be between us?"

Casey sighed, her shoulders slumping. "Fine. Let's do that. Where are we going again?"

Mike pointed. "This way." He waited for her to step alongside him and they resumed their walk, not touching, not talking.

Eventually, they stopped in front of a gray stone building on the corner. Casey looked up and saw the name of the business. "Museum of Sex?" she asked, turning to Mike. "This is our date?"

He nodded, grinning. "It's supposed to be a laugh."

"Ok," Casey replied grimly, stepping through the doors without waiting for him.

Inside, they entered what appeared to be a gift shop. There was all manner of sex toys and strange contraptions on display. Mike picked up a few items and showed them to her, grinning. She smiled back, but the expression never reached her eyes. They went downstairs to the museum, and came out an hour later. Mike seemed very entertained; grinning and ushering Casey along with an arm around her shoulders; but Casey's smile was wan and she made no effort to touch him.

When they stepped out onto the sidewalk again, Casey turned to him. "Did you have anything else planned for our evening, Mike?"

He put one hand on either side of her waist and pulled her to him, looking into her eyes. "I was thinking I could take you back to my place and show you around."

She rested her hands on his arms, but shook her head. "I'm sorry, Mike - I'm really not feeling that well. I think maybe all the travel is getting to me, but I'm just worn out. If it's all the same to you, I'd rather go back to my hotel and get to bed early."

He smirked, leaning in closer. "I can put you to bed early at my place, if you need to lie down."

She shook her head, grinning. "Nope, I don't think that would result in me getting the rest I need." Before he could say anything else, she stood on her tiptoes to give him a quick kiss on the lips, and then freed herself from his grasp, stepping away to hail a cab. Mike started after her, but she smiled and waved, stepping into the waiting taxi. "Goodnight, Mike! See you at the cocktail party." She closed the door behind her without waiting for a reply, and sped off.

* * *

When she got back to the hotel, hours later, she found the production crew huddled in the large living room in her suite. Vince, in person for once, gave her an unreadable look, before one of the other aides grabbed her and pulled her over to the couch, roughly shoving her down.

"What the Hell do you think you were doing?" asked a man whose name she didn't even know. His small frame practically quivered, as his nostrils flared and his helpless eyebrows rode the tide of his anger. "You do NOT get into an unsanctioned vehicle, ever, and drive away from our crew! You are not allowed to leave your handler, ever. And you've been gone for hours, without supervision or authorization. This is a serious breach of your contract!"

Casey took a deep breath before replying calmly: "Look, I'm sorry if I've worried anybody -"

The man held up a hand in her face, stalling her protests. "Worried? You think we're worried? We're pissed off! This is unacceptable! You cannot behave like this. You've signed an agreement. We OWN you for the duration of filming. You do NOT get to go off and leave us alone. Your time belongs to US."

Her eyebrows scrunched together as she frowned at him. "I hear what you're saying, but Mike was -"

"I don't care what Mike was doing!" the man shouted. "He could have been goddamn raping you for all I care, but we get it on film and you do not get to walk away from our crews, ever!"

Vince stepped up and grabbed the guy's shoulder. "Alright, Javier, you've made your point. Although, for the record, the show cannot condone the intentional harm of any of its participants, and that includes rape. So maybe you should take a walk and cool off for a bit. We'll impress upon her the seriousness of this breach."

A woman stepped up and took his arm, and he suffered himself to be led out of the room while the rest of the hovering production crew drifted away from the couch. Vince sat down next to her, his face grim.

"Look, Casey, I've tried to have your back, as much as I can, during this process. But just going off like that is way outside the bounds of the kind of slack we can cut. We didn't know if you'd just left the show, or if you'd gotten kidnapped on your way back to the hotel - or if you were intentionally violating your contract by talking to a news outlet, to one of the other contestants, to your family or to - anyone, really." He shook his head. "Javier is pissed, but mostly that's because he might be fired as a result of you going off like that. And he's not the only one. If the network thinks we can't keep tabs on you, they'll clean out your whole crew and find someone can. And these people all rely on their jobs to feed their families, pay their bills - all that."

She sighed. "Look, Vince, I really am sorry. I wouldn't want to get anyone in trouble. Honestly, I wasn't thinking. Mike just..."

He held up a hand to stall her response. "Hold that thought, Casey. You might be able to go a little way toward making this up if you've got a good confessional to offer. If we can play it up like we knew you were bailing, and we had it all under control - we were giving you an out after a horrible date with Mike, and you were really just going around the corner to where the crew was waiting for you - we might be able to brush this under the rug. If Javier can keep his cool. Let me grab a camera and get your confessional set up. We good?"

She nodded, perplexed, but willing enough to go along with what he offered. He had the crew set up the camera for her to make a confessional, and piped himself back into her earpiece - an earpiece which had stopped working as soon as her cab drove out of range of the production equipment. Now that she was back with the crew, his calm voice was back in her ear.

"Ok. Tell the camera what made you so unhappy about your date with Mike, and why you had to run out of there."

Casey took a moment to school her face into a sad smile, and launched into an explanation. "Just got back from my date with Mike, and... it didn't go as well as I would have hoped. I've been wondering, lately, if he really likes me and Niko - or if it's just about the idea of me - the woman who got away - and the son he never knew. Like we're some kind of missing piece he can just slot into his life, and everything will improve. Except it won't, because Mike is still the Mike he was way back then - and it was never going to work between us." She shook her head, the smile fading.

"I think, after tonight's date, I know the answer to that. Mike was just trying to buy his way into Niko's affection, after missing potentially nine years of his life - like he had to get him gifts to make up for all those missing years. Even though those years weren't his fault at all. And he didn't even bother to tell his parents about Niko - he doesn't really care about Niko at all, unless he turns out to be Mike's son. I don't think Mike even really wants a son - he's just looking for something to fill some hole in his life, and thinks we're it."

She shook her head again. "Anyway, his choice for tonight's date just shows that Mike and I are very different people. He took me to the Museum of Sex." The corner of her mouth twisted up in a wry smile. "Don't get me wrong - I'm as human as the next woman, and I'm not afraid of the idea of sex." Her smile faded. "But this is his big chance to make an impression on me in his hometown, and that's how he chooses to do it? That's just not... me." She sighed. "I realized that I can't imagine Niko and I trying to make a life here. I don't miss Manhattan, and Mike isn't going to leave here." She looked directly at the camera again.

"I went for a long walk in Central Park after I left Mike outside of the Museum of Sex. I had to see what it was like to be back in the city, and think about what it would be like to raise my son here, and how I'd feel about being here with Mike - or even just near Mike, if it turns out he really is Niko's dad - and far away from Neil and Richard. And I realized, Mike isn't it. I don't want to be with him. I don't want to be here. If he is Niko's dad, we'll have to find a way to make something work for Niko's sake, but it won't be living here. But all Mike was interested in was getting me back to his place and into bed... I had to get away. Thank God the crew had that taxi ready, and I was able to bail so easily."

"Nice save, Casey," Vince said softly in her ear. "Now don't do that again, and I'll see if I can smooth things over with the rest of the production staff and make nice for you."

Casey took a deep breath of the fresh air as she stepped out of the van on a picturesque farm in Vermont. Nicholas climbed out behind her, looking around enthusiastically. He spotted Neil first, and ran to greet him. Neil scooped him up in a bear hug and spun him around, using the momentum of his ebullient greeting, then set him gently back on the ground, groaning. "Man, you're way too heavy for that! You're gonna break my back."

Niko giggled, and Casey stepped up for a greeting of her own; a long, quiet hug, followed by a short but heartfelt kiss. "It's so good to have you here," Neil said, smiling widely.

Casey returned his smile, looking around. "So where is here?"

"Welcome to Boorn Brook Farm," Neil said with a half bow, waggling his eyebrows at Niko, who laughed in response. "We're here today for something I think you're both really going to like: a falconry lesson, followed by a hawk walk!" Nicholas squealed and jumped up and down enthusiastically.

Neil knelt in front of him. "I'm glad you like my idea! I totally agree with your enthusiasm, but there's something very important you should know: hawks are pretty picky. They're not big fans of loud squealing, laughing, squeaking or any sort of sudden, loud noises. Or sudden movement." He tilted his head and looked at Niko speculatively. "I wasn't going to tell you this, because I didn't want to scare you, but I think you can take it. Do you scare easily?" Nicholas shook his head, his eyes wide and solemn. "Ok. So here's the thing: if you move suddenly, or squeal, or squeak - the hawk will think you're dinner!" He reached out suddenly and 'got' Nicholas's nose. "That's what happens when they hunt rabbits and squirrels and other small rodents. And then - they eat them up!" Neil mimed eating Nicholas's captured nose, and the boy giggled, and Neil smiled. After a moment, though, his expression turned serious. "So. Do you think you can stay quiet, and remember not to make any squeals or squeaks or laughs?" Niko nodded. "And do you think you can move slowly - like you've got weights tied to your arms and legs to keep you from flying off?" Niko nodded again.

"Good! Ok, then, let's go meet the hawks!" He took the boy's hand and walked toward the barn, throwing Casey a smile over his shoulder. She smiled back, bemused.

When they entered the stable, they met the Master Falconer who would be conducting their lesson. He sternly repeated Neil's caution about noises and sudden movements, and Niko nodded carefully, his face serious. Then, the falconer walked them through the stable and showed them the birds, several Harris Hawks and a Tawny Eagle. He explained how birds of pray catch and eat their pray, much to Niko's delight. He showed them the powerful claws, dangerous talons and piercing beaks, making sure that Nicholas in particular understood that these were serious predators, not pets, and must be respected as such.

Once it was clear Nicholas was ready, they walked back to the stable doors and went over the equipment they'd be using. They tried on gloves, and the falconer showed them how to use the jesses and hoods. He cautioned that he would be the only one using the hood, but that they would all be expected to use the jesses to help control the hawks. Then, he instructed them to take their gloves and wait in the field outside while he brought out a hawk.

A few minutes later, the falconer brought out one of the Harris Hawks and showed them how to fly him. They each tried several launches and recalls, and even Nicholas got to do a couple of launches and recalls. The falconer explained to them how the lure would work, and went over the basics of how one would fly a hunting hawk. When they were all comfortable handling and being around the hawk, the falconer took the hawk back inside, put it away, and brought out a different hawk.

"That one is too full, now, from what we just did. They need to be hungry to fly and hunt - otherwise, they might not come back to the glove, and that's a fast way to lose a hawk. Sometimes, they come back after a few days if they get hungry or tired of being out in the weather - but not always. So we'll take Elmer for our walk."

For the next hour, the three of them walked the trails around the property. They went in and out of the woods, and practiced flying and recalling the hawk in the trees and in the open field. They didn't flush any small game, so when they got back to the stable, the master falconer fed the hawk. After he was fed, the hawk even submitted to a few light caresses from Niko before the falconer took him back inside.

Once the hawk was safely away, Niko looked around once to be sure, then ran up to Neil, pumping his fist in the air. "That was so cool!"

Neil chuckled. "I thought you might like that. Now that you've had the basic class, you can always come back another time for another hawk walk. But we always have to remember the rules about how to behave around the hawks. Now do you understand why?"

Nicholas nodded. "They're like raptors! They hunt little animals, and if I sound like a little animal or move like a little animal, it'll try to hunt me!"

Neil chuckled again, smiling. "That's right! And in fact, they are raptors, but I think the raptors you're talking about are the ones in Jurassic Park, yeah?"

Niko nodded enthusiastically. "We saw a T-rex yesterday by the Jurassic Park display at Toys R' Us. I thought it would have been better if it was a pack of velociraptors. But then Mike bought me a cool Meccano robot building kit. I can't wait until we're in one place long enough for mom to say it's ok for me to build it."

Casey grinned apologetically. "Sorry. Clearly he's excited about it."

Neil shrugged. "No worries. But now I'm wondering if I should have bought you something cool."

Casey shook her head emphatically. "No. We already had to give Mike the lecture about how giving is something you do out of generosity, not obligation."

Niko nodded, wanting to be a part of the conversation. "Yeah. He didn't even know how important it is for me to work for the toys and cool stuff I get!"

Casey burst out laughing. "Well, there's a bit more to it than that, but yeah."

Neil looked back and forth between the two of them. "Well, I can see that must have been an interesting day. But today is our day! So. Are you ready to have lunch - and meet my family?"

Casey and Niko looked at each other and nodded excitedly. "Come on, then!" Neil grabbed one of Nicholas's hands, and one of Casey's, and lead them across the farm toward a picturesque red barn standing off by itself. They walked around it until they got to a small wooden door in a beautiful chest-high stone wall, and Neil opened it, motioning them through. Then he closed the little wooden door behind them, and led the way up a garden path, between beautiful wildflowers, to the white front door.

When they opened it, they found a friendly-looking older couple standing on the other side. "These are my parents, Elizabeth and David," Neil introduced them. They stepped forward in turn, smiling, to take first Casey and then Nicholas in a warm embrace.

"And obviously, mom and dad, this is Casey - and Nicholas. She calls him Niko for short."

"Such a pleasure to meet you both," Elizabeth gushed, kneeling down to look into Nicholas's face. She smiled at what she saw there, and beamed up at her husband, giving him a single, small nod. He repeated the greeting, and then waved them through the mudroom and into the large, charming living room. There, they found a slender woman in her mid-30s, who smiled when she saw them.

"This is my sister, Rebecca," Neil offered, following them into the room. She shook Casey's hand, and she waved at Niko, who was suddenly bashful. "Becks, this is Casey and Nicholas."

Rebecca nodded, and Casey smiled in return.

"So, we've got a lovely lunch all ready for us in the kitchen," Elizabeth said as she stepped into the room, smoothing over the moment of awkwardness. "I'll bet you're hungry after your lovely walk in all this fresh air. Did you have a nice time on your hawk walk?"

"Yeah!" Niko cheered, then proceeded to follow them into the kitchen and launch into a stream-of-consciousness recap of the past two hours. Elizabeth deftly guided him to wash his hands and then set up a plate, all the while asking questions and making appropriate responses to his gushing. David followed them, assembling plates for himself and his wife, while Casey hung back and watched the scene.

"Is something wrong?" Neil asked, coming up beside her and gently cupping her elbow.

"No," she answered, shaking her head and dashing the back of her hand quickly across her eyes.

"Aww," he took her in his arms, pulling her against him. "What's the matter?"

Casey sighed against his chest, sniffling. "Just... this. I always wanted him to have this. My parents dote on him, but now your parents have jumped right in, and it's like they know exactly what to do and say." She leaned back and gazed at him without breaking the embrace, her eyes sparkling and moist. "And you. You're so awesome with him. That was just a perfect thing for us to do. And you didn't buy him some stupid, expensive toy... and you didn't take us to some overblown commercial Mecca..."

He smiled, wiping his thumbs under her eyes to clear away the moisture. "I'm just sorry this couldn't happen sooner. It's long overdue. But now that you're back in my life... or I'm back in yours... whatever happens, I'm going to make sure he isn't left wondering about his dad. I'll be around."

She sighed. "But what if... his dad isn't you?"

Neil grinned, his eyes sparkling mischievously. "Well, you did say you put my name on the birth certificate. Who's to say?"

Casey couldn't help grinning in response, but she tilted her head as she looked at him. "But there's the paternity test. If Mike's the father, he's got parental rights. He can assert those."

He shrugged. "My sister is a lawyer. I've already talked to her about it. Whatever happens, we'll find a way to deal with it. I'm not going to let the two of you go without a fight," his voice dropped as he gazed deeply into her eyes.

Although neither of them seemed to move, they were suddenly kissing, their arms sliding around one another in a tight embrace. The kiss continued, growing more passionate, before Neil's sister finally broke the spell by lobbing a dish towel at them with an amused "All right, get a room, why don't you, you two?"

Casey grinned shyly and giggled, but Neil raised an eyebrow as he gazed at her. "Well, there *is* a lovely four-poster bed in the master bedroom, just over there..."

"Alright, now, you two," Neil's mother chided gently, but she was smiling at them. "We've got a lunch to eat! And I want to get to know my new friends."

The six of them sat down at the big, sturdy farm table. They seated Casey at the end, with Neil on her left and Nicholas on her right. Next to Niko was Neil's mother, Elizabeth, and his father sat at the other end of the table. He sister sat on his left, across from his mother.

Elizabeth made small talk for a few minutes, and they politely worked their way through their lunch. Before they were even halfway through, though, Neil's sister broke in, her tone less than friendly. "So, Marie," she began, and then paused.

"Actually, it's Casey," she interjected, glancing at Neil.

"Oh. Right. Not Marie. Casey. The woman my brother spent an amazing day with, who utterly captivated him - apparently to the point of conceiving a child - and then vanished off the face of the planet by the time he came looking for her, taking said child out of his reach for nearly ten years, gave him a fake name. I slipped."

Casey, stricken, glanced over at Nicholas. He was staring down at his plate, shoving his food around, his lower lip quivering like he was about to start crying. Noting her gaze, Elizabeth looked over and saw the situation. She put a hand on his shoulder, asking "Young man, do you like dogs?" Niko looked up, nodding, his face hopeful. "Neil does, too. I brought along one of his favorite books from when he was your age. It has pictures of all of the breeds of dogs, and descriptions so you can get to know their personalities. Why don't we go take a look at it in the living room?"

Nodding happily, he stood and followed her out of the room, hand-in-hand. David glanced at the three of them, and then followed her out.

Neil fixed his sister with a stony gaze. "Rebecca, play nice."

Casey shook her head. "No, she's got something to say, so I want her to say it. Let's get all this out into the open and clear the air so we can move forward without a bunch of pent-up animosity." She turned to Rebecca. "So let's hear it."

The other woman shook her head. "You are unbelievable. You just suddenly turn up out of the blue, ten years later, and now there might have been a son all this time? Not only has my brother been dealing with the disappointment he's carried around all these years since you vanished, and the idea that maybe you were never even real to begin with - just a figment that sprang from his coma - but now we find out he may have had a son all this time, and you denied him nine years of that boy's life?" She slammed her hand on the table. "And now you just expect to bat your eyelashes at him, say 'sorry,' and move on like none of this ever happened?"

Casey sighed. "That's not how it is."

"Then how is it? I want to know! I want to hear from your own mouth how you could possibly justify putting him through seven kinds of hell and then just expecting to play nice and pick things up again all these years later?"

Casey looked down at the table. "You're right that Neil deserves better than this. You all do. I was so busy protecting myself all these years that I didn't do what was right by my son, and didn't give Neil the chance to be a part of his life." She looked up, her expression serious as she gazed into Rebecca's face. "I know I can't make it up to him, or to all of you. All I can do is say that I'm sincerely sorry, and do what I can now to make things right. I can't undo what I did."

Rebecca shook her head in disgust, but Casey continued. "But. I'm not trying to excuse my actions here - just give you an explanation. From my perspective, I had this magical day with this amazing guy, and then he just vanished. He never called me. He never came back to my place. I never saw him in the park. The only explanation in my head was that he was intentionally avoiding me."

Rebecca exploded. "Bullshit! My poor brother almost died, coming home from your apartment. He was in a coma. It took him months just to get out of the hospital. Which you would know if you hadn't just hared off to who knows where when things got serious. Or if you'd ever bothered to come looking for him."

Casey held her hand out in a placating gesture. "That's true - I didn't come looking for him. But were you ever a young girl who thought a guy was totally into you, and then he never called? How did that make you feel? Either you act like a stalker and look like some sort of sorry, desperate wreck trying to hunt him down and get him to talk to you again - or you feel like a fool for getting attached, but suffer in dignified silence, and accept that 'he's just not that into you.'" Casey shook her head. "I had my pride. I thought I was doing the right thing by taking my medicine like a grown-up and letting the guy go when he clearly - to me - didn't feel the same way I did."

Rebecca sighed loudly, frustrated. "Fine, whatever, but first of all - my brother isn't like that. And second of all, you may have thought you were doing the right thing at first, but what about maintaining radio silence when you found out you were pregnant?"

"Umm," Casey looked at Neil. "Not to put you on the spot, but when you were younger, did you ever have a date with a chick who seemed to really like you - and then not call her again?"

He shrugged. "I don't remember off the top of my head, but probably. If it was just one date, and I wasn't that into her, I might have blown her off. I wasn't immune to doing dumb stuff, especially in college."

Rebecca shook her head. "Whatever. But when you were pregnant, you should have tried to get in touch with him."

Casey nodded. "Now that I've had a chance to talk to Neil, and the idea of Niko's dad isn't so abstract, I agree. I should have. But at the time, I thought I was letting some guy who didn't want to be with me off the hook. I thought it would be easier for me if I didn't have to see him constantly, as I still had feelings for him and I knew it would tear me up to know he didn't want to be with me. But I also thought it would be easier for him to never know. He'd never feel obligated to pay child support, or potentially 'do the right thing' and offer to marry me for the sake of an unborn kid. When I was younger, I thought it was a win-win for both of us."

Rebecca shook her head again, still frustrated. "But..." She sighed. "Ok. Fine. You thought you were handling things in the best way you could, even though it was completely shitty for us. But damn, I wish you'd had someone around to talk sense to you."

Casey shrugged. "I didn't. That's why I moved back home. The girls I lived with in Manhattan were completely clueless. They were nice enough, but they were so concerned with the next party and whether the guy they liked would call back, and whether they'd get the job they wanted, that they totally couldn't relate to a girl their age who was suddenly pregnant and on the verge of motherhood. I never even told them. I just said that Manhattan wasn't working out, and I was moving back home."

"But surely they told you later that Neil had come looking for you?" Rebecca probed.

Casey shook her head. "Nope. They forwarded me mail twice after I left, but aside from that, I never heard from them again."

"Well, shit," Rebecca finally said, staring at the table. After a long moment, she looked back up at Casey. "You know, I really want to hate you." Casey bit her lip, but remained silent, nodding. "And a little part of me always will," she added, putting a hand over Neil's. "Thoughts of you gave him the strength and the courage to fight his way out of that coma, and work through his injuries in rehab. The doctors weren't even sure if he'd be able to walk again. It was a hard, hard time for him." Neil put his other hand over Rebecca's. "But you got him through it. He even started running again, because of you." She shook her head. "But then, when he couldn't find you, he broke apart into a thousand pieces again. But this time, it was somehow worse, because we couldn't see his injuries; there wasn't some sort of physical ailment that we could treat medically. He was just..." She shook her head again.

"Hey, now, I wasn't that bad," Neil interrupted, smiling wryly. "I may have been a little morose for a while, but I got over it. I moved on."

Rebecca shook her head. "No, that's the thing, Neil. You never did. You eventually dated again, and you acted like everything was fine - but she's the reason you haven't held down a serious relationship. She's the reason you never married."

He snorted. "Yeah, and how well did marrying work out for you?"

Rebecca leveled a glare at him that could melt ice. "Out of bounds, Neil." Her voice held a dangerous edge.

He sighed. "Sorry. I shouldn't have said that. I didn't mean it. It's just frustrating to have you picking apart my entire relationship history, and to have you telling the woman I want to be involved with how much of an emotional mess I've been."

His sister rolled her eyes at him. "'The woman you want to be involved with?' Oh, dear brother, why get all circumspect now? Just tell her you want to jump her bones, and spend the rest of your life with her, and have lots and lots of babies, and let's all move on."

Neil blushed a deep scarlet. He tried to counter Rebecca's words, but he just kept opening and closing his mouth, like a fish, while nothing came out. A slow smile spread over Casey's face as she watched his discomfort.

Rebecca chuckled, eyeing her brother and then giving Casey a wicked grin. "Well, ok, then. I guess my work here is done." She shook her head again, sighing as her smile faded. "I'm not quite ready to let go of all my anger over this," she told Casey, standing. "I've spent ten years cultivating it, and it's not going to go away overnight. But I think you and me are good. Or we will be, anyway." She squeezed Neil's shoulder, and then turned toward the living room. "Thanks for talking," she threw over her shoulder as she walked out.

Casey stared after her for a moment, then turned to Neil. He was looking a little more composed, but still couldn't meet her gaze. "So. That was... enlightening."

He nodded, then sighed and turned toward her, his voice brisk. "Yeah. I guess I should have expected that. She hasn't had much time to deal with all this, and... well, she's a good sister. But I'm sorry she was so..."

"Direct?" Casey offered.

"Hostile," Neil responded.

Casey smiled sadly, tilting her head. "Well, I suppose I had it coming. Most of it, anyway. I did screw up a lot then, but I was just a kid and I didn't really know what I was doing. I tried to do the best I could, but I made a mess of it."

He shook his head. "I know it's a lot - and I feel like I should still be angry at missing out on so many years of my son's life - but I think I've come to understand why you did what you did." He turned toward her, reaching out to take her hand in both of his. "Casey, I forgive you. I want you to know that." Tears sprang to her eyes as he continued. "I wish we could go back and do it all over again, and get it right from the beginning... but better late than never. I just want to get it right now, this time, and go forward from here with no regrets."

"Oh, Neil." She bent down and gently kissed the backs of his hands. "That's so much more than I deserve. I can't tell you how much this means to me, really."

He stood, stepped around the corner of the table, and gently guided her to her feet. He wrapped one arm around her waist, pulling her close, and used the thumb of his right hand to wipe away the tears that were beginning to spill from her eyes. "Don't do this to yourself, silly girl. I forgive you, so you have to forgive yourself. Stop punishing yourself. It's time to move forward."

Casey wrapped her arms around him as she started sobbing, dripping tears on his shirt and clinging to him helplessly. He held her while she cried, gently rubbing her back in soothing circles. Neil's father started to come into the kitchen, but noted the scene and quickly turned around again.

Eventually, her sobs quieted and Casey cried herself out. She pulled away, sniffling and wiping her face, but he wouldn't let go of her entirely. "I'm serious, Casey. I want to move forward. With you. And Nicholas. I want us to be together. I want us to be a family."

She smiled tremulously. "Can we start by finding me some tissues so I can clean up?"

He led her to the bathroom. "Take your time. We'll be entertaining Niko in the living room." Before he closed the door behind himself, he gave her a smoldering look, but didn't say anything else. When he had gone, Casey stared at the closed door for a long time.

Everyone was resplendent in formal evening wear for the last cocktail party in the mansion. Anastasia wore a stunning gold sheathe dress and matching stiletto heels, and her hair was styled into an elaborate updo. Casey wore a sparkling midnight blue gown with silver accents; cut low in front, and with a plunging back. Her hair was styled into a sophisticated french braid.

The men had made an art of looking dashing. Neil wore a simple black Armani suit with subtle black pin striping, expertly tailored to show off his slim, toned body. Mike wore a dark grey suit that hugged his muscular torso, although it looked a little too tight across the chest, shoulders and arms. Richard also wore a black suit, but it was very no-frills and solid; just like him.

As they milled around in the main living space of the mansion, Nathan May strode into the room. They greeted him, smiling and automatically forming a small group in front of him. "This is the last time you'll all be together," Nathan began without preamble. "I advise you very strongly to use this time to ask any remaining questions you might have, and to say anything you need to say, before tomorrow's vote. With hometowns, it's been a big week, and pressure is on to really search your feelings and determine who you want to be with. Next week will be the exotic dates abroad, and only four of you will be going. And the week after that will be the final week, in which America chooses its Favorite Couple. So get to it, guys and girls - and I'll see you tomorrow for the vote." With a wave, Nathan walked out again, leaving the five of them standing around, staring at each other in silence.

"Well, this is awkward," Casey observed, staring around at the group with a shy smile. Anastasia looked annoyed, and Mike shot her a glance.

"Can I borrow you for a few, Casey?" Richard asked. Casey nodded and took his arm, and they headed to a secluded seating area in front of the mansion.

Once they were out of sight of the house, Richard wrapped her up in a tight embrace, his hands resting warmly on her bare back. "Mmm, it's good to see you again." Without waiting for a response, he tilted her head up and kissed her, his lips massaging hers and his tongue probing her depths. When he released her again, he sighed, resting his forehead against hers. "It's getting harder and harder to be away from you."

She smiled, leaning back to gaze up at him and caressing his face softly with her hand. Suddenly, she winked, pressing her hips against him. "That's not the only thing getting harder," she teased him, and he chuckled.

"Now none of that, or we're going to get carried away again," he chided gently. His eyes roamed over her. "You look ravishing, by the way," he added, stepping back to admire her more fully. Gently, he lifted her hand and twirled her, catching her in his arms after a few rotations. "Alright, maybe we can get a little carried away," he amended, moving in to kiss her again, one hand roaming across her bare back, while the other crept down to cup her ass.

She returned the embrace, sliding her arms inside his jacket and pulling him firmly against her. The kiss escalated, grew more passionate, until they both broke apart again, breathless.

"Maybe we should have a seat," he offered, guiding her the few steps to the padded bench and waiting for her to sit. Then, he sat next to her, wrapping an arm around her shoulders and pulling her against him. "I cannot wait until this is over," he told her, his voice low. "Because I need to get you all to myself for a few days while we get some of this tension out of our systems."

She smiled, leaning her head against his shoulder. "That sounds fabulous. Just a few more weeks."

He looked down at her. "Do you mean it? We'll be together at the end of this, in a few weeks?"

She stared into his eyes. "I mean this is over in a few weeks. And then all of us will be free to pursue our heart's desires."

"And what does your heart desire?"

"A lot of things. But this is a good start," she pulled his head down to hers, licking his lips lightly and then kissing him sensuously.

"Incoming," Vince said in her ear, and Casey pulled away just in time for Neil to come around the bushes toward them. Casey sighed deeply, and Richard fixed Neil with an unfriendly stare.

"Can I borrow you, Casey?" Neil asked, taking her hand without waiting for a reply. She glanced helplessly at Richard, but then she was on her feet, following Neil through the main entryway and out the back toward the pool. As they crossed through the main living space, they saw Anastasia and Mike in an intense conversation, but didn't stay long enough to hear what they were discussing.

When they got out to the pool area, Neil led her to the same cushioned bench where she and Richard had their stolen moment a week earlier. "My turn," he whispered into her ear, before taking the lobe into his mouth and nibbling gently. Her head lolled back, and he attacked the side of her neck, kissing and suckling his way down to the hollow of her throat.

She struggled to catch her breath, panting and hanging limp and helpless in his grip. "Not that I'm complaining," she whispered, "but what's this all about?"

He pulled far enough away to stare intently into your eyes. "I know you have some sort of insane chemistry with *him*," he answered, his brows pulling together in a frown, "so I wanted to remind you that we have a fire that can burn just as bright, although that's not all we have." He kissed her lips, then her chin, then began working his way down his jaw to her other ear. "I also know that you have some sort of bond as parents, but you and I will have that, too," he whispered, his voice fierce in her ear. "Because I believe that Nicholas is my son, and I pray that you and I are going to raise him. Together." He nibbled on her earlobe, then suckled the tender spot on her neck just below her ear.

"But mostly," he pulled back to look into her hooded, desire-filled eyes, "I think you are a beautiful, amazing person, I adore everything about who you are, and I want to spend every minute with you." He leaned into her, staring intensely into her eyes, his breath mingling with hers as he whispered against her lips. "Because I am in love with you, and I can't bear to let you go." He kissed her passionately, and she returned the kiss just as fiercely, her arms snaking around him to pull him tight against her.

Eventually, he pulled away far enough to gaze into her eyes again. His voice broke as he spoke again, deep and throaty with emotion. "Even if you end up with him, I will always love you, forever. I am lost. I am yours. Utterly, and completely." He kissed her again, but this kiss was sweet and tender, offering everything, not taking; carrying his heart on his lips.

Mike chose that moment to walk out into the pool area, clearing his throat awkwardly. "Sorry if I'm interrupting, but I was hoping to chat with Casey for a few minutes."

Neil didn't even bother to look over at him. He continued to hold Casey, one arm securely wrapped around her waist, the other gentle at the back of her neck. Without breaking his gaze with Casey, he replied: "Not a good time, Mike." He kissed her again, softly, and then again, in a persistent series of kisses that built in passion and intensity. She matched him kiss for kiss, returning everything he gave her.

Mike continued to stand there awkwardly, and then he cleared his throat again. Neither of them paid him any attention. Finally, he stepped closer and spoke. "Dude, I'm not going away. Have some respect, man. I'm trying to form a relationship with her, too, and it's not cool for you to carry on kissing her like I'm not even here."

Neil took his time about ending the kiss, letting its momentum fade gently while the two of them slowly came back to reality after the emotional exchange. Eventually, he released her lips, but the two of them stood locked in an embrace, gazing into one another's eyes, for a long moment after. Finally, Neil stepped away, releasing her but continuing to hold her hand. Smiling slightly, he turned to Mike. "What, now?"

Mike shook his head. "Seriously, not cool. Scram. I need to talk to her." His look shot daggers at Neil, but the other man didn't seem bothered. He returned his gaze to Casey and smiled slowly at her, evoking an answering smile from her in return. At last, he raised her hand to his lips and kissed it, lingering, before releasing her and turning to head back indoors. She stared after him until Mike cleared his throat.

"Hey. Earth to Casey. Is that it? Have you chosen him, and the rest of us can just screw off?" Annoyed, he stepped closer. Casey instinctively backed away from him, sitting heavily on the padded bench seat behind her.

She shook her head, her expression still dreamy. "No, sorry, Mike. You just caught us in a... moment."

"Yeah. I noticed." His tone was thick and sarcastic. Without waiting for an invitation, he sat beside her. "So? Is it him? What if the kid is mine?"

Casey blinked, finally seeming to really notice him. "Sorry, Mike. I was a little preoccupied." She shook her head. "As much as he might think - or hope - otherwise, no, I haven't made a decision. And yes, Nicholas's parentage is still up for debate until we get the paternity results. But how much does that matter to you?" She tilted her head and looked at him, pursing her lips. "I thought you said you had come looking for us? That we were what you were missing? Is that only if he turns out to be your son after all?"

Mike looked away. "Well, no, I didn't mean it like that. I do want to give things a try again with you and me. I think we ended things prematurely back then, and I think we have a lot of potential." He looked back at her. "And when I first came to the house, I thought you felt the same. You seemed to enjoy the time we spent together early on. But lately..." he shook his head. "I don't know. I just get the sense that you aren't really into it."

She sighed, reaching out to place her hand on his. "I'm not going to lie, I was a little disappointed by our hometown date. You must be picking up on that. I'm sorry I didn't say anything about it at the time - I just felt like I couldn't complain because you had gone to the effort to plan that stuff for us. But it wasn't really the stuff I would have planned. It didn't show me that you and I share similar values or interests. Honestly, I think we'd have our work cut out for us if we were trying to raise Niko together."

Vince's voice spoke in her ear. "Hey, just a reminder here, kiddo, but we need a show. Mike is a big part of that show. Can't dump the potential baby daddy just yet. You can doubt, but it's gotta look like there's still a chance."

She tilted her head, giving him an appraising look. "Maybe it was just an off day. We did have fun together early on, that's true. And you've been at a disadvantage since you got here, because I had already spent more time with the other guys." She nodded. "Maybe it's just that you and I have more catching up to do."

He clasped her hand. "So what does that mean? Are you willing to try to get there? Or do you just want to focus on the other relationships you're building, and let this go?" He seemed so sincere that Casey reached out and caressed his face, smiling gently at him.

"I think I'd be doing us both a disservice if I did that. If you are Niko's father, it would be selfish of me to not at least try to find out whether there could be a relationship between us. I owe that to you, and to myself, and to Niko." She smirked. "And then there's the fact that you're hot, and we did have fun together." She winked at him, and he laughed out loud.

"Now there's the woman I remember!" He grinned and leaned in closer, sliding his arm around her shoulders. "I thought you had lost your sense of humor." He kissed her, confidently, the kiss of a man who knows where he stands. She slid her hand up his arm, squeezing his bicep. He broke away and grinned. "You like?"

She chuckled. "Yes, Mike, it's very clear you've been taking care of yourself."

He grinned wickedly at her and then stood, sliding one arm under her knees and tightening the other around her back, and picked her up lightly. She squealed, and her arms flew around his neck. He hefted her easily in his arms, tossing her up a few inches and then catching her again. "It does have its advantages." He tilted his head down to hers, his voice lowering seductively. "I could carry you back up to my room and we could forget the rest of this stupid party." He put his lips to her ear and whispered. "With all these muscles, I can do some pretty athletic positions... maybe you want to try something new?"

She giggled. "As interesting as your invitation is, I don't think the others would appreciate us leaving the party early." She wiggled as she felt her dress slipping, and lightly slapped his chest. "Now put me down, you big oaf - I think I may be about to have a wardrobe malfunction."

He didn't budge. "I could help with that. Maybe take you someplace more private so you can address it? Or just remove the dress entirely?" He deliberately eyed the low-cut chest. "I think there's far too little of it. You should probably take it off before you have an embarrassing incident."

She snorted at him. "That's what I'm trying to avoid. Now kindly put me down - I happen to like this dress."

He grinned lazily, but obliged her. "Fine. But I want you to remember my offer. If you feel like you want to revisit this conversation, you know where to find me. I know you'll enjoy it."

Casey smirked as she tugged at her dress, trying to make sure it was all safely back in place. "Why don't we leave something to anticipate for the overnight dates?"

He shook his head. "Man, you really know how to make a guy work for it, don't you?"

She tilted her head at him. "Careful, Mike - you're starting to sound like a womanizing misogynist."

He frowned. "Ahh, you know I mean it in good fun, Case. It's not like it's anything we haven't done before. And we both agree we're good at it."

"Mmm," Casey replied noncommittally. "Let's not make assumptions, shall we? It's been a while. I seem to remember good things, but I've had more experience since then." She grinned broadly. "If you play your cards right, maybe you'll have a chance to show me again." As he stepped toward her, she shooed him away. "Not right now! Back to the house."

He sighed, but obediently led the way back into the party.

"Nice work," Vince praised her. "He seems to think he still has a chance, anyway, so maybe America will buy it, too."

When they entered the main living space, Neil and Anastasia were sitting on a couch together. Anastasia was leaning against him, her breasts pressed against his chest, as she spoke into his ear. He smiled at whatever she said, but the smile faded as he saw Casey come into the room.

She turned back to Mike. "Umm, actually, I am a little concerned about this dress. It doesn't feel quite right; I think maybe it's about to cause problems. Make my excuses to everyone, will you?" She kissed his cheek, squeezing his arm as she turned toward her room. "Goodnight."

When it was time for the voting ceremony to start, the participants filed in, one by one. Mike went first, followed by Anastasia. Neil was next, then Casey, holding Nicholas's hand, and finally Richard and Cassidy. Nathan May was already standing in the front of the room when they filed in, and his face was serious as he greeted them.

"Good evening. As you know, the stakes are higher than ever this late in the process, and another one of you is going to be going home today. We've watched your relationships grow in the past eight weeks, and it's clear that you're forming real attachments and there are real feelings involved - which makes this process even harder. But tonight, it's time to say goodbye to one of you."

One of the production assistants walked over and handed Nathan a sealed envelope. He nodded his thanks, then turned back to the group. He opened the envelope, looked at the card inside, and then looked up at the group, dropping his hand to his side.

"Alright. This is a very important elimination. After this week, there will only be four of you left, and next week you're going on our exotic getaway dates. America has spoken, and this week, we'll be saying farewell to..." He paused dramatically and looked at each of them in turn. "Anastasia," he finally said, his eyes resting on the stricken woman. "It's time to say your farewells."

She turned to look at the group, her eyes going back and forth between Neil and Mike. Finally, she stepped up to Neil and gave him a big hug. He returned the embrace, whispering something in her ear. Then, she stepped over to Mike and wrapped her arms around him. He gave her a squeeze, and kissed her forehead in a surprisingly tender gesture. He left one arm wrapped around her waist. "Can I walk you out?" he asked. She nodded, using her thumbs to wipe away tears from the corners of her eyes.

The two of them left the room, Anastasia completely ignoring Richard, Casey and the kids. Richard, Casey and Neil exchanged glances, and Nathan remained standing at the front of the room. After what felt like a long time, Mike returned, resuming his place among the men. Nathan looked at each of them in turn.

"Ok. Casey, you're the last woman standing, so no matter what happens in the next few weeks, you will be one half of America's Favorite Couple." He offered a smile. "Congratulations." His face turned serious again, and he looked at Richard and Casey. "Now as you know, next week you'll be having the exotic getaway dates. Richard and Casey, Cassidy and Nicholas will not be accompanying you on the next leg of your journey, due to the difficulties and logistics around traveling internationally with children. So they'll go home and stay with your families, while you focus on finishing this journey."

He looked to the four of them in turn. "Because Casey is the last woman standing, we know the final week will be dates in her hometown of Philadelphia with the final two men. And then, at the big reveal, we'll find out if there will be a proposal from one of you - and if she'll accept."

"So it's very important that you use this next week to really cement your relationships, and think about whether you want to propose - and how you'll respond, Casey. To this end, we're having one final two-on-one date, and then three one-on-one dates - and each one-on-one date will include an overnight portion where you can choose whether you want to forego your individual rooms and stay together in a camera-free suite."

He smiled. "So are you ready to find out where you're going?"

They looked at one another, smiles growing as the excitement of the moment sank in.

"For your exotic adventure, we're going really exotic this time, as you'll be traveling to Japan. Specifically, Okinawa." He smiled broadly. "We've got a lot of fun activities lined up for you, so we hope you have a great time as you explore your relationships and the island."

"For tonight, prepare to say farewell to your kids, pack up and get ready to head out tomorrow on the next phase of your journey!"

CHAPTER SIX

Week Nine

"Welcome to gorgeous Okinawa," Nathan greeted the four of them. "We've got plenty of fun adventures planned for you, but today is your final two-on-one date." The guys exchanged glances, but Casey refused to look at them. "Today's date is for Richard, Casey... and Neil." Casey stared down at the floor, while Richard and Neil traded an intense stare.

"Ok. The kids aren't here, but we've planned the first part of today's date in honor of one of Nicholas's favorite pastimes: karate. Out of respect for local customs and the incredible culture surrounding karate, we won't be visiting any of the local dojos while we're here. Instead, we've made arrangements with the International Karate Study Center, which hosts many international students, to host a session for you there. You'll spend a few hours learning the basics, and then you'll spar. The winner of the match will go on to the evening portion of the date with Casey." He smiled at Neil and Richard in turn. "Guys, best of luck - and enjoy your day!"

With that, Nathan turned and left the room. Casey sighed, then turned to the two men. "Ready?" she asked.

Mike grinned broadly. "What I wouldn't give to be a fly on the wall for this date," he teased.

The three of them piled into the nearby van without speaking. When they got out again, an awkwardly silent ride later, they had arrived at the International Karate Study Center. Casey's eyes were wide as she took in the large stone blocks that formed the wall framing the entrance arch. Without waiting for the guys, she waked through the archway and into the complex, turning slowly as she admired the red tile roofs, the high walls and twisted trees. "This place is so cool," she said, to no-one in particular. "Niko would have loved it."

Richard chuckled as he stepped up behind her. "I'm sure he'd be envious that we're going to learn some moves - but I bet it would have entertained him to watch us bashing away at each other."

She turned and smiled at him, her smile including Neil who was just walking up. "Actually, he wouldn't be envious about you learning karate. He'd be super psyched about it. Although he might ask you to spar - a lot. He's an orange belt, though, so he might kick your asses." She winked.

Richard smirked. "Hmm, a nine-year-old orange belt versus a thirty three year old white belt... he might have the moves, but I'm pretty sure I'd have him on reach and physical strength."

Neil glanced at Richard, then focused on Casey. "I'll bet he's a little spitfire. I might have to let him win."

She shook her head. "Don't do that," she cautioned. "If he figures it out, it undermines his confidence. Plus he'd never let you live it down. You might go a little easy on him to make it fun for him and help him stay motivated enough to improve - so he can beat you someday - but letting him win is a bad idea."

Neil nodded. "Good to know." He took Casey's arm, walking with her toward the training hall. "You're such a good parent, Casey. How did you learn all this stuff? I know they don't come with a manual. But I feel like I should know more than I do, coming in so late to the game."

She shook her head. "Don't worry about it. You'll pick it up as you go along. And Niko's pretty forgiving, as kids go. Mostly, it's important for us to be on the same page on the big stuff, so he's getting a consistent example and response from both of us." She looked at him shyly out of the corner of her eye. "I'm new to this whole co-parenting thing. I've been used to doing things my own way all these years, so I'm sure I'll have to adjust to letting someone else have a say."

Richard stepped up on her other side, giving her a big smile and nodding empathetically. "That was a tough lesson for me and Lavinia. Especially since she dropped out of Cassidy's life for so long. As the primary parent, I'm the one who's most likely to get my say, but I do have to listen to her side. When it comes to girl stuff, sometimes she knows better than I do." He shrugged. "You'll work it out over time."

Casey nodded. "That makes sense," she replied, turning her attention to him and dropping Neil's arm. "I feel like I've got all this extra baggage, though, because it's my fault Neil missed out on so much of Niko's life.

So I feel extra sensitive about considering his parenting perspective..."

Neil placed a gentle hand on her shoulder, stopping her in her tracks. "Casey, I know we're going to have to feel our way through this, but I really do want you to stop blaming yourself. We'll figure it out. But I don't want you to give extra weight to stuff I say, or do something you wouldn't want to do ordinarily, just because you're struggling with guilt over what's happened."

She sighed. "Thanks." Then she glanced ahead to where Richard had continued walking a few feet, so as to give them space for the sensitive discussion. "This is really weird," she said loud enough to include both of them. They both grinned at her, but carefully avoided glancing at each other.

"Weirder than the two-on-one last week with Mike?" Neil asked.

Casey nodded. "Yeah. Which I guess says something about my relationship with him." She looked at them each in turn. "Well, let's not waste all day - time for the two of you to get a crash course in karate!"

With a smile for both of them, Casey charged ahead, stepping up to the training center and through the open doors. Beautiful wood floors stretched before her. A man, slightly taller than her, stood in the center of the floor, a small smile on his face. "Greetings," he offered, bowing to her. She bowed in response, and Richard and Neil followed suit as they stepped up beside her. "Today, I will show you a few kata we use in our Shōrin-ryū karate. Shōrin-ryū is one of the oldest forms of karate, and is one of the major martial arts in Okinawa today. Things that make this style different than other forms of karate include a more natural breathing style, more natural high stances, and circular rather than direct movements that help you evade violence more effectively."

He looked between the two men. "As this is a short demonstration only, I do not have time to instruct you in the cultural history and importance of martial arts among my people. But please understand that we take this very seriously, and what I show you today is but a small glimpse of a path that would take you a lifetime to tread to mastery."

He motioned for them to remove their shoes and move further into the room, while another man stepped up next to him. The two men bowed low, and then executed a series of smooth, fluid movements that led them back and forth across the room; a series of strikes, evasions and redirects that moved so gracefully it was almost as if they were dancing. The entire exchange lasted less than a minute, and then the two men bowed at one another once more. The second man left the floor, and the instructor turned back to them.

"Today, I show you Fukyugata Kata. You will not master this kata. But we will work until you know how to execute the moves - and counter-moves - and can mimic the demonstration I just provided." He held out a hand, indicating a third man standing in the open doorway behind them. "My assistant will take you to don your karategi, and then you will return and we shall begin your instruction."

Casey followed them to the building next door, where they each had a full karategi waiting. A female assistant helped Casey don her gi, while the guys worked with the male assistant to properly put on the gis and tie the belts. A short time later, they returned to the training arena.

"This is really comfortable," Richard offered, smiling at Casey. "I might have to get one of these to take home and wear around the house."

Casey smiled back, but the instructor frowned at them. She quickly donned a more serious expression as she looked to the instructor for direction. The men followed her lead, the three of them standing together in front of him. He looked at them for a long moment, but then began the instruction.

First, he led them through the series of movements that composed the kata. He showed them each movement one by one, then waited as they moved to mimic him. After they had gone through the movements once, he repeated the sequence, stringing them together without pause. Casey was able to follow most of it without missing too much, but the guys were soon hopelessly lost.

After three repetitions, the instructor called over his assistant, who was waiting at the side of the room. He took Neil aside and began teaching him a different series of movements; the poses necessary to block, redirect and evade the strikes in the kata, and deliver strikes of his own. The two of them began to work intensely with the two men, while Casey popped back and forth and practiced some of each. She generally picked up the movements faster than the men, which she attributed to watching Nicholas's classes when Neil remarked on it.

They drilled in the kata for nearly two hours. By then, the three of them were ready for a break, so they paused for a short lunch. They managed to make small talk, but it was halting and strained. Afterward, they returned to the training hall, where the sensei ran them through the kata a few more times.

"We have done as much as is possible in our short time together," he said, bowing to the three of them. "It is my hope that you have glimpsed the beauty, utility and passion of this lifelong pursuit."

He stepped to the side of the room, motioning for Richard and Neil to step forward. "Richard, you will begin the Fukyugata Kata. Bow to your opponent, then run through the form twice, please."

Richard nodded, then stepped across from Neil, standing the appropriate distance as demonstrated by the instructor. They each bowed to one another, precisely, a shallow bow in which both were careful to go no deeper than the other. Then, Richard turned to the starting position, prepared to begin the kata.

As the two men ran through the first few steps, it was clear that their performance was clumsy, but they made a decent showing for themselves. Casey smiled as she watched them, noting their fumbles but applauding their willingness to try the demonstration even though they lacked skill.

Then, without warning, things went horribly wrong.

Richard executed a strike, but Neil wasn't prepared for it. Instead, he was transitioning into a turn-step combination, and Richard's strike caught him in the shoulder. He knocked Neil off-balance, and a flash of irritation blinked across Neil's face. The runner lunged forward to stabilize himself in the stumble, and ended up launching himself into Richard's mid-section. The bigger man went down under the unexpected tackle, and rolled to gain the advantage, assuming he'd just been assaulted. As Richard fell on top of him, Neil's fist moved automatically, launching itself into Richard's jaw in a mean left hook, shoving the man away. Then, Neil was on top of him, punching at his face while Richard grappled with him, trying to throw him off and simultaneously block the other man's blows.

Casey stood by watching, her mouth fallen open in a horrified "O." Before the sudden fight could escalate further, the sensei and his assistant leapt into action, the former dragging Neil off Richard, and the latter standing in front of Richard, his hand on his chest, holding him back as he sprang up and sought to pursue Neil.

"Stop it!" Casey finally shouted, surprising all of them. The two men immediately relented, both turning to gaze at her in various states of chagrin. "What are you doing?" she asked in disbelief.

Richard and Neil exchanged a glance. Neil stepped forward, motioning his peaceful intent to the sensei before grabbing Richard's hand in his. "Hey, man, sorry about that," he offered, one hand shaking Richard's, while the other came up to pat his arm awkwardly.

Richard nodded, anger still simmering in his eyes, but he reached up with his free hand to work his jaw. "You've got a mean left hook," he offered, the awkward compliment his way of accepting the apology.

Neil grinned ruefully. "Reflex. I probably couldn't do it again if I tried. I thought you were trying to drop me, and when I tried to correct my stumble, I may have overcompensated a bit..."

Richard nodded again. "Yeah, I haven't been tackled like that since my football days. You caught me off guard a bit. I normally wouldn't make it that easy." He offered a wry grin.

Casey still stood staring at them, jaw open. She shook her head in disbelief. "I can't believe you two just got into a brawl like a couple of schoolboys. Instead of showing proper reverence and respect for tradition, you've belittled this place and this experience." She turned and bowed deeply to the instructor. "Please accept my sincere apologies, sensei. I pray they have not caused enduring offense."

He fixed all three of them with a stern look, but a moment later, he lightened, chuckling and gracing them with a small smile. "Two men. One woman. Under such trying circumstances, one can, perhaps, forgive any offense." He looked at the two men in turn, his expression becoming serious again. "Under formal instruction, the two of you would learn control. Perhaps you should study karate more deeply when you return to your home."

Neil nodded, chagrined. Richard glanced over, but he gave the sensei a small bow in acknowledgement.

"I believe we are finished for today," the sensei told them. "You should leave the training hall before you encounter another misunderstanding."

The three of them walked out of the building, Casey still shaking her head and walking apart from the men. A production assistant waved them over toward the room where they had changed into their karategis at the beginning of the lesson.

"The 'winner' of the demonstration was supposed to be the person to go on to the evening portion of the date with Casey. Things have turned out a little differently than planned, though. Casey, do you have a preference to decide who will accompany you this evening?"

She looked at each of them in turn. "Okinawa is a beautiful place. I was really looking forward to seeing what we'd be doing this evening, and sharing an amazing and unique experience with one of you. But in light of what just happened... I don't feel I can reasonably continue the date with either of you."

She stepped closer, lowering her voice. "I am not going to reward that kind of behavior. Nicholas may watch this show someday - maybe even this weekend when it's aired - and I would not want him to look up to or admire this sort of behavior. I don't want him to see one of you getting to go off and have a great evening after the display you just put on." She put a hand on her hip, giving them a saucy look. "And that aside, I don't know how I'd look at either of you without getting annoyed over and over again all evening."

She shook her head. "I suggest the two of you spend the evening licking your wounds and thinking about what led you to such childish and immature behavior. Hopefully, you'll be better behaved on our one-on-one dates later this week."

Without waiting for a reply, she headed in to change out of the gi, leaving the two men alone to sort out their troubles.

Before the sun had even risen, Casey and Richard found themselves on a charter boat, heading out into the dark seas around Okinawa. "How does the captain even know where he's going?" she asked Richard, gazing vainly into the dark but unable to see more than a few feet away from the boat.

He chuckled at her. "I'm pretty sure he has a GPS at the very least, and probably some other equipment to guide him." He tiled his head at her, reaching out to steady her as the boat swayed and she wobbled uncertainly. "Is this your first time on a boat?"

She shook her head. "Not the first time, but the first time I've been on a boat in the ocean. Especially a boat this small. I used to go fishing with my grandpa, but we generally stuck to lakes. The water was a lot less active most of the time - except before or after a big storm." She stepped away from the side of the boat and sat on one of the padded benches running around the perimeter of the inner cabin. "He had fish finders, which could show you how deep the fish were - and I guess they also showed things like stumps and obstacles along the lake bed, now that I think about it. It's been so long, though, I'd mostly forgotten." She looked back at him. "How about you?"

He grinned. "I'm a water rat. My pa used to take me fishing all the time in these small metal boats. We'd fish lakes, rivers - wherever we could float the boat. When we got older, and he got a little more successful, we started taking trips to the coast a few times a year for charter fishing expeditions. Hunting was never really his thing; it was fishing. Which is just fine by me. Somehow fishing just seems a lot more peaceful to me than hunting ever could."

"Have you ever been? Hunting?"

He nodded. "Sure. My uncle was big into hunting. Our granddad did both - hunting and fishing - but the boys each had a favorite so they both just sorta started doing their own thing. My uncle would take me, along with his sons, a few times a year. And my dad would take my cousins fishing with us sometimes, too. I guess they wanted us to be well-rounded."

She tilted her head at him. "Did you ever kill anything?"

"Hmm. Will that change your opinion of me?" He shook his head. "Don't answer that. You're an omnivore. I've seen you eat meat. So I know you wouldn't be so hypocritical of me to think the less of me because I've killed critters, when you eat critters yourself."

She winked. "I just want to know if you're a good shot." He laughed aloud. "No, I wouldn't think less of you - my grandma had friends who lived on a working farm, and she'd make me go help out on the farm sometimes to learn about where my food came from. She said it would teach me proper appreciation for the food I put on my plate everyday." She shuddered. "Mostly, it taught me to fear farm animals. Those things can be mean! And life on the farm isn't for the squeamish. But I have killed a chicken and helped to clean it and cook it for my supper, so I know all about the circle of life. I'm not some pampered woman who thinks my food comes from a sterilized, shrink-wrapped package in the supermarket."

He grinned. "Good. Because I've been told we're going to go spearfishing this morning. That's why they made us come out here so early."

"Spearfishing?" She looked at the water passing under the boat, which she was beginning to be able to make out as light was slowly building in the pre-dawn twilight. "Are there sharks in these waters?"

He laughed again. "Don't worry - spearfishing is a big thing around here. I was reading up on it on the flight over. I'm sure they wouldn't let tourists do it if they were constantly getting attacked by sharks."

She raised an eyebrow at him. "Are you? Because I'm pretty sure tourists die doing stupid things all the time."

He leaned in and winked. "So maybe you're hoping we don't get fresh sushi for lunch, then." He chuckled. "Don't worry. I hear it's a pretty tough thing to do, so I doubt we'll actually hit anything."

The boat slowed, and a few minutes later, they were in the water. The light was growing quickly, and the dive instructor gave them a quick rundown of how to look for fish, which fish to target and how to use the sling spear. As the sun was staining the eastern sky with beautiful yellows, oranges and reds, Casey and Richard swam away from the boat and began looking for fish to target.

By the time the sun had risen, Casey could clearly see the ocean floor. The water was fifteen to twenty feet deep, and the floor was dotted with beautiful coral formations. They quickly spotted some bright, colorful fish, but they weren't the ones that the pair had been told to target, so they held their fire. Richard gave Casey a big thumbs-up, though, to indicate his enjoyment.

At this time of day, the ocean was teeming with life. Spearfishing aside, it turned into an amazing snorkeling experience. They spotted a pair of rays, dancing gracefully across the ocean floor. A little further away, Casey saw what looked like a shark, but it didn't seem interested in them, eventually swimming off in the other direction.

After a while with no shots, they surfaced. "I'm not seeing the fish we're supposed to be looking for," Casey offered, spitting out the snorkel.

"Yeah, we might have to try diving down and checking under ledges and overhangs. The instructor said they might be hanging out in hidden spots," Richard replied. "Let's take a look." Without waiting for a response, he prepared his gear and dived down again, swimming deeper and leaving Casey behind. She moved to follow, and by the time she had reached him, he had already shot his spear at something she couldn't see in a hole. As she swam up, he shook his head, indicating a miss.

The two of them spent hours combing the ocean floor, poking into underhangs and holes, and generally admiring the beautiful and diverse ocean life. As a spearfishing trip, it hadn't been so successful, but as a snorkeling trip, it was amazing. Eventually, they admitted defeat, swimming back to the boat and boarding. The dive instructor took over, jumping into the water. As the two of them were drying off and getting settled, he reappeared, carrying a mesh bag containing several fish he had just speared.

Casey shook her head in amazement. "Either we really suck, or he has some kind of magic trick. We were down there for hours with nothing to show for it!"

The instructor flashed her a grin. "Years of practice, honey. We bring tourists out here almost every day, and no-one wants to go hungry."

He vanished into the cabin, and soon the smell of cooking fish wafted out on the breeze. Richard and Casey sat in companionable silence on one of the padded benches, side-by-side, his arm wrapped around her, as the water lapped gently at the boat.

"This is one of those moments," Richard quietly observed. "I'm real happy to be sharing it with you, Casey. But I want a lot more of them." He swiveled his head around to face her. "I want all of them, for the rest of my life." He tenderly kissed her forehead.

"Somehow, you always seem to know exactly what to say," she replied, twisting around to kiss him thoroughly.

They were still kissing, several minutes later, when the dive instructor came to lead them to the back of the boat. A feast had been set out for them; the freshly-speared fish, both cooked and sashimi-style, as well as some rice and a variety of colorful looking vegetables.

After they'd finished lunch, one final dish was put before them; a covered dish with a large metal dome on top. Casey looked at Richard, and then lifted the dome to find a sealed envelope inside. She took it, handing it to him. He opened it, but then handed it back to her. She grinned, and pulled out the card, reading its contents aloud.

"For the afternoon portion of your date, you'll be visiting the historical Shuri Castle, a UNESCO World Heritage Site, and the only Okinawa castle that has been restored to its former glory. You'll enjoy a guided tour, and we've arranged a special dinner for you on-site. After dinner, we'll have one more surprise for you. In the meantime, enjoy your time at this historic landmark."

By mid-afternoon, Casey had traded her bikini for a swishy knee-length skirt and a fitted, sleeveless top. She was wearing a comfortable pair of flats for the tour, but her hair had been twisted into a neat bun, and she wore a beautiful pair of earrings and matching bracelet.

"As usual, you look beautiful," Richard smiled, enfolding her in a short hug and giving her a quick kiss. He'd traded his own swim trunks for a pair of loose khakis and a loose dress shirt, tucked in at the waist but unbuttoned at the neck.

"You clean up well, yourself," she replied with a grin. "In fact, that's one thing I admire about you: you never seem to be overdressed, and you never look like you're trying too hard. You always manage to dress appropriately while still seeming casual and approachable. I like that you don't put on airs."

He laughed. "You mean I'm shabby and don't know how to dress myself like those tailored suit boys?"

She giggled. "They do have some very nice clothes. But I don't begrudge them; working in a competitive professional setting day-in, day-out will leave anyone feeling like they have to dress to impress. And in New York, you do. They won't respect you if you look like a country bumpkin."

"Ohh, and it don't matter so much for a landscaper in South Carolina, huh?" he prodded, in a prolonged Southern drawl.

She narrowed her eyes at him. "That's not what I mean." She shook her head. "Anyway, let's not argue. This place looks really amazing - I'm looking forward to the guided tour!"

They spent the next two hours exploring the site with the guide; a native historian who spoke passable English. He took great delight in showing them each of Shuri Castle's several gates, and giving them a history of the original construction, destruction and restoration of the site. As they entered the inner structure of Shuri Castle itself, the guide filled them in on the history of the Ryūkyū Kingdom, and translated the signs and information stations for them. It was a fascinating site, and the central castle itself was full of interesting exhibits that provided good insight into the cultural significance of the site.

By the time they finished the tour, shadows were getting long and many of the visitors who crowded the site earlier were gone. The guide smiled, and led them to one of the roped-off areas of the castle. Nodding for them to follow, the guide unhooked the red rope, hooking it again behind them. Then, he led them across the room, opening a door in the wall and again motioning them through. He closed the door behind them, and they found themselves in a steep stairwell. At his insistence, they climbed, coming out into a long hallway with polished wooden floors. He guided them down the hallway, and through another door into a wide, airy room.

The room contained a raised platform, and upon that platform had been laid out a short table piled high with Japanese delicacies. Casey could see more kinds of sushi than she could name, various bowls of curries and soups, and stranger dishes she couldn't identify. The dais was piled high with pillows, and the guide motioned to the spread. "Here is your specially prepared dinner. In two hours, we will bring you your final surprise for the evening." He bowed to them, and then left the room.

Casey and Richard looked at each other. "That is a lot of food," she observed. "I really hope they don't expect us to eat all of it!"

Richard chuckled and stepped over to her, putting one hand on each of her arms and gazing into her face. "I'm sure we'll do it justice, but this is the first time we've been alone all day. I've been dying to do this." He slid one hand to the back of her neck and placed a tender kiss on her forehead. Then, he gently kissed each of her eyelids. With his free hand, he caressed her cheekbone with his thumb, tracing the lines of her face before moving to kiss her lips, the gesture soft and full of emotion.

Casey took a deep, shuddering breath. One hand came up to the side of his face while the other wrapped around his waist, pulling him tight against her. She returned the kiss, but there was nothing soft or gentle about it; she kissed him deeply, passionately, like she was drowning and his kiss was the only thing keeping her alive.

He responded in kind, the hand that had been gently caressing her face sliding down her body to rest on her ass. He gave a little squeeze, pulling her against him.

She grinned against his lips, breaking the kiss. "Ok, tiger. I can see what you've got on your mind." She leaned her head back to gaze into his eyes, her own sparkling with mischief. "Maybe we shouldn't rush right to the finish line? Why don't we take some time to enjoy this dinner they have so thoughtfully provided, and spend some time together, and see where that leads?"

He shook his head from side to side, grinning ruefully. "I didn't intend to attack you right here and now. I was trying to show you the softer, gentler side of lovemaking. But have I mentioned that you do things to me, woman?"

She sighed softly as she released him, but she was still grinning. "I don't think that's a bad thing, necessarily. As long as that's not all there is between us."

His gaze turned serious as he took her hand and led her over to the dais, helping her sit down in the nest of pillows and making sure she was comfortable before sitting beside her. "I wouldn't want you to think that, Casey. I think you're an amazing woman, and I am in love with you - all of you. Casey the mom, Casey the fun and adventurous woman, Casey the seductress, and Casey the person who knows how to live in the moment and be grateful for life. There is so much about you that I admire and appreciate. And while I am deeply attracted to you, I'd never want you to think it's just sex."

Her smile had turned soft, and her eyes glistened. "Thank you. That means a lot to me."

He took her hands in both of his, his expression serious and sincere. "Listen. I know we're nearly at the end, and you need to see this through. So I'm not going to talk to you about running away with me now, or what's going on with that other guy, or say anything that would be pressuring you in any way. But I need you to know how real my feelings are for you, and that I'm ready to spend the rest of my life with you. And I hope to ask you formally next week to do me that great honor. But now we can drop that subject," he finished, giving her a small smile.

She tilted her head as she looked at him. "So I'm curious. What would our life together look like, to you?"

He nodded. "That's a good question. I've thought a lot about it. You already said you'd picture yourself moving to Asheville, if we ended up together. So I'd picture us living together with the kids in Asheville. Cassidy is real settled in our home, so I think it would be easiest for her to get used to the idea if we could keep living there - but if you don't like the house, we can shop for a new home together. It's a four-bedroom - right now I've got it set up with the master for me, Cassidy has her room, one of the bedrooms is an office, and the last one is a guest room. We can easily turn the guest room into a room for Nicholas, for the moment, and I can build on an office on the side of the house so we can turn that last bedroom into the new guest room. I could even make it two offices; one for you and one for me; if you think you might do any working from home. I've got the landscaping business in its own building on the edge of town where real estate is cheaper - we have a lot of equipment and supplies to store - but I do work from home sometimes, so it's important for me to have the space."

He paused and glanced away from her. "You could find a marketing job in Asheville, I have no doubt. Or maybe you could start your own firm. I think you've got all the skills you need to run a shop yourself. But if you didn't want to start that right away, I make a pretty good living. You wouldn't really have to work at all, unless you wanted to. So if you were interested in maybe having a few kids of our own together, you could take as much time as you wanted to with them when they're born..."

She raised an eyebrow. "You want more kids? Even though between us we've got two already?"

He turned his head back to meet her eyes. "I love Cassidy dearly, and nothing and no-one will ever take her place in my life. And I'd be proud to be a father to young Nicholas, although I know he'll need to have a relationship with his own dad, now that things are out in the open. But the idea of having children with you, Casey... little pieces of you and me running around in the world... it just makes me feel all lit up inside, like a Christmas tree." He grinned, but his eyes shone with emotion. She couldn't help smiling back.

"Just how many little pieces of you and me do you think you'd want?" she asked, her voice thick with amusement.

"As many as you'd have," he answered honestly, his smile growing bigger.

She choked. "I was afraid you were going to say something like that." She shook her head. "I realize this is a little late to be asking this question - but are you Catholic, Richard?"

He laughed aloud, a hearty, booming sound that echoed around the room. Then, he shook his head in response. "No, darlin', I'm not. But I'd become Catholic if that's what it took to get four or five or six or seven little ones out of you..."

She coughed again. "Six? Seven?" She shook her head. "My God, man, I can't even begin to imagine what that would do to my body... or how the two of us could possibly handle eight or nine kids..."

He leaned in close, putting a warm hand on the side of your waist. "I have no doubt that your body would become even more lush, beautiful and womanly after bearing our kids, however many there were. But I would worship it, and you." He placed a little kiss on her collar bone, and she playfully shoved him back.

"Hold your horses there, cowboy. I'm not done talking about this." He grinned, then leaned in close and breathed a soft sigh across her lips before kissing her intently. After a moment, he released her and leaned back again.

"You were saying?" he teased as she gazed at him breathlessly.

She shook her head to clear it. "Kids. Babies. Lots of them. What if I'm not interested?"

His expression turned serious again, and he took one of her hands and squeezed it. "If you're not interested, that's it. I might not be able to help asking now and again if you've changed your mind, but I promise I wouldn't pester you. We've already got two great kids - I'm sure we'd have a happy life together even without adding more of our own to the mix."

She nodded. "Ok. Right answer." She grinned at him. "So here's a very important point: where do you stand on the dog question?"

Richard laughed. "Personally, I love 'em. I've always been a dog person. But Cassidy is very particular, and she thinks dogs are messy and smelly and would introduce too much chaos into her life. It's safe to say she's a cat person."

Casey grinned. "She's probably right, but she's never lived with a nine-year-old boy before. *He's* messy and smelly and is going to introduce a ton of chaos into her life. Maybe a dog would help her come to accept it a little easier." She tilted her head, smiling. "Or one of each?"

Richard chuckled. "I'm sure she'd say yes to a cat in a hot minute, but are you planning to clean the litterbox? Because that's not something I'm very interested in doing."

Her grin deepened. "I'd clean the litterbox if you'll pick up all the dog poop in the yard. Oh, and is it fenced? If not, we'll need one."

He reached out his hand for her to shake. "Deal. Done. One cat and one dog it is."

She giggled. "Pleasure doing business with you," she answered, shaking his hand.

He leaned into her, wrapping his arms around her and pulling her against him. "You know, I've gotta say, that was a very pleasant negotiation. Makes me want to try another one. About those babies?" He kissed her before she could answer, deeply, slipping his tongue into her mouth and holding her in a tight embrace. She kissed him back, their tongues dueling and their breath coming loudly in the quiet space.

Some time later, they came up for air again. "Ok. I'm willing to entertain the idea. Let's save the negotiation for a more private setting, though," she offered.

He grinned. "I have some thoughts on that." He released her and righted himself, turning his gaze to the table. "Do you suppose any of this is still warm? I find I've worked up a bit of an appetite."

She smirked. "We definitely want you well-fed." Turning her attention to the table, she leaned over and opened a few of the dishes. "Seems reasonably warm. Shall we enjoy our feast?"

Nodding, he followed her lead. They tucked in, sampling various dishes and going back for the things that were particularly tasty. Casey really enjoyed a yellow curry with chicken, and helped herself to a large bowl of it. Richard fed her a piece of decadent-looking sushi, topped with avocado and something crispy and some kind of sauce, and she proclaimed it delicious. They took turns feeding each other and feasting, and by the time they were finished, they'd done justice to the meal. The table was a long way from empty, but they'd eaten their fill and enjoyed a bit of almost of all the dishes - even the ones they couldn't identify.

As they were leaning back in companionable silence, feeling stuffed and enjoying their evening, the guide from earlier popped his head into the room. "I have your final surprise for the evening. May I enter?"

Richard stood and waved the man in, and Casey followed suit. "First, I ask that you come with me," the guide requested, turning and leading them back the way they had come to the main part of the castle. "The castle is now closed for the evening, so you are the only guests who still remain on the property," he told them, walking them through the quiet corridors and out the front door of the main structure. When they turned back, they could see all of the buildings of Shuri Castle were beautifully lit against the dark; a shining beacon of beauty visible from much of the city. If they walked out into the park, the view would be even more impressive.

"Each night, the restored Shuri Castle shines through the darkness, a beautiful sight that lifts the hearts of many. Few get to see this from inside the grounds, so you are enjoying a great honor and a rare sight. Now I am asked to give you this card, and remain while you read it." He bowed and produced a card from his jacket with a flourish, handing it to Casey. She bowed back and took it, opening the envelope and sliding the card out.

She turned toward Richard, reading it aloud. "We hope you have enjoyed your time in Shuri Castle. If you like it here, we've arranged a special surprise; a private suite here in the castle has been prepared for you to spend the night. If you choose to forego your individual rooms in the resort where you've been staying, we invite you to stay here together as a couple and enjoy a magical evening - with no cameras." She looked up at him. "What do you think?"

He stepped closer and took her hands in his. "I think I would never turn down a minute with you. But I know it's a big decision, and I'll respect whatever you want. I wouldn't want you to feel pressured into something you're not comfortable doing."

She nodded. "I appreciate that." She looked down at her hands in his. "I think because we're getting so close to the end, and we've got a big decision coming up, it makes sense for us to spend all the time together that we can. I'd enjoy spending the night here with you, and having some time without the cameras where we can just relax and be ourselves and continue the important conversations we've been having."

He smiled. "That sounds wonderful."

She turned back to the guide. "We would like to stay for the evening. Can you show us where to go?"

He bowed again, smiling at both of them. "I think you will be very pleased. Follow me." He took them back into the main structure, retracing their steps, taking them through the ropes to a restricted area and up a set of stairs. He led them down the same long corridor, past the room where they'd enjoyed their dinner, to a room along the front of the castle. A large, ornate four-poster bed stood on a dais on one side of the room. A few small chaises and couches littered the room, and a table on one side of the room contained an assortment of snacks. On the wall opposite the door, a tall, floor-length window was opened, the vertical slats on the outside of the building visible from where they were standing. A gorgeous view of the city spread out below the castle greeted them through the window.

The guide bowed again, then left the room. "This is beautiful," Casey observed, looking around at the room and smiling at Richard. He smiled back, and slid the door closed behind him.

"Looking good, mama." Mike winked by way of greeting when they met on the white sand beach. The early morning sun was kind to him, setting his even tan aglow, his muscles making him look like some sort of Greek god. He caught her looking and flexed, winking at her again.

Casey laughed. "Alright, you're looking good, too, this morning,

Mike." She pulled up her hair into a loose ponytail and walked toward him, slightly self-conscious in her bikini-clad state to be the focus of his intense gaze when it was just the two of them, alone. When she reached him, he pulled her into his arms, sliding his skin along hers with a low, satisfied hum. He kissed her, but kept it light, releasing her with a little squeeze.

"So! Are you ready to go surfing at White Beach? I've wanted to surf Okinawa for years - it's really cool to finally be able to do it."

She turned and eyed the waves. "Well, there's one minor problem with that, Mike... I don't know how to surf."

He grinned and shook his head at her. "You're kidding! Badass dune buggy driver like you doesn't surf?"

She stuck her hand on her hip, giving him a raised eyebrow. "Hey now. The two are not related."

He chuckled. "Well, in Baja, they are. I'll have to take you, sometime." He rubbed his hands together, satisfied, looking at the waves. "Fortunately, you're in luck. I happen to be an excellent surf instructor. Let's get started!" Without waiting for her response, he wrapped an arm around her waist and picked her up, carrying her down the beach and into the water like a sack of potatoes under his arm. She squealed and wiggled, but he ignored her, grinning as she tried in vain to escape. As the bottom started to drop away more, he snagged his other arm under her legs and hefted her up, then tossed her out into the water.

As she came up, sputtering and laughing and wiping water out of her eyes, he smiled. "That's done. Let me go get the boards."

He jogged up the beach, then jogged back down a moment later with two surfboards. "This is a big board so it should be easier for you to learn on," he offered, sliding one into the water next to her. The other board was slightly narrower, and he slid himself onto it, sitting up with his legs on either side. "First, you're going to want to leash up." He showed her how to fasten the leash around her ankle, and demonstrated the quick release functionality. "Now we're going to paddle out a bit, and once we're in deeper water and there aren't so many people around, we'll work on the pop-up." He helped her lie down on the board, and showed her the best way to paddle without creating drag. Then, he led her out to a deeper area where there weren't too many people around.

"This will do," he offered. "I'm going to show you the pop up. Then we'll work on helping you get the right position and have you practice a bit before we try to catch a wave. Ready?" When she nodded, he demonstrated the pop up, talking her through it as he placed his hands, pushed himself up, and got to his feet. "Ready to try?" She nodded. He stepped off his board, making a surprisingly small splash as he entered the water, then came up next to her. "I'll steady the board so you don't have to worry about it right now. Remember where I showed you to place your hands? Go for it. Steady as you get your feet under you - you've got it!" He cheered her as she managed to pop up on her first try. "You must have great balance," he offered. "Usually it takes a while for beginners to get up."

She grinned at him. "Boxing."

He coughed. "Right, then. Why am I not surprised? Well, hooray boxing." He motioned for her to sit down again, then resume the paddling position. "Try again. One more time with me holding the board, then I'll let go and see if you can get up without my help."

She managed to pop up again without much drama, but the first time she tried it after Mike let go, the board bobbed with uneven weight distribution and she lost her balance, falling over the side. When she came up, sputtering, Mike was grinning at her. "Try again."

After they'd gone a good dozen times in a row without her falling off, Mike nodded. "Ok. Good enough. Things change when you're in moving water trying to catch a wave - but you can't really practice that until it happens. Now we've gotta paddle out further, and push through the surf. The waves here are small enough that you can probably do a push-up." He demonstrated the technique. "But if that doesn't work, or if you see an out-of-control surfer or a loose surfboard coming toward you, try a turtle roll." He demonstrated. "Now I want you to try both of these. We need to make sure you understand how to do it before we get out to the breaking surf."

Casey followed his instructions, practicing the moves a few times before he was satisfied. Eventually, he nodded. "Alright! Let's get to it. We're going to paddle out past the breakers, I'm going to find you a good wave, and then we'll see I few can get you up." She obediently followed him deeper into the ocean, using the push-up technique to get past the breakers and into a good spot.

"Ok. I was watching the waves a while before you got here, and I think this is a good spot for the break. Now the idea is to spot a good swell, figure out where it's going to break, and be there, ready to pop up on your board and ride it. This part really just takes practice. We'll try to find you a good wave and see what you can do." They sat in silence, letting the waves roll under them for a few minutes. Eventually, Mike said: "That one! Not the next swell, but the one after it. Start paddling into it and I'll tell you when to pop up." Casey moved, paddling as Mike instructed. "Pop up!" he shouted, and she did just that, in one fluid movement.

The breaking wave startled her and she fell off the side, coughing and sputtering as she came up again. "Good job! Your first wipeout," Mike grinned.

"Thanks," she said, smiling wryly as she climbed back onto her board. They tried it a few more times, and on the third try, Casey managed to turn into the wave and surf it for a few feet before she wiped out. When she surfaced, Mike was still waiting where they'd started out, so she paddled back over to him, pushing through the break again.

"Ok. I think you're getting there - maybe a little demonstration will help. Why don't I surf the next one, then paddle back out here and meet up with you again?" She nodded, so he returned to watching the waves again, then picked a good swell and paddled into it. Moving with the fluid grace of an expert, he popped up, keeping his center of gravity low and turning into the wave. She watched him shift his hips and shoulders in constant, minute adjustment as he rode the wave, surfing it most of the way in toward shore. Without waiting for him to paddle back out, she turned toward the incoming swells again, watching the waves break for a few minutes before picking one and paddling into it. As Mike was paddling back out toward her, she popped up and caught the breaking wave, surfing it clumsily, her expression determined. She actually managed to ride the wave all the way in, passing Mike as he paddled back out, but unable to spare him any attention as she struggled to remain upright. Eventually, the wave broke again a few feet from shore and she stepped off the board, her momentum spent.

Grinning broadly, she turned to face Mike, who had sat up on his board and watched her surf the rest of the way in. She waved to him, and he waved back, motioning for her to come out. She turned the board around in the water and paddled back out to where they started, and they repeated the whole cycle over again, taking turns surfing as Casey improved. Eventually, her muscles weak and wobbly and fatigue making her clumsy, she rode a final wave in and stumbled onto shore, untethering her leash and collapsing onto the sand. She tried to watch Mike surf in, but she was too tired, giving in to the siren call of being horizontal and flopping down to lie on the warm sand. She closed her eyes, soaking in the warmth, salt and sand drying on her skin. She might have dozed off a little.

She started awake to a wet arm snaking around her waist as Mike laid down in the sand next to her. He leaned into her, kissing her awake as he doodled little patterns on her skin with his wet hand. He rubbed his wet length against her side, kissing her harder, and finally she shoved him off. "You're wet. And cold."

He grinned. "Warm me up, then. You've been lying here in the sun, soaking up heat. Give me some." He leaned into her again, resuming the kiss.

A moment later, she shoved his shoulder again. "Alright, alright, let me up! I'm exhausted, but I itch all over and I seem to have sand places where sand was never meant to be. I need a shower."

He chuckled. "Fortunately, I think they've got you covered." He motioned toward where a small tent had been erected, with a large, open, airy pavilion next to it. "Changing and shower area, and lunch, babe. A little food will help. I forgot how much work it is for a beginner, and how wiped out you'd feel." He got off her and then stood, reaching out a hand to help her up. She stumbled to her feet, legs wobbly and sand coating her from head to toe where she'd been lying down. He laughed aloud, and she couldn't help but join him.

"Yeah, I definitely need a shower," she confirmed, wincing as she walked toward the tent and the sand chafed her in unpleasant places.

"I'll let you go first," he grinned. "Unless you want to speed things up by going at the same time, and I can help you get that sand out of... everywhere."

She smirked. "Tempting. I really hate to think of missing any of this sand. But let's preserve the mystery a little longer."

She ducked into the small tent. Mike wandered over to the food, nibbling on some of the snacks as he waited for her. A short time later, she emerged, her hair still pulled back but the coating of sand gone. She wore a white, wispy blouse that billowed in the breeze, and a short skirt. Her feet were bare. "Your turn," she offered, waving toward the tent.

Mike strolled off for a quick rinse, and returned a few minutes later, wearing a different, dry pair of board shorts, but still not bothering with a shirt. They sat down together under the pavilion, digging into the lunch with a good appetite.

"So what did you think of your first surfing experience?" Mike asked her with a smile.

"It's a lot of work," she returned, grinning ruefully. "But fun. I don't regret trying it, but not sure I'd go out of my way to do it again."

"That's a shame," he responded, popping a sushi roll into his mouth, chewing and swallowing before continuing. "I was hoping to take you. This is a beginner beach. The big waves are a real blast, and I know some great spots."

She shook her head. "I think you're on your own. I'm pretty sure the big waves would just pulverize me."

He tilted his head as he looked at her. "So, I know you like driving dunes. But what else do you do for fun?"

"I spend a lot of time with Niko, doing stuff he likes to do. It's easier than fighting with him to get him to do stuff he doesn't enjoy, although I do try to get him to step out of his comfort zone now and again." She gazed off at the distant waves as she thought. "We stay in and watch movies a lot. On a nice day, we'll go for a drive and try to find someplace to hike. I'm thinking about getting him a dog, so I'm sure we'll be taking the dog to the park when it's nice out." She shrugged. "In the winter, we like to play in the snow. Sledding and building snowmen and having snowball fights, and then coming inside to warm up with a cup of hot cocoa - that's one of my favorites."

"That's a lot of stuff that revolves around the kid," Mike observed.

Casey nodded. "That's what being a parent is about. I still have some of my old interests - like running, for example." She looked at him, her expression serious. "But you learn to enjoy new things - things that make your child happy. We like to build stuff, for example. If I had more space, I'd put together a real shop for us, but for now, we stick with Technics and kits and stuff like that. He's getting into electronics, so we've built some simple electrical circuits. We made a motion detector, and rigged up some Christmas lights to turn on when he opens the door to his bedroom."

Mike shook his head. "You build stuff? For fun? And mess with electrical circuits?"

Casey chuckled. "Yeah. Not what you expected?"

Mike looked away. "Maybe not. I love living in Manhattan. I have access to so many things to do - right outside my door. I can catch a flick, go out to a great restaurant, hang out in a favorite bar, go clubbing. We've got art galleries and shows and stuff if that's what you're into. Some people I know even go do drunk painting - it's some sort of wine and painting club. Whatever you want." He sighed. "Staying at home with a kid? That's... not something I've really thought a lot about."

"And if it turns out you're his dad? Or if you and I end up together at the end of this?"

He looked back to her. "Well, I did say I'd been looking for something. Something was missing with my ex wife, and maybe it's this part of my life I'm missing. Staying at home. Cooking dinner. The simple life."

She tilted her head. "What does life look like, if you and I end up together?"

"Well, Hell, I don't know... I guess you and the kid move to Manhattan. We give it a go and see how it works out. I'm sure it won't take you too long to find a marketing job there, but maybe we take our time about it and you do some interviews and get something lined up before you move? I'm not in that much of a rush. It's been this long - it's probably better to make sure things are solid before taking a big step like that."

"What would a weekend day be like?"

"Hmm. Wake up, spend the morning in bed having glorious sex," he winked. "Grab a late brunch - we've got a ton of great spots. I know how you ladies like your brunch." He tilted his head. "Then... I don't know... something with the kid? Maybe take him to Central Park or the Zoo or something? What do kids like to do in Manhattan?"

She shook her head. "I don't know. That's part of why I left Manhattan when I found out I was pregnant." She reached out and laid a hand on his arm. "But, Mike - your romantic view of life with a child is nothing like reality. You can't leave a kid to his own devices until after a late brunch. Nicholas is pretty easygoing, but even so, he's up early - and he has to be fed breakfast and entertained. Sometimes, on a Saturday morning, I let him do cartoons for a while, but even then he only gets limited screen time, so we have to find something else to do. And he's in a lot of activities, so it's pretty normal for a weekend day to be taking him to an activity, or a play date with a friend, or having a friend spend the night, or taking him out to do something special as a reward or... it's a pretty endless list."

He shook his head. "How do you have a life of your own?"

She smiled sadly. "I don't have much of one. It's hard to find time to date. And if I do, I'm careful not to bring the guy around Niko until I know if he's gonna stick. I don't want a rotating cast of men in and out of his life. That's part of why I came here - it's hard for me to find someone out in the real world, so I was hoping I might leave here with a good, solid relationship I can take into my life afterward."

He sighed. "It's a lot, Case."

She nodded. "I know."

They lapsed into an awkward silence, deep in thought. A production assistant came over to where they were sitting. "For the afternoon portion of your date, we've got a whale watching cruise planned - which will turn into a sunset cruise. Then, we've got dinner and a special surprise arranged for you." They both nodded, following the production assistant to a car that took them to the harbor. The show had chartered a whale watching boat for them, so they had a private cruise. The cruise guide told them about interesting spots they were passing on the island as they glided through the water, and they did come across a pod of whales - as well as a playful group of dolphins. They smiled and laughed and had a good time, but the serious conversation from lunch hung over them.

As they sat through dinner in an oceanside restaurant at the harbor, flitting around from topic to topic without touching on anything of substance, a production assistant delivered a sealed card to them. Casey opened it and read aloud. "We've arranged a special suite for you to stay together as a couple, if you should choose to forego your individual rooms. If you take this key, you can enjoy an entire night together - with no cameras - to get to know one another better and take your relationship to the next level."

Casey sighed and looked up at Mike. "What do you say?" he probed, grinning suggestively. "We could have fun."

She smiled sadly and shook her head. "I'm sorry, Mike - surfing this morning really wore me out, and it's been a long day. I don't think I'm up for anything else. I'm ready to go back to my room and crash."

His smile softened. "I could give you a massage. Great for sore muscles. And we could just see what happens."

She shook her head again. "Sorry, Mike. I'm going to head back now." She put the card on the table and stood, kissing his cheek and heading outside to the waiting car.

Casey stepped into the airport to begin her one-on-one date with Neil, following a guide to a small gate where her handsome suitor was already waiting. He smiled when he saw her, reaching out to enfold her in a warm hug, then releasing her with a nervous look. "Sorry - I didn't think. Are you still mad from the other day? I know that afternoon didn't unfold exactly as planned."

She grinned at him. "Maybe. But I'll make you suffer later. Do you know why we're at the airport?"

He nodded, grinning back. "Yup. Our date today will take a little work to get to, but I think it's going to be worth it. We're starting with a short flight to one of the nearby islands. From there, we're taking a high-speed ferry to Iriomote Island. I've been reading up on the great jungles, beautiful waterfalls and amazing mangrove trees. I think we'll really enjoy our day."

She chuckled at his enthusiasm. "I can see you're excited. You remind me of Niko when he's all in a tizzy about something." She tilted her head and looked at him speculatively. "Maybe he gets that from you."

He flashed her a boyish grin. "Well, at least he comes by it honestly."

Laughing, Casey slipped her arm through his and followed the guide onto the small airplane. "Ok. Let's do it."

A few minutes later, they were belted in and taxiing down the runway. The cockpit door wasn't even closed, and the one flight attendant was still closing overhead bins and checking seat belts. "This is a lot less formal than I'm used to," she noted to Neil.

He nodded. "I've flown on a lot of puddle jumpers for work - and for my leisure travel, too, I guess. This seems pretty normal to me."

"Maybe the more regimented style of the major airports I'm used to flying is a bit contrived... but I admit I feel a little uncomfortable here with everything so informal. What if they cut corners on maintenance? Or the pilot?"

He placed his hand over hers. "Don't be nervous. These guys fly hundreds of flights a month. Nothing to worry about."

She smiled. "If you say so. Maybe I'll just focus on something else for a while." She tilted her head as she looked at him. "I had a lovely time in Vermont with you. But I was surprised the hometown date took us there. When did you leave Manhattan?"

"Ahh, yes. Well, the thing is, I haven't precisely left Manhattan. I have a lot of meetings there for work. So I keep a loft there, for when I'm in the city." He sighed, leaning back in his chair. "I kinda got tired of

Manhattan a while ago, though. It's a great place in limited quantities, but I wanted a quieter place where I could work and easily connect with nature without having to drive hours to get upstate. Central Park is nice, but... it's so busy and it's just not the same."

He glanced over at her out of the corner of his eye. "And I sort of hate Central Park now. I looked for you there, a long time. I may have become a little obsessed, running different parts of the park and switching to different days and times to try to find you there. But you never were. Eventually, I told myself that I'd given up... but even so, I'd always find myself straining to catch a glimpse of you, or turning because I saw a woman who might have been you, only to discover she looked nothing like you. It became an ongoing reminder of my failure to find you. I needed to get away."

Casey gave his hand a little squeeze. "I guess I can understand that. It sounds a little maddening."

Neil nodded. "It was. I can't really tell you how amazing it is to have you back in my life. I know there are no guarantees at the end of this, but at least we've gotten to spend more time together, and neither you nor I will vanish unexpectedly - whatever happens, we'll be able to discuss it and we'll have closure." He leaned a little closer, and gave her a charming grin, flashing a dimple at her. "But I hope we don't need closure."

She grinned, and shook her head at him. "Tell me how you really feel," she teased, but then she grew more serious. "Really, though, thank you for being so straightforward with me. After all these years, and all the time I've spent wondering about you, I don't think I could take it if you decided to play games now." A wistful look stole across her features as her eyes grew distant. "I can't tell you how many times I've wondered about you through the years. I wish I'd had the courage to reach out to you." She focused on him again, smiling widely and squeezing his hand again. "But we're here, now, and I, for one, intend to make the most of it."

"So tell me about your work?" Neil probed. "What's your favorite thing about it, and what do you hate?"

Casey laughed. "Umm, that's tough. I think my favorite thing about it is when a campaign comes together and a client loves it. It's always gratifying when it performs well, too, but the tough part is the clients. Sometimes they don't even know what they want. Sometimes what they want absolutely isn't what they *need* to help them reach their goals. Then we have to convince them to change their minds. But when you find the right angle, and the campaign just comes together - and the client loves it - my job is awesome."

She stared at the bulkhead ahead of her as she thought about the second part of the question. "I guess the thing I hate about my job is related... it's when you think you have an awesome campaign that will absolutely kill - and it flops. We're good, so it doesn't happen often, but when it does..." She shook her head. "Sometimes, people lose jobs. We always have to do a post-mortem to figure out where it went wrong. If we can trace it back to someone not doing their job right, we don't dick around. It's human to make mistakes, but when those mistakes slip through all the channels - due to incompetence or negligence - and impact the client directly, we have to take action. Fortunately, that's not the case most of the time, but I remember every time it has happened. I remember each of their faces when we told them. And I remember one particularly vitriolic speech someone made at us when he felt we were being unfair."

"That must be hard for someone with your compassion," Neil observed.

Casey barked a short laugh. "I've been called a lot of things, but I can't remember the last time one of them was 'compassionate.'"

He grinned. "They just don't know you that well, then." His smile grew wistful. "I remember a conversation we had that day, ten years ago. You were pissed at the way I walked right past the bums and panhandlers without even looking at them. You told me that whatever else was going on with them, they were human, and they were entitled to the dignity of being acknowledged like a human being." He smirked at her. "And then you bought the next panhandler we saw a bagel, to prove a point, and he threw it at your head, yelling 'What the hell am I supposed to do with that?'"

She laughed. "Was I really that naive?"

He smiled. "I found it charming."

She shook her head. "Gosh, I was so young then."

"I hope your values haven't changed too much. You were right, then. And I'd want Niko to grow up feeling the same way."

She smiled, her eyes shining with pride as she looked at Neil. "He's such a good boy. You'd be amazed at how thoughtful and sweet he is. We started with charitable stuff when he was young, and it has become a cornerstone of his childhood experience. We volunteer at a soup kitchen once a month, and a food bank every other month. He's so willing to give away excess - if he gets too many toys at Christmas, or if people ask him what he wants for a birthday. We've had entire parties themed around raising money for his favorite charities, like our local animal shelter."

She chuckled. "Of course, when he really does want something, I may be a little too quick to give in, since he's so good about being generous and giving most of the time. I make him 'work' for expensive stuff, by getting good grades, doing community service projects, taking classes and joining clubs and things. But he gets pretty much everything he wants. Which I guess is why he was so upset when I couldn't celebrate his birthday the way he wanted to this year, and why he took off on his own to go see the circus."

Neil leaned his head back against his headrest, thinking back to that day. "You must have been so worried about him when he vanished. If I'd have known who either of you were, I would have been a nervous wreck, too. Especially if he's so good most of the time - you must have feared the worst when he turned up missing."

Her face grew pinched as she thought about it. "I was worried. It's the first time he's ever done anything like that. I know he's going to be acting more independent as he grows older, but I wasn't ready for him to take off on his own. I just kept thinking about the fact that it was a house full of people and cameras, and surely someone had seen where he'd gone. I hoped they'd be able to bring him back to me. But it was hard to be patient and not panic."

He squeezed her hand. "I'm sorry you had to go through that alone. But I can't be too upset that it happened, because it led to me finding out the truth about you and him." He turned toward her, fixing her with a serious gaze. "Were you planning on telling me? When?"

She sighed. She met his gaze squarely, but the corners of her lips were turned down and she looked uncomfortable. "I wanted to talk to you about it. But I also wanted to get to know you. I wanted to see if there was anything between us naturally, instead of forcing a connection because we might have a son together and because I couldn't stop thinking about you all these years. So I don't know when I would have brought it up, if Niko hadn't let it slip."

He frowned. "I guess I understand why you'd say that. But I don't like it. I'd rather know you would have told me on your own. Or I guess if I'm telling the truth, I wish you'd have told me on night one so we didn't lose out on weeks when we could have been getting to know one another."

"I'm sorry. I thought I was doing the right thing."

He grinned as he looked out the window. "Well, at least we got you through the flight." He pointed, and Casey saw that they were making a final approach to the runway. His expression turned serious again as he continued. "I meant it, though, when I said I didn't want you to feel guilty or keep blaming yourself for the past. I just want to move forward together. I'm kind of sorry I brought it up, but sometimes I can't keep myself from asking uncomfortable questions. I think it's part of what makes me a good interviewer - I don't pull punches and I tend to get good, honest answers from the people I'm talking to - but it can be a bit of a liability in my personal life."

"Do you do interviews often?" she asked, squeezing his hand as they bumped down the runway, but then relaxing as the plane gently taxied to a stop.

He shook his head. "Not so much anymore. These days, I do more travel writing, and I've had pretty good luck with my novels. I do still interview people sometimes for my current event pieces, but it's been ages since I've written a real profile on anyone."

She tilted her head at him. "Novels? I don't remember seeing anything written under your name. What kind of novels?"

He grinned. "A little bit of everything. And I write under a pen name. Ask me later, and I might tell you what it is." He smirked as they stood to deplane, and Casey found herself watching the way his lean muscles rippled under his shirt as he squeezed out of their row and headed down the short aisle.

They climbed down from the small puddle jumper, and caught a quick car ride to the port where the fast ferry was waiting. Everything caught her attention; the smell of the water and the bustling activity of the port combining to captivate her. She felt like she was in a fairy tale. The surprisingly speedy ferry looked more like a sport boat than a large people carrier. Dolphins rode the bow wave as the ferry carried them to Iriomote, and Casey clung to Neil's hand as she watched them frolic alongside of the ship.

When they reached Iriomote, they met Ken, the tour guide who would take them up the river through the mangroves and into the island's interior. Ken gave them a quick lesson in using a stand-up paddle board - something Casey laughingly confessed that she enjoyed more than surfing with Mike - and then they set off up the Urauchi River into the island's lush interior.

What felt like mere moments later, they had left the hustle and bustle of the travel behind them, and they were paddling up a narrow river corridor, mangroves growing thick along the river. The tide was low, but rising, and Casey was enthralled by the way the rising water slowly hid the iconic mangrove roots as they paddled. The trees grew thick and dense over the river, filtering the light through a canopy of green and creating a magical, otherworldly feel.

"This is amazing," Casey finally said to Neil in a low voice, breaking the silence that had blanketed them since they had begun paddling the river.

He smiled over at her. "Yeah. I've seen mangroves before, but never like this. What an experience."

They lapsed into silence again, enjoying the enchanting scene. Ken occasionally pointed out a bit of wildlife, or a particularly interesting plant, but otherwise, he simply let them enjoy the morning.

When they stopped for a picnic lunch, Casey flopped onto the blanket with a theatrical groan, not even waiting for the crew to set out the food. "Everything ok there?" Neil asked, giving her a glance that was half concerned, half amused.

She grinned sheepishly. "Yesterday was my first time surfing. Let's just say I'm a bit more out of shape than I realized."

He chuckled. "I'm kinda surprised you're up for stand-up paddle boarding the day after your first surf lesson. I hope you popped a lot of Ibuprofen with breakfast this morning."

She shook her head. "I didn't, but I'm wishing I had. Maybe we can scare some up to go with lunch." Rallying, she gave him a plucky grin. "No big deal, though. After childbirth, anything else is a breeze."

He laughed aloud. "The childbirth card. Yeah, my mom plays that one sometimes. I'm kinda surprised Becks hasn't popped out a few little tykes so she can do the same - she's tough as nails and she'd probably be back at work again by lunch time."

She tilted her head. "You implied that marrying hadn't worked out too well for her when we had lunch with your family in Vermont. Can I ask what the story is there?"

"It's pretty simple: her husband is a certifiable asshole. He cheated on her. With his secretary. Apparently he felt the need not only to violate his marriage vows and break my sister's heart, but also to become a walking stereotype." He shook his head, his face hostile. "That dude is not getting a Christmas card."

Casey giggled. "I'm sorry - I know it's not funny, but the way you talk about it is." Her face became serious again. "So are they divorced now? When did all this happen?"

"Twice. The first time was a few years ago, but Becca said she wanted to work through it because she still loved him, and every marriage faces a few rough patches. But he did it again, and she caught him - on Valentine's Day. She filed for divorce pretty much immediately, and she told me it went through while I've been here. But she's still pretty raw about it."

Casey sighed. "That's awful. Poor woman. I take it they didn't have kids, then?"

He shook his head. "She wanted to, in spite of being a high-powered lawyer. Like I said, she's tough as nails, but she has a warm, gooey center and I think she's secretly dying for kids to love and spoil. They actually tried for a few years, before and after he cheated on her the first time - she thought the stress of trying might have been part of what drove him to cheat. But she found out when things went down that he had secretly had a vasectomy years ago, before they ever started trying to have kids, and he just never told her. Kids were never going to happen. He's such a dick." Neil looked like he wanted to hit something.

"Yikes," Casey cringed. "I didn't realize people were actually that horrible in real life. I thought stuff like that was just made up for movies."

"I wish. I'd give up a lot to have spared Becca this pain. But there's not much I can do about it." He grinned evilly. "But, I have decided that I'm going to write him into every one of my books from now on, and find new and inventive ways to make him suffer horribly."

Casey laughed. "You have a twisted mind. And I kinda like it. I hope your sister appreciates the gesture." She sighed, growing serious again. "How old is she?"

He frowned. "She's thirty-five. Not ancient, but it's getting kind of late for her to start all over again, find a husband and then still try to have kids. I think she might be looking into having her eggs frozen, but I don't know how viable things will be by the time she's ready to use them."

Casey leaned forward, placing a hand on his forearm. "She should find a sperm donor and do it now, while she's young enough to enjoy it. If things work out, she can still have a few kids before forty, and then there's no pressure to find a man right away. If I could raise a son as wonderful as Niko on my own, I'm sure your badass sister would find it a cakewalk."

He tilted his head as he looked at her. "You think so? You'd advise someone to intentionally become a single parent?"

She nodded. "If they wanted kids bad enough, and they had the ability and understanding to deal with being a single parent - sure. Plenty of people become single parents by accident, and it can suck, but we're clearly capable of dealing with it. You just do the best you can with what you have. It might be a little harder to choose it - it makes dating more difficult, and what happens if you find the right person but you've already got kids? But it sounds like your sister is more than capable, and she shouldn't have to wait around, hoping for the right man to come along. Plus, right about now, she's probably wondering if she can ever trust another man again - it'll take time for her to be in the right place to accept a new relationship. But in the meantime, she could be pouring all of her love and affection into a new little life. Things are even easier if your parents are willing to help. I don't know where I'd be without mine."

His face took on an odd look. "You value being close to your parents. You'd want to stay in Philadelphia, then?"

"Well..." she trailed off. "I'm not sure." She sighed. "I'm sorry for bringing this up, but you asked... if I ended up with Richard, I know I'd have to relocate to South Carolina. He owns his own business there, and he's tied to the geographical space, so there's no way he could relocate for me." Neil's face turned sour and he looked away.

"But with you..." she leaned in closer, giving his arm a squeeze where her hand still rested on it. "Would I have to leave Philly? You said you don't normally stay in Manhattan, anyway - just when you have meetings - how tied are you to Vermont?"

He sighed. "I own my place there, and I bought it with the intent of staying there for the rest of my life. I hoped that if I raised a family, it would be there. The space is great, the schools are great - we've got a few Montessori schools that aren't too far away, and there are some great private schools for when a kid gets older. It's peaceful, the air is fresh, and it isn't so crowded and busy. I really like it, and I find it gives me the space to think and the quiet to write. I'd have a hard time giving that up for any city."

He focused on her, placing his free hand over hers. "But I know you and Nicholas are established in Philadelphia. I'm sure moving him would be disruptive, and I don't doubt your parents value being close to him - mine sure would. And I can work from anywhere, whereas you have an actual physical office you work from in Philly. If you felt it was important for you to stay there, I could understand that. I'd do my best to fall in love with it, because I want to be with you - wherever you are." He flashed her a brilliant smile.

She giggled. "Is it hard work, always finding the perfect thing to say? Or is it just a gift you writers have?"

He laughed. "I wish I could take credit for it, but my friends would tell you I often say 'I'm a writer, not a speaker.' The truth is, I sometimes mangle what I'm trying to say - like, really badly. If you think otherwise, maybe you're being easy on me." He leaned toward her, his gaze dropping to her lips. "Or maybe you just make it easy." He kissed her, lightly, tenderly, tasting her lips but giving her the chance to pull away. When she didn't, the kiss deepened, his hand slipping behind her head and working its way into her hair as the kiss turned demanding and sensuous. She returned it fervently, her hand sliding up his arm to rest on his shoulder, then snaking behind his neck.

Some time later, Neil broke away, pulling back a few inches and gazing into her eyes with a small smile. She was smiling, too, the corner of her lips turned up and the grin becoming girlish as he continued to stare at her. Eventually, she shook her head shyly, breaking the look and leaning back, taking a deep breath.

"Wow. You really know how to make me feel like a kid again. I feel like I'm in high school and I just made out with a guy I like, and now I'm all shy and don't know what to do with myself. I should be handing you a note that says: "Do you like me? Circle one: Yes, No." She grinned at herself, but refused to meet his eyes, staring absently at the food laid out on the blanket.

He tucked his fingers under her chin and lifted it gently to look at him. "We're way past that," he grinned. "That's a firm yes. And by now we've definitely graduated to making out on my parents' couch in the basement, paranoid about getting caught but unable to resist the temptation."

She laughed. "Ok. How did we end up getting to potentially having a son together?"

He chuckled. "We were young, then. Full of hormones and emotions.

I'm sure we didn't take ourselves so seriously. Nothing seemed to matter as much back then, and everything was easy."

She nodded. "You've got a good point. I know the stakes are high, but let's stop being so serious and try taking it easy." She smugly smeared a piece of soft cheese across his flawless cheekbone, raising an eyebrow at him with a wicked grin.

He sputtered, his mouth dropping open. He stared at her for a beat, watching her lick the rest of the cheese off the end of her finger while she smirked at him. "Oh, you asked for it," he finally pronounced, grabbing a small bowl of grapes and dumping it over her head. She squealed and grabbed for whatever was closest, tossing a handful of crackers at him before going back for something more messy. He leaned over to smash some sliced kiwi against her face, and ended up losing his balance, getting her collarbone instead and knocking them both over. They rolled around on the ground for a while, laughing like school kids and covering each other in picnic foods.

Eventually, smeared in peanut butter and smashed fruit, Casey called out "Mercy!" Neil laughed as he looked at her, but he'd taken the brunt of the cheese and crackers, which had become pulverized into small crumbs that now adhered to him in odd patches. She laughed out loud as she took in the state of him, the noise startling a pair of nearby birds, which set them both off into another fit of giggles.

Suddenly, he was on her, pinning her down where she lay amidst the ruins of their picnic lunch. He kissed her hard, demanding and promising in the same breath, his hand on her hip and the weight of his torso pressing down on her. Her hands came to the sides of his head, fisting in his hair and holding him there as she returned his kiss passionately. One of his hands slowly slipped up under her t-shirt, the fingers tickling her skin and coming to rest on her rib cage. He pressed the length of his body urgently against her. Her hands slid down to rest on his lower back, her fingers tucked under the edge of his waistband as she writhed against him.

"Hate to interrupt, but this is a prime time, network show," Vince pointed out in her ear.

Neil got a similar reminder and broke the kiss with a sigh, but he stayed where he was, lying half on top of her and sliding his free hand up to caress her face as he gazed deeply into her eyes. "Casey, you're it," he whispered to her, his voice hoarse with emotion. "You're everything I want. You've been missing from my life for ten years, and it'll never be complete without you."

She sighed, her eyes closing and her lips twisting into a small smile as she basked in the warm emotions his words inspired. Her hand at the small of his back slipped around his waist, pulling him tightly against her. They lay in silence, Neil dropping small kisses on her face and hair.

The sound of a drip of water near her head broke the spell. Casey opened her eyes to see Neil still staring at her, and she smiled at him. The lone drip was followed by another, and then another. Before they could finish disentangling themselves, the rain was pouring down, and the crew had raised a pop-up tent roof to protect the remains of the picnic.

Casey laughed, noting once again that she was still covered in food, and waggled her eyebrows at Neil. "Shall we?" she asked, shoving herself up and then holding out a hand to him. He took it, rising to stand next to her, and the stepped out from under the tent and let the rain pour over them, rinsing away the food debris. She scrubbed a little at the peanut butter, but it came away, leaving her skin smooth and soft in the rain.

Their clothes were quickly plastered against their skin, so Casey unbuttoned the loose blouse she'd worn over her bikini top and took it off. Neil grinned and followed suit, much to Casey's delight. She gave him a very deliberate look up and down, admiring his lithe frame and toned body, and smirked at him. He laughed and stepped toward her, wrapping her in his embrace and kissing her again. They stood in the rain and kissed for a long time, skin sliding wetly against skin as their hands roamed freely.

Eventually, a production assistant stepped up and tapped Neil on the shoulder, motioning for them to step back under the pop-up tent once he got their attention.

"The afternoon was supposed to be cliff diving, but the guide says the rain makes it too dangerous. You might slip, and the canyon system we'd be traversing could flash flood. So we'll take you by boat back down the river, and we'll get you to your evening destination early. Since we're cutting the next portion of your date, I guess I'll give you this now." He handed Casey a sealed envelope.

She quickly dried her hands on a towel that another PA handed her, then took the envelope. "Casey and Neil: we hope you've enjoyed your time in the Iriomote jungle. If you want this magical date to continue, we've booked a unique treehouse suite where the two of you can spend the night together, alone and free from cameras. If you choose to forego your individual rooms at the resort, we hope you enjoy this one-of-a-kind experience as a couple."

She looked up at Neil with a shy smile. "It sounds amazing. I'd really like to spend more time with you, and I'd have a hard time passing up something as unusual as a treehouse suite. What do you think?"

He smiled, taking her hand and bringing it up to his lips in a kiss. "It sounds magical, but even if it was a glorified outhouse, I'd never pass up a chance to spend more time with you."

She laughed. "That was the perfect blend of romantic and disgusting. Forgive me if I say I'd turn down an outhouse. This, on the other hand, sounds enchanting. Let's do it."

The production assistants packed away the remainder of the picnic debris, as well as the stand-up paddle boards and guide Ken, and loaded everyone and everything into a large river boat. They took a leisurely trip back down the river, Casey and Neil spending time on the outside deck in the rain for a while, admiring the mangroves as Casey stood wrapped in Neil's arms. Eventually, the wet grew too cold for them, and they came back inside, wrapping themselves up in fluffy robes that the crew provided as they snuggled up together on a padded bench. They talked quietly, the noise of the boat drowning out their conversation.

A few hours later, they had boated, driven and taken a short hike to their evening destination. They stood hand-in-hand as they admired the amazing structure. A small balcony enfolded the base of a giant tree, with a few steps leading up to the base. The balcony wrapped around the tree, and on one side, a staircase began, spiraling around the tree as it led to the upper level. The main structure was large and airy, with a wide, sloped roof overhanging beautiful wood support beams. Gauzy drapes stood open to reveal a bed, a small table and a few chairs. A small bamboo room held a shower, toilet and sink. The table was piled high with covered dishes, concealing a delicious-smelling gourmet dinner. The entire structure glowed with twinkle lights, giving it a magical, fairy-land ambiance.

"This is like something out of a fairy tale," she confessed to Neil, her voice low and reverent as she admired the beautiful structure.

He nodded. "I can't think of a more beautiful place to spend some quiet time together - away from the cameras and the hustle and bustle."

Sharing a smile, they walked up the path and stepped into the treehouse, closing the gauzy curtains one-by-one as they walked around the majestic structure and shut themselves away from the world.

Nathan May walked into the small room where they were all waiting, Casey standing carefully apart from the three men but chatting amiably with them. Nathan smiled as he greeted them. "Hello, everyone. Are you enjoying Okinawa?"

They nodded, smiling in return. Mike offered an enthusiastic "yeah!" Nathan chuckled, but then motioned for them to sit down. The three men sat together on a carefully-positioned couch. Casey sat at one end of the couch in a comfortable chair, and Nathan sat opposite her at the other end of the couch in a matching chair.

"This week is a little different. Because Casey is the final woman, she's safe through the remainder of the show. No matter what else happens, she's going to be a part of America's Favorite Couple. Congratulations, Casey!" He offered her a smile, but his expression turned serious as he looked back at the men.

"Now, the three of you are not safe. One of you is definitely going home this week, while the other two will be going to Casey's hometown next week, where one of you might be proposing."

He leaned back in his chair. "We also have a little housekeeping to do. This has been an extraordinary season, as one of our women revealed that the father of her child might be among our pool of potential men. So, as you know, we conducted a paternity test, and we invited the other potential father - Mike - to join us here on the show."

"Before I reveal the results of this week's vote, we've invited a special guest to come and personally deliver the results of the paternity test. Doctor Teddy, please come in and join us," Nathan called out, and the doctor strolled into the room, stepping across to sit in an empty chair next to the host.

"Doctor, you've got the results of the paternity test?"

He nodded to Nathan. "As you know, four weeks ago, we took samples from the child, Nicholas, as well as the mother, Casey, and the potential father, Neil. When Mike made the trip to join you, I also personally took a sample from him. I've run the results, and I can confirm the paternity with a ninety-nine point four percent certainty. This is the highest possible potential certainty in a paternal match, and is completely accurate according to the court of law. These results are admissible for establishing parentage, pursuing custody and child support, and other legal paternal issues."

Nathan nodded. "Thank you for your diligence, doctor. And thank you for coming all the way to Okinawa to deliver the results in person. Let's get right to the moment we've all been waiting for: why don't you tell us who is the father of Casey's child?"

The four of them stared intently at the doctor. Casey held onto the arms of her chair, gripping them so tightly that her hands were turning white. Richard glanced back and forth between the two men flanking him, then returned his gaze to the doctor. Mike looked queasy, while Neil's brow was furrowed and his expression was intense.

The doctor nodded, glancing over his glasses at the two men, and then at Casey. "Certainly. The father of Casey's child is..." He trailed off, letting the suspense build. After a long beat, and then another one, he finally finished with: "Neil."

Casey and Neil jumped up, grinning foolishly at one another and hugging each other tightly. Mike slumped back into the couch, letting out a deep breath and looking relieved. Richard looked mildly annoyed as he watched Neil and Casey embracing, their eyes brimming with moisture. After a long moment, she pulled away, but she held his gaze as she smiled and they returned to their seats.

"Thank you so much for sharing the news with us, doctor," Nathan smiled. "As you can see, I think you've made them both very happy."

Neil and Casey nodded, smiling hugely, and Nathan gallantly handed Casey his handkerchief as she sniffled and blotted at unshed tears with her fingertips.

The doctor nodded and smiled at the two of them. "Congratulations," he offered, standing and walking across to shake each of their hands before stepping out of the room.

"Well," Nathan began, looking at the group. "That was a big moment. How are the three of you feeling? Why don't we start with you, Mike?"

He sighed, looking at Nathan and then over at Casey. "Well, honestly, Nathan - I'm feeling a bit relieved. Nicholas is a great kid, and his mom is very dear to me, but the idea of unexpectedly becoming the father to a nine-year-old boy - just being plopped down into his life without any practice or training or warning - has been making me feel pretty freaked out. I definitely would have done right by both of you, Casey," he pointed out, turning to face her directly and getting a smile in return. "But I think

I'd like to try fatherhood the traditional route - making a baby, finding out she's pregnant, getting nine months to get used to the idea and prepare, and then having a forgiving little thing that isn't as hard to figure out to start with."

Casey laughed. "Oh, poor Mike. You have no idea what lies down that route..." She smirked and winked at him. "But seriously, no hard feelings. I know it was a lot to take in, and I never anticipated dragging you into this. I've just had a feeling it was Neil all along. I'm glad you're not disappointed!"

Nathan smiled. "Neil, what do you think of this news? I take it from the look on your face that it isn't unwelcome?"

Neil nodded, smiling and dashing the back of his hands across his eyes. Casey tried to hand him the handkerchief, but he laughed and waved it off. "I was completely floored by the idea when Nicholas let it slip that day on the train that I might be his father. I thought for sure he had gotten something wrong. But when Casey told me who she was, and admitted that Niko was probably mine... first I was angry at her for not telling me sooner, and potentially making me miss years of my son's life. I've effectively missed half his childhood." He shook his head. "But then, the more time I spent with both of them, and the more Casey and I talked... I realized what an amazing child he is, and I came to understand her position and accept her reasons for not reaching out to me sooner. I still wish I hadn't missed out on so many firsts - his first steps, his first words, his first day of school - but I'm just so grateful to be a part of his life now. Whatever happens here and in the future, I feel blessed to have him in my life, and I'll make sure he'll never have to be without his father again."

Casey reached over and squeezed Neil's hand, dabbing at her eyes with the kerchief again. He beamed at her.

Nathan turned to her. "And Casey - I take it you aren't surprised by this news? Is it everything you were hoping for?"

She shook her head. "Everything, and more, Nathan. I've thought about contacting Neil so many times over the years. But I wasn't one hundred percent positive that Niko was his child, and I felt like such a fool, and the more time passed the harder it was to make myself do it - until it became habit. Coming here - and meeting Neil again here - has been so amazing. We've had the chance to spend time together, talk about everything that has happened, and he's gotten a chance to get to know

Nicholas - without the pressure that might come from us making contact privately. It was all a part of our journey here, and somehow that's made it easier. But now that I know for sure it's Neil, I can't imagine it being anyone else, and I know Niko is going to be so happy when he finds out."

Nathan nodded, his gaze becoming somber as he turned toward Richard. "What about you, Richard? I saw you react when the doctor gave us the news - how do you feel now, knowing that Nicholas is Neil's son? Does that change how you feel about Casey, or what you hope to get from your experience here?"

Richard took his time as he thought about his response. "Those are good questions, Nathan. Yes, I did react when I heard the news." He turned toward Neil. "No offense, man, but I know you and Casey have a close bond, and something like this can't help but pull the two of you together." He swiveled to face Casey. "That being said, I have learned to work with my daughter's mother to co-parent without having a romantic connection with her, and I know Casey and Neil can do the same thing, given time." He shrugged. "Nicholas was never going to be my son, and Casey isn't the mother of my child. But knowing that he has another father - regardless of who it is - doesn't change how I feel about him. I'd be proud to have Nicholas in my house as a part of my family, and I'd do my best to provide a positive male role model and a loving parent in spite of the fact that Neil is his dad. Just as I know Casey will do for my daughter, in spite of the fact that she's not her mother."

His voice turned husky with emotion. "I am in love with Casey, and I know what an amazing parent she is to that boy." Neil's head spun around toward Richard, and he fixed the other man with a steely glare. Richard plowed on, ignoring him. "I still want nothing more than to be with Casey at the end of all this, and I'm sure we can work out amicable co-parenting arrangements with Neil."

Neil's nostrils flared, and he squeezed his hand into a fist. "If you think I'm going to let you take my boy to South Carolina and let him live in *your* house-"

Casey interrupted him with a gentle hand on his. "Neil, all of that is still ahead of us. Let's just enjoy the good news now, and we can talk about all the details and legal arrangements later."

He turned to face her, but his eyes were unfocused and a little wild. "No, Casey, what I want-"

She squeezed his hand. "Doesn't matter. Not to be insensitive, but I think Nathan has some more business for us." She released his hand and turned to look at the host. "Nathan, I believe we've still got a Vote this week?"

He nodded. "Right you are, Casey. And now that we've taken a moment to digest this news, I think it's time to move on to the other question on everyone's mind: who's going through to next week?"

He looked at each of the three men in turn. "We tallied the results of the Vote before we revealed the results of the paternity test, so the question of who's the father wouldn't bias people when making this week's choice. I know there are real feelings involved now, and this is certainly the most difficult elimination of the season to date - if not the most difficult elimination in the history of the show, with the added factor of Nicholas's paternity."

"As you know, one of you will not be going through to the hometown dates and potential proposal next week, and that person is..." He paused, but didn't drag it out too long. "Mike." He nodded to the man, his expression somber. "I'm sorry, Mike. You will not be a part of America's Favorite Couple. Please say your farewells, and prepare to head home."

All of them stood, and Mike shook hands with the other two men. Then, he stepped over to Casey. He enfolded her in a tight hug. "I'm not all that surprised by this. The writing was on the wall. I think you've got your hands full with those two." He leaned back, staring into her face. "It's been good to see you again, Case. You've turned into a pretty incredible woman, and I'm glad I got to spend time with you again." He gave her a big kiss on the lips.

She smiled, grabbing his biceps. "Mike, Mike, Mike." She shook her head. "I never thought I'd see you again in a million years. Seeing you has brought back a lot of fond memories. We did have fun. I hope you get what you want out of life - to have fun - and I hope you're able to find whatever you thought you were missing with your ex wife." She kissed his cheek.

As Mike turned to leave, Nathan cleared his throat. "Mike, one more thing. When you get back stateside, Anastasia will be flying out to Manhattan to spend some time with you. While you might not have become a part of America's Favorite Couple, it seems maybe you did find love on this journey, after all."

Mike gave Casey a sheepish look and a rueful grin. She laughed aloud. "Good for you, tiger. Go have fun. And do lots of things I wouldn't do."

She winked at him, and he flexed his muscles, grinning, before walking out of the small room.

Nathan turned back to the three of them. "We're down to the end, now, lady and gentlemen. Next week is the final week. You'll each have a hometown date with Casey, where you'll get to meet her family and spend a day on a date of her choosing. And then it'll be time for the final decision. Will one - or both - of you propose to Casey? Will she accept? And who will be voted America's Favorite Couple?"

CHAPTER SEVEN
Week Ten

Casey greeted Richard with a big hug and a kiss as they met outside the Philadelphia Zoo. She gave Cassidy a more reserved smile and a wave, but Niko jumped in with a hug for the girl, which she returned with a sweet smile. "Welcome to our hometown!" Casey offered, grinning at the two of them and leading the way into the zoo.

The kids quickly bonded over the adorable and interesting zoo animals. Niko dashed from exhibit to exhibit with his usual unbridled enthusiasm, and Cassidy followed, running along with uncharacteristic abandon. Richard and Casey smiled at each other as they followed at a more sedate pace. "That looks promising," she offered at one point.

Richard nodded. "I love my girl, but she's a little prim and proper... and *old* for her age. It might be nice for her to have someone a little more playful around. She can have a hard time relating to kids her age, so maybe he can bring her out of her shell a bit and help her figure out how to be a kid."

He grinned at her. "On a lighter note, how did Niko react when he heard about the karate date? Did he hate to miss it?"

Casey made a face. "I didn't tell him. I didn't really know how to explain that you and Neil got into a real fight. I kinda glossed over the two-on-one entirely, and just told him about the individual experiences I had, and how awesome Okinawa was. Although I did bring him back a few mementos, including a couple of karate-related tchotchkes, and he just thought that was the best."

Richard nodded. "So... how did he react to the big news about his paternity?"

Casey tilted her head at him. "I'm kinda surprised you're asking."

He smiled ruefully. "I'm not a monster, Casey. I've made it clear that I'm not a big fan of the guy - which I think is understandable given the circumstances - but I know this is a big question in your life that has gone unresolved for a long time, so I'm sure it was an important moment for the two of you." He reached out and gave her hand a squeeze. "That means it matters to me, too. So how did it go?"

She smiled, stepping close and giving him a quick hug and kiss. She pulled away before it could turn into anything more serious, but she squeezed his arm and offered him a grateful look. "I appreciate that. I think it's very thoughtful that you asked - especially given the difficulty of the circumstances."

They kept walking to where the kids had dashed ahead. "Nicholas was really happy to finally have an answer. It's something he's asked me about more and more often as he's gotten older, so I think it was important for him to know for sure - more than I realized. And he likes Neil a lot, so he couldn't be happier. I know he's looking forward to seeing him tomorrow." She glanced over at Richard. "I know this complicates things, but I think you're right about being able to co-parent with him even if we don't share a romantic connection. He seems happy with the news, and I know Nicholas is, so we'll work together to figure it out even if it's you and I who end up together at the end of this."

He smiled, reaching over to grab her arm and spin her around into an embrace. "I don't like the sound of that 'if,'" he said in a low voice, before locking her into a deep, sultry kiss.

A loud "Ewww!" from Cassidy brought them out of the moment, and Casey grinned apologetically even though it was Richard who initiated the display. He turned to Cassidy.

"Sorry, honey, but you're going to have to get used to me showing affection to the special woman in my life. I know how you feel right now, but I promise one day you're going to want to kiss someone of your own, and you wouldn't want me - or anyone else - 'Ewwing' at you."

She scrunched up her face at him. "Aww, dad, I wish you wouldn't say things like that. I don't want to kiss anyone. Especially not a boy - they're gross and messy and smelly and dirty... only you and mom and grandma and grandpa get kisses, because I love you and it's ok to kiss your family." She nodded decisively, and Casey restrained a laugh.

Niko turned to his mom. "Yeah. Kissing girls is gross."

Casey shook her head at him. "No you don't. You're just saying that because Cassidy said it, and you want to get on her good side. Trust me, son, kissing is the least of what you're gonna want to do someday. But that talk is not for today! Today we're here to have fun and check out all the animals!" She grabbed his shoulders and spun him around, pointing him at the nearest exhibit. "So what do you think of that..." she glanced over at the sign. "Madagascar giant jumping rat. Isn't that cool?"

Richard's head whipped around, and he squeezed Cassidy's shoulder, pointing her toward the exhibit and nodding. She nodded back.

"Yeah!" Niko agreed, stepping close to the display.

Casey glanced over at Richard, but he was staring intently at the rat and didn't notice her gaze. After a moment of admiring the giant rodent, Niko stepped over to the next display in the Small Mammal House, pointing and gesturing for them to come check it out. Casey followed, and the two of them made their way around the rest of the building, checking out the lemurs, aardvarks and other small mammals. As they were finishing up and preparing to head back out into the main zoo, Casey looked around for Richard and Cassidy. They were just coming toward them, having lagged behind.

The four of them went out together and explored the rest of the zoo. Niko particularly enjoyed the reptiles and the polar bear, although he was a little disappointed that many of the large animals were lounging around, inactive in the middle of the day. They stopped at the 34th Street Market for lunch before heading out, and then went back to the Kelly family home to meet Casey's family.

"Now this isn't my house," Casey cautioned them as they stood on the walkway in front of the large, rambling structure. "This is where my parents live, and where my brothers and sisters and I grew up. Niko and I live in a much smaller row house about fifteen minutes away." She looked back and forth between Richard and Cassidy. "I've got a large family - I have two brothers, and two sisters - and we can be kind of a lot, so they've left their significant others and kids at home. It's just the immediate family. But Niko has 5 cousins right now, and another one on the way. And maybe more soon if Auntie Bridget ever gets hitched," she winked at Nicholas, who giggled.

With that, she opened the front door, calling out "We're here!" in a loud greeting. Her brothers appeared first, and she introduced them as Patrick and Liam. They smiled and shook Richard's hand, but Cassidy was so reserved they didn't quite seem to know how to greet her. Then the sisters appeared; Bridget and Fiona. They greeted Richard warmly, but then they cooed over Cassidy, admiring her hair ribbons and her dress and her beautiful eyes. By the time her parents appeared, and Casey introduced them as Susan and Hugh, Cassidy seemed right at home, sitting comfortably on an oversized chair between the two sisters and having her hair braided while they chattered.

"Did you have a good time at the zoo?" Casey's mom asked, her green eyes crinkling as she smiled, deepening the network of fine creases that spoke of a lifetime full of smiles.

Niko nodded enthusiastically. "Yeah! We saw tigers and aardvarks and lemurs and bears. And there were some really cool alligators and crocodiles, but my favorite was the Gila monster. The word 'monster' is right in his name! He was living with a rattlesnake, and didn't seem scared at all, so he must have some sort of super powers or just be really scary to other animals, too, so they leave him alone."

Susan smiled and led him off to one side of the room, asking him more questions about things they'd seen at the zoo and occupying his attention so the rest of the adults could talk.

"So let's cut to the chase: do you want to marry my sister?" Patrick asked. Bridget and Fiona burst out laughing, while Casey's jaw fell open and her face turned bright red. Liam raised an eyebrow at his younger brother's lack of tact, and their father looked around at all of them, shaking his head.

"Well, I might have led with something a little lighter to break the ice, but that did the trick," Richard chuckled. "I haven't formally asked your sister that question - so it might be a little rude for me to answer before I've had that conversation with her." He stepped over to her and took her hand in his, bringing it to his lips and giving it a small kiss before holding it at his side. "But I am falling in love with her, and I could absolutely see a future where we spend the rest of our lives together."

She beamed up at him, the blush fading as he handled the question with such aplomb.

"So, with that out of the way, maybe we should move on to some meaningless small talk?" He winked, and Liam laughed aloud, while Patrick looked slightly annoyed.

"I like him," Liam declared.

"I'm reserving judgement," Patrick pronounced, crossing his arms across his chest.

"Boys," their father chided. "Didn't we teach you better manners than that?"

"I don't know, dad," Patrick retorted. "Aren't you the one who literally chased away Fiona's first boyfriend with a broom?"

Hugh coughed. "I don't remember it quite like that."

Fiona nodded. "He did." She leaned toward Cassidy, adding conspiratorially: "I hope your dad is a little better behaved when you start bringing boys around."

Richard shook his head. "Oh, no, Cassidy won't be bringing any boys around."

The girl nodded. "That's right. Boys are gross."

Bridget grabbed the top of her head and held it steady as she finished the braid. "We'll talk again in a few years. I think you'll change your tune." She grinned.

"So, Richard," Susan interjected from where she had redirected Niko's attention to a puzzle. "Why don't you tell us a little about your family. Are they as much as a handful as this lot?"

He smiled. "They can be, in their own way. We men are a little outnumbered by the women. I've got two sisters, Charlotte and Lucinda, and three nieces, Penny, Betsey and Avalie. And Lucinda's married to a woman, so she didn't even bring another brother-in-law to the family. Although her wife is wonderful, so I can't complain too much. But it's just me, my dad Boone, and my brother-in-law Wade. And just between us, I don't care for Wade all that much - he has a little ego problem. But at family gatherings, it's just us three guys against what seems like all the women in the world. So it's nice that your family is a little more balanced."

He grinned at Niko. "It would be nice to have another guy in the mix to help us even the numbers a bit." He winked at the boy, who giggled.

Cassidy shook her head. "We don't need more boys."

"Agree to disagree," her father told her.

"I can see we've hit on a sore spot here," Susan smiled. "Having my boys has definitely made things more chaotic. But I think girls are harder. All those emotions."

Fiona chuckled. "We were a nightmare. You can say it, mom. We know we tortured you, and we're sorry." She looked at Bridget and Casey in turn. "Well, I am, anyway, and they will be, too, if they ever have girls of their own."

"Mind your own business," Bridget chided Fiona, turning her nose up and looking away.

"What are your thoughts on the matter, Richard? Do you think you'd like more kids?" Fiona asked.

He looked at Casey, grinning a slow, wide grin and squeezing her hand. "I've filled Casey in on my thought about more kids. Which is: the more, the merrier, if she's involved."

Casey blushed deep crimson again, staring at the floor while biting back a grin. Her brothers exchanged a glance, while her sisters grinned and giggled at each other. "Well, that tells us a lot," Bridget smirked at Casey.

"All right, now, children," Susan interrupted. "We have little ears in the room, so be nice and keep in mind that we don't want to make them feel awkward. Or invite any difficult questions."

"Like what, gran?" Niko perked up. "What kind of questions?"

"Like how is it that you can pick up on things we don't want you to notice so quickly, but you can't hear me calling you when it's time to finish something fun you're doing and start your homework," Casey replied, pouncing on him and tickling him mercilessly. He dissolved into fitful giggles, and subsided as Casey stood again and went to sit next to Richard.

"So would you mind telling us, son, what you think about our Casey? You've said you have feelings for her, and have implied that you're hoping for a serious future with her, so I'd like to know what it is you like about her and hear a little bit about how you've come to this place." He shook his head. "This process is so unusual, it would make me feel better about the whole thing if I know you've got good reason to admire her, and that you're saying these things for the right reasons."

Richard nodded. "I understand what you're saying, sir. Honestly, I get almost sick to my stomach sometimes when I think about Cassidy's future. As a father, I feel very protective toward her, and I know how men think, so the prospect of her growing up kind of terrifies me. And I agree that this process is unusual, so I can see why you'd feel concerned."

He turned his head to look at Casey, and a soft, affectionate smile spread over his face. "Realistically, when this whole thing started, I didn't really expect to find love. And that's God's honest truth. I was open to the idea, because it's hard for a single parent to date, but it's such a strange situation - a bunch of people who don't know each other living together in a house and dating multiple people - I didn't have high hopes. But Casey struck me right away as one of the people worth getting to know. She just had such a way with Nicholas, and she seemed so genuine and honest and had such a great sense of humor, that I took pains to spend time with her, even when we weren't on dates."

He gave Casey's knee a squeeze and turned back toward her family. "We hung out together a lot in the house, with the kids. They encouraged us single parents to mingle with the non-parents, but we sorta naturally divided ourselves because we were always taking turns looking after the kids while the others were on dates, or getting together meals for the kids, or dealing with their schooling, or entertaining them. The more time I spent around Casey, the more I could see that she was something special, and the more I became interested in her romantically."

He grinned, nodding his head to Hugh. "I think I started to fall in love with your daughter before we ever even kissed, sir. But it was when we had a romantic dinner together at Six Flags after spending a day with the kids that I think I really started seeing a future with her, and began to realize how deep my feelings were growing. It's the first time we were away from the kids and I could spend time with her as a woman, and not just in 'mom mode.' And you've raised an amazing woman."

Susan blotted tears from the corners of her eyes. "That's good enough for me, young man. Whatever happens between the two of you, you have my blessing."

"What about you, Cassidy? Has anyone asked you how you'd feel about having Casey and Niko as a part of your life?" Fiona gently stroked the girl's head.

Cassidy looked at her father, and then at Casey. "I think it might be ok," she finally answered after a long pause. "I don't care for boys too much, but Nicholas isn't so bad. I'm sure I could show him how to behave better. And Casey's nice. She watches movies with us sometimes, and has cooked dinner for us, so I think she'd be ok to have around. As long as she doesn't think she's my mom and doesn't try to tell me what to do," the girl qualified, her tone stern.

Casey nodded seriously. "I would never try to replace your mother, Cassidy," she confirmed. "But if I were to get together with your dad, we'd be sharing parenting responsibilities, which means sometimes I might have to tell you what to do." The girl frowned, her expression becoming pinched. "We can talk about it when we get to that point, so we all understand what's expected and what's reasonable."

Richard nodded. "And that's that, Cassidy. No need to drag it out." His voice held a warning, and the well-behaved young woman subsided.

Richard looked at the clock. "Well, it looks like that's about it. Cassidy and I need to head out. We've got a few things to discuss, and I've got a lot of thinking to do before the next time I see Casey." He stood, and Cassidy followed suit. "Casey, will you walk me out?" he asked her.

Casey nodded and stood, smiling. Nicholas waved farewell while the three of them walked out the front door. Casey closed it behind her for privacy. "They're probably watching us out the window anyway," she warned Richard as she indicated the big windows on the front of the house.

He sent Cassidy to wait in the van that was there to take them back to their hotel. Then, he grinned, stepping close to Casey and wrapping her up in a big bear hug. "I've been waiting to do this all day," Richard whispered in her ear. Without waiting for a reply, he took her chin gently between his fingers and lifted it to his face. He kissed her, lightly at first, tasting her lips, but the kiss quickly grew more demanding. One of his hands slid down to cup her ass over her jeans, while his other slipped under her shirt at the small of her back, sliding up to rest against her bare skin as he pulled her against him.

She returned his kiss passionately, her own hands quickly sliding under his shirt to lightly scratch her nails along his bare back. He growled and nibbled on her lip, and as she arched her head back, his lips slid to feast on her neck and collarbone.

Eventually, he tore himself away. "If I don't let go of you right now, woman, I'm going to do indecent things to you, right here in your childhood front yard, in front of your parents and siblings and who knows who else might be watching."

Casey chuckled, but she looked disappointed to let him go. "Your daughter?"

He sighed hugely. "Oh boy. Yeah, I told myself I'd be a good example in front of her, but I guess that ship has sailed."

He squeezed her hand, bringing it to his lips for a lingering kiss. "I had a lovely day with you today, darlin'. It was a pleasure to meet your family and spend some time in your hometown. I look forward to speaking with you again this weekend. Be ready for the conversation."

She nodded, and stared after him as he turned and walked down the front path, climbing into the van and closing the door behind himself. She continued to stare after the van as it drove off, before reluctantly turning back to the house to face her family.

Bridget gave her a knowing grin as she stepped back into the house, and Casey returned the look with a guilty smile. Patrick noticed the exchange and catcalled, summoning the rest of the family into the well-worn living room. Liam and Fiona came strolling in, smirking at her, and her parents followed shortly after. Niko was conspicuously absent.

"We settled him down with a movie in the family room," Susan offered, noting Casey's gaze scanning the assembled crew. "We all need to have a serious chat."

The seven of them perched on various chairs, couches and footstools scattered around the room, Casey at the center. They looked at her expectantly.

"Well," her mother started, "first thing's first: do you love him?"

Casey smiled and looked down at the floor. "I *am* falling in love with him. He's just so solid, and dependable, and he knows exactly what to do with the kids - he's a great dad to his own daughter. He seems to have it all figured out."

"And?" Bridget probed. "So far, all ye've described is a dog, or a cousin, or a spinster uncle. But I saw the two of you outside. My God, girl, you could have lit the house on fire with all the heat coming off the two of you!"

Patrick whooped again, and Casey coughed, looking around the room for rescue. "What exactly do you expect me to say in front of our parents, Bridget?"

Her parents gave each other a knowing smile, but Bridget shot back a reply without missing a beat. "Why don't you start by saying he sets your knickers on fire, and then give us details?"

Casey sputtered, grinning hopelessly and shaking her head. "I can't decide whether you make me want to laugh or throw up, Bridget! You guys have never given me this hard a time before when I bring around a new guy."

Her mother leaned in. "That's because it's never been this serious before, dear heart. You're talking about a potential proposal at the end of this, and moving to South Carolina if it's Richard - so we need to have a candid discussion and make sure you're making the right decision for the right reasons."

Casey sighed. "I love you all dearly, but I fail to see why I should let you have a say in my love life."

Her father spoke up. "Casey, you know I haven't always been happy with your decisions. We had a big fight when you came home pregnant with Nicholas, and I know how tough that must have made things then. But now we love that boy to death, and it's hard to imagine not having both of you in our lives." He cleared his throat. "In all these years, you've never been serious about a man before. I didn't mind so much, because it meant I got to be selfish and keep you and Niko nearby, and I got to meddle freely in your life. But now marriage is on the table. And this is a guy you just met a few months ago, and the circumstances under which you've been dating aren't exactly conducive to making such an important decision with a clear head." He squeezed his wife's hand. "We feel like it's our job to help you look at things with the clearheadedness and perspective that will help you make the right decision - a considered and informed decision - in spite of the unusual circumstances." Susan nodded in agreement.

"All right, all right, no need to play the guilt card. You're a wonderful family, and I appreciate your meddling. So lay it on me." Casey sat back, waiting for their questions.

"Do you see a future with this man?" her sister Fiona asked, speaking up for the first time.

Casey nodded. "I do. In spite of what you say about the circumstances not being optimal to approach this decision with a clear head, I've really tried to do that every step of the way. Richard is a good, responsible man. Any woman would be lucky to have him. He's great about telling me - and showing me - how he appreciates me, and how he feels about me. And he makes me feel..." she looked at the floor, unable to meet the gazes of her assembled family. "Like a woman, not just a mother."

Patrick catcalled again, and Liam threw a couch pillow at him. "Lay off, loony."

Casey's cheeks flamed scarlet, but she looked up again, continuing. "Well, it's true. Most of the guys I've dated are either one or the other, but Richard is the full package."

Fiona nodded. "And what does a future with him look like? Tell us where you would live, where you would work, what a day would be like."

Casey smiled. "We've already talked about it. Niko and I would move into his house with him and Cassidy. He's got plenty of space, and he can build on to add more. We'd turn the current guest room into Niko's bedroom, and he'd build on two new office spaces - one for me and one for him - so the fourth bedroom that he's currently using as an office could become the new guest bedroom. Or maybe a room for the kids." She blushed and paused, and Patrick started to open his mouth, but Liam shook a fist at him in warning. Patrick shut his mouth again, and Casey continued. "He's got a successful business, so there's no rush for me to find a job right away. I could either look for a firm in Asheville, or if I don't want to start at the bottom again and can't find the right fit, I can start my own firm. I think I've got most of what I need to run a shop of my own."

"It sounds like you've given all of this a lot of thought," her mother praised, nodding gently at her. "What do you think a day would be like in that life with him?"

Casey gazed off into space, thinking. "Hmm. I guess we'd get up, feed the kids, get them off to school. Richard would head to work. If I were working from home, I'd head to the office and get started - otherwise, I'd go to work myself. I'd come home, one or both of us would cook dinner - probably Richard, as he tends to come home earlier for Cassidy and he's actually quite a good cook, and we'd hang out with the kids. Maybe we'd go horseback riding - Cassidy is really into horses, it's adorable. Or maybe we'd take Niko to karate, or just... hang out." She shrugged.

"Who does the dishes?" Liam asked. "Or the laundry? Cleans the house? I don't want you to find yourself in a glorified housewife situation. You deserve better."

Casey smiled at him. "This is why you're my favorite brother." Patrick began to object, and Liam raised his fist again. At a sharp look from their mother, the two of them subsided. "I really don't think it would be that way," Casey continued. "He does pretty well for himself already. With my income, too, I'm sure we could hire someone to come in and clean. Or we could do a chore chart and split things up, like Niko and I do at home. I think it would be fine."

Her mother nodded, then moved from her spot on the couch to kneel down in front of Casey. The older woman took her hands, gazing up into her face. "It sounds like you've given due consideration to what it would be like to live in the real world with him - not just in a fairy tale mansion with magical dates planned all the time. I can see how real your feelings are for him, and I'm so proud of you for valuing his stability and his suitability as a father and a partner - not just a romantic fling. If you decide you want to marry this man, you have our blessing."

Casey's eyes filled with moisture as she gazed at her mother, and then looked around at the smiling faces of her family.

Casey smiled as Neil jumped out of the van, beaming as he hurried up to them. He gave Casey a big hug, but he settled for a quick kiss before turning to Nicholas. "Hey, man," he greeted the boy, holding out his arms to him.

Suddenly shy, Niko turned toward Casey and wrapped his arms around her waist. "Aww, it's ok, little man - you know Neil. I know the news that he's really your dad is exciting and makes things a little different, but he's still the same guy you've gotten to know in the past ten weeks."

Nicholas nodded solemnly and released Casey. Neil reached out for a slightly less intimidating handshake. "It's good to see you, Nicholas. I've been really excited about hanging out with you since we got the news. I know it's going to be an adjustment, and I've got a lot to figure out as I learn how to be your dad, but I'm really happy about it."

Niko smiled shyly. "Me, too," he finally ventured.

"So where are we hanging out today?" Neil asked, looking around at the funky mosaics and eclectic colors. "This place looks pretty cool."

Casey nodded, smiling. "I hope you think so! It's Philadelphia's Magic Gardens. It's this really cool outdoor art installation that became sort of a community project when the property owner decided to sell it, and the locals fought to preserve it. It's a cool place with a cool history. Did I mention cool?" Her smile turned to a rueful grin. "I know you live in Manhattan, and we can't really compete with that, city-wise. But we do have a few unique things here, so I wanted to show you a little piece of Philly that wouldn't exist without creativity and the local community coming together to support a common goal."

He gave her a sad smile. "Casey, you don't have to try to impress me or make me fall in love with Philadelphia. I'm already in love with you. If you decide you feel the same way at the end of this, we'll figure everything else out. It's just details."

She bit her lip as she smiled, reaching out to give his hand a squeeze. "Thank you. But I'm still gonna try, because I want you to see a little bit of what I love about this place."

With that, she led them into the Magic Garden, holding Neil's hand on her left and Niko's hand on her right. All three of them were smiling as they took in the space around them, craning their necks and swiveling their heads constantly as they noticed new things. Niko made it a game to try to recognize items the artist had repurposed, like bicycle wheels and glass bottles, pointing them out every time he was able to identify something new. Casey and Neil smiled at his enthusiasm as they took in the installation with a more relaxed pace, pausing frequently to admire an element or read some lettering. It wasn't long before Niko had abandoned Casey entirely, dashing around the space and looking at things closely to try to identify them. This left Casey and Neil largely on their own; she kept an eye on Niko out of the corner of her eye, but was able to enjoy the scene with Neil.

"I wasn't expecting him to be quite so shy when I saw him again," Neil remarked, watching Niko. "He hasn't been like that with me before."

Casey shook her head. "Me, neither, to be honest. He told me on our zipline date that he really likes you. I kinda figured he'd be overjoyed to see you after getting the news, and would be dragging you around here like a shiny new toy, but I guess he's not quite sure how you fit into our lives yet."

Neil glanced over at her. "Neither am I. But I know how I want it to be." He stepped closer to her, pulling her into his arms and stroking her hair back from her face in a tender caress. "I want the three of us to be together. I want us to live together, like a real, proper family. Once I figure out the basic dad stuff, I think I'll actually be a big help. Since I work from home, you wouldn't have to worry about getting home from work so early, or dealing with logistics if he has any after school activities and needs rides. I could even do stuff like getting dinner on the table, so you wouldn't have a bunch of household chores waiting for you when you got home from work."

Casey laughed. "You can cook?"

Neil scoffed. "Quite well, in fact. Just because I've been a bachelor all these years doesn't mean I've been living off hot dogs and ramen noodles. I've traveled a lot, which means I've eaten a lot of interesting foods from different cuisines - and I like to incorporate all of that into my cooking when I'm at home."

She laughed again. "That sounds wonderful, but I'm guessing you've never cooked for kids. Niko isn't as bad as some of his friends... but feeding a child isn't the same as dining with an adventurous adult who will try every exotic thing to come along. You can't put just anything down and expect him to eat it. We still tussle now and again over veggies, although he's gotten better about that as he's gotten older. But if it's something that's not in the normal rotation? It's a toss-up whether he'll give it a try or flat out refuse it."

Neil grinned at her. "Challenge accepted. I'll bet I can get him to at least try anything I put down in front of him. And if I've cooked it, there's a pretty good chance he'll eat it."

Casey shook her head, laughing at him with a note of pity. "You're on. I know my son. I'm going to enjoy seeing you trip on your overconfidence, buddy."

He nodded, smiling mischievously. "Alright. Stakes?"

Her grin matched his, as she whispered something quietly into his ear. His face turned red and his smile took on a sheepish expression, but he nodded. "Done."

Nicholas ran up at that moment, yelling "Mom! Mom!" but stopping short of grabbing her hand as she was still locked in an embrace with Neil. "Mom! I need to show you something really cool," he said impatiently.

Casey laughed and shared a grin with Neil. "Alright. Let's take a look!"

They spent the next few hours exploring the Magic Garden in great detail. It was only half a city block in size, but they stopped frequently and talked about a lot of the images and mosaics with Nicholas, who was enjoying the adult attention so he kept encouraging them to continue talking.

Eventually, they'd seen everything and Niko had gotten tired of hearing them talk, so they decided to head off for lunch. Casey led them a few blocks away to the Morning Glory Diner. "Niko loves breakfast foods, so a diner is always a safe bet for him," she explained to Neil.

"Monkey french toast!" Niko exclaimed after reviewing the menu.

Casey looked at it, then looked at Neil. "Not a good idea, kiddo. That's got way too much sugar. Why don't we compromise: you can get a pecan waffle - that's got whipped peach butter for topping - and I'll split my veggie omelet with you."

Neil wisely remained silent for the duration of the negotiation. Niko raised an eyebrow at Casey and stared at her a moment, as if deciding how intently she was going to stick to her guns, before surrendering with a reluctant "Ok."

Neil ordered the garden keeper frittata, with a side short stack of pancakes topped with fruit. He looked at Casey. "If your mom says it's ok, I might share some of my pancakes and fruit with you," he offered. Niko brightened and looked at Casey hopefully. She nodded.

"But only after you eat some of my veggie omelet," she reminded him.

The three of them ended up sharing all of their food, eating off one another's plates and enjoying a tasty lunch. Niko ate too much, and was stuffed by the time lunch was over. When they climbed into the van to head over to meet Casey's family, Nicholas passed out. Neil carried him into the house, and laid him gently across the loveseat on one side of the room.

Casey smiled. "You're sweet, but he's a pretty sound sleeper when he goes down. Still - my family can be loud, and I have no doubt they will be once they get wind that you're in the house, so I think I'll take him upstairs to nap in a quiet bedroom." She picked him up and headed up the stairs with him.

While she was gone, one of her sisters wandered out, and gave a little shriek when she saw Neil standing in the living room. He held out a hand to placate her while the rest of the family dashed into the room, drawn by her exclamation.

"I'm Neil," he quickly explained to the alarming number of family members crowding into the room. "Niko's tired and fell asleep, so Casey took him upstairs to nap."

The older woman stepped forward, taking his hand with a warm smile. "I'm Susan, Casey's mother," she introduced herself. "This is my husband, Hugh. And these are Casey's brothers and sisters: Bridget, Fiona, Patrick and Liam," she pointed them out as she made the introductions.

"Hi everyone," he gave a little wave, smiling awkwardly.

"Have a seat, have a seat," Susan ordered, guiding him over to a worn-looking but comfortable chair. The rest of the family followed her advice, perching on various pieces of furniture as they eyed him.

"So," Fiona began, breaking the silence. "That whole coma story - is that true?"

Patrick grinned widely, while their mother sputtered and their father looked stern. The rest of the siblings looked vaguely aghast, but all of them were waiting for Neil to answer.

"Umm, yeah, that's true. It happened about a block and a half from Casey's apartment, when I was crossing the street for the train station."

Fiona tilted her head at him. "And you were in a coma for how long, again?"

Casey came gliding down the stairs just then, and turned a look of outrage on Fiona. "Look here, sister dear - I know you're the oldest girl, and you've taken it upon yourself to be my personal guardian, but you have no right to be asking those sorts of questions - or more importantly, making those sorts of intimations."

"Well, dear sister, the lad vanished after getting you with child. You've been pining after him ever since. Of course I'm going to question it when he suddenly appears in your life again with a magical explanation that lets him off the hook for disappearing on you. And you should, too!"

Casey shook her head, frustrated. Before she could say anything, though, their mom interrupted their spat. "Alright now, girls - Neil is our guest, and you will be civil in front of him. Not to mention, he's the father of our Niko, so I expect we'll be seeing a lot more of him, whatever happens with him and your sister. So let's not get off on the wrong foot by being unkind at our first meeting." She turned back to Neil, smiling apologetically. "I'm sorry, Neil. That must have been a very trying period in your life; I can't imagine the struggles you went through as you fought to regain mobility and get back to your life. And Casey has told us that you were upset when you weren't able to find her." She leaned in conspiratorially. "My children mean well, but they can be a bit clannish, so I apologize for Fiona's impertinent questions. She's trying to look out for her baby sister, but she shouldn't do so at your expense."

He nodded, smiling in return. "No hard feelings. My sister did the same thing when she met Casey. From my family's perspective, Casey is the woman who took my son away - and who I've been pining over for ten years. They used those exact words, in fact. So I think we have a little bit in common, and I can understand how you all feel."

His expression turned sober. "If I can be candid with you all, I am in love with Casey." Liam grinned, while Patrick looked uncomfortable. The girls smiled. "Now that I've had some time to adjust and get used to what happened - and the fact that I've missed so many years of his life - I couldn't be happier to find out I'm Nicholas's father. I know you all have played no small part in raising him, and helping him to become the engaging young man that he is now, and I owe you a big debt of gratitude for that. But I'm here now, and I want to be a part of his life the way he deserves. I'm absolutely ready to get to the end of this, and I pray that Casey chooses me, because all I want is for the three of us to be a family."

Bridget spoke for the first time. "Are you saying you want to be a family because of the lad, or do you genuinely want to be with Casey even if there wasn't a child?"

He looked over at Casey, who was staring at the floor, uncomfortable. "I know this probably sounds crazy, but I've felt a connection to your sister since the first moment I met her. That hasn't gone away in ten years of not being able to find her. Sometimes, I've even wondered if I made her up; if she was something I dreamed in my coma. But I've always felt her out there in the world somewhere, and I've never been able to have a serious relationship in all that time because none of them were her." He shook his head. "Even now, I can hardly believe she's real and she's right in front of me. But the same way I've felt this connection to her all these years, I know I always will. Whether you want to call it soulmates, or love at first sight, or... whatever... I feel it for her, and there's no doubt in my mind that I'd do whatever I can to make a relationship with her work. Because I never want to not have her in my life, and I don't believe I'll ever feel this way about anyone else."

The room was silent. Casey's family looked around at one another, exchanging glances. Casey herself remained staring at the floor, but her face was red and the corners of her lips were curled up in a small smile.

"Right, then," Fiona finally said, breaking the silence with her businesslike tone. "Do you want more kids? A chance to start at the beginning? Or do you think Niko is enough?"

Casey shot her a venomous look, but Neil smiled, his eyes warm. "I'd like to spend some real time with Casey, and figure out the best way for the three of us to move forward as a family, before we go adding to it. But I'm not opposed to more kids; if one came along while we're still figuring things out, I know for sure that he or she would be loved, and cherished, and welcomed with open arms." He looked toward Casey. "Also, the question you're asking takes two of us to answer. What I want isn't all there is to it; what Casey wants also determines how we move forward. But for my part, I'd love to add to the family, and be there for every blessed day."

"What's there to figure out? You're Niko's father, and you say you're in love with Casey - isn't that all there is to it?" Bridget's tone was vaguely annoyed.

He shook his head. "Not at all. Casey lives here and loves having all of you nearby, and I split my time between Vermont and Manhattan. My family is in New York. I don't know where we'd live, really, or what our lives would look like. Casey's established here with her work and you guys, and Nicholas, too, with school and his friends, but I need to be in Manhattan for work a fair amount, and I really love living in the countryside in Vermont. And it's nice to have my family just a couple of hours away."

He sighed. "I guess it makes the most sense for me to give up my home in Vermont, but it makes me sad to do it. Philly isn't too far from Manhattan, so I probably wouldn't find it too difficult to get up there for work when I need to. But I really do love living out in the country - maybe I can convince Casey and Nicholas to try a compromise and move somewhere a bit more rural with me, and commute. Or maybe we get a country house, and live in the city during the week and the country on the weekend." He shook his head again. "I just don't know what life looks like that takes all of our needs into account."

"And then there's the fact that I just don't know how to be a dad, really. I want to jump right into the deep end, but I don't know the first thing and I'm sorta worried I'll screw it up. I'd feel better if Casey is around to help. And I worry I'll bite off more than I can chew, and disappoint Nicholas - or Casey - or both."

Hugh spoke up. "It speaks well that you're thinking about all of these things, son. That tells me that you're taking a more realistic view of things, in spite of the unusual circumstances of this dating process. But those are big, tough questions to answer. Questions like that can make or break a relationship."

Neil nodded. "I know. I want to do whatever it takes to make this work. But I also don't want to end up resenting Casey or Nicholas for giving up something that means more to me than I realized. I think, for the moment, I'd probably keep my places in Vermont and Manhattan and look for something around here. Maybe I can rent something rural and convince Casey and Niko to try it out with me, see how it all works. Or I can just move in with them in their place and see if maybe it doesn't chafe as much as I worry it would. But all of these are questions I can't answer right now." He shook his head. "Regardless, I want to be with them. That's my bottom line."

Susan stood, smiling warmly as she stepped toward Neil and reached for his hands. "Thank you very much for taking the time to sit down and talk with us a little while, Neil. I know we'll be seeing a lot of you, whatever happens, and I look forward to getting to know you better. But for now, my family and I need to talk, and I know you've got a lot of thinking to do, too."

He nodded, giving her hands a squeeze. "Thank you, Mrs. Kelly. It's been a real pleasure to meet all of you."

She grinned. "Please, call me Susan. Casey, would you like to walk your young man out?"

Casey nodded, not looking at her family as she slid her arm through Neil's and walked with him to the front door.

"Wait. Shouldn't I say goodbye to Niko? Won't he be upset if I'm just gone when he wakes up?"

She smiled. "Don't worry. He'll be passed out for a while. He knows you had to go, and I'm sure you'll be seeing him in a few days regardless of what happens with us." She opened the front door and led him through it, closing it behind them.

"I'm so sorry for how hard my family grilled you, Neil. I wasn't expecting them to be so pushy, and ask so many tough questions."

"It's ok," he offered, giving her a warm hug. "I like that they look out for you. If I can't do it, I want someone to have your back, so it makes me feel better to know they'll look after your best interests."

She slipped her arms around him, pulling him tight against her. They held one another for a long moment, her face against his neck as she breathed in the scent of him. "I don't want this to end," she finally whispered.

"It doesn't have to," he replied in a low voice. "In just a few days, all of this will be over, and if you choose it, we can be together then."

She sighed. "I wish it was that easy. But you were there, talking with my family - you know all the hurdles in front of us, even if we make it through this one. We'd have a lot to figure out."

He smiled softly at her, tilting her chin up to look into her eyes. "So we will. We're two successful, competent adults. I have no doubt that we can figure out whatever comes our way and find a way to be happy together." His smile faded as he gazed intently into her face. "I want to be with you,

Casey. I want us to be together. I promise we'll find a way to make it work. We're meant to be with each other." He rested his forehead against hers, closing his eyes. "I just don't work without you," he whispered, his voice breaking with emotion. "You're the only woman I want to be with. Let me be with you. I'll try every day to make you happy."

Her lips found his, softly, at first, but soon the kiss grew more serious. He returned it tenderly, cupping her face with his hand as he put his heart and soul into the kiss. He kissed her like he might never have another chance, because he knew she could pick someone else and break his heart the next time he saw her.

"I hope to God this isn't the last time I kiss you," he finally said, pulling away to gaze into her eyes.

She sighed, her eyes brimming with moisture as her fingers traced his cheekbones. Suddenly, she jumped back. "Wait! I almost forgot! I have something for you. Stay right there," she commanded, turning and dashing into the house, closing the door behind her.

Neil waited on the porch, staring at the door where she'd vanished. A few minutes later, she came running out again, out of breath, holding a wrapped package out to him. "I made this for you."

He took the gift, staring down at it, feeling its weight. "Should I open this now?"

She nodded, her eyes bright and her face full of anticipation. He slipped his thumbs under the corners of the wrapping paper, tearing it neatly and sliding out the package inside. It was the bottom of a book with a padded cover. He turned it over, reading the title aloud. "Our Son."

"I put this together for you. It's all those firsts you were talking about missing. A picture of his first steps, a copy of his baby footprint from the hospital, his first words, his first day of school, his first fight, his first friend..." As she spoke, he flipped through the album, touching the precious pictures and words on each page, tracing them with his fingers. "I know it doesn't make up for missing all those years... but I wanted you to have it."

Tears dripped from his eyes as he reached out to pull her to him, crushing the album between them. "I love you so much, Casey." He held her, breathing in her hair. Eventually, he pulled away again, carefully holding the album against his chest. "Thank you for this. It means more to me than I can say." He dashed the back of his hands across his eyes, and gave her hand a squeeze before stepping down off the porch.

Casey watched as he walked out to the van. He turned to stare at her for a long moment before opening the door and climbing inside. Then, he was gone, leaving her standing on the porch with her arms wrapped around herself to ward off an uncharacteristic late-season chill.

"Oh, girl, you're in trouble," Bridget shook her head and tut-tutted at her when she came into the house.

Casey's cheeks flamed, but she stiffened her spine and raised an eyebrow at her sister. "Oh? And why is that?"

The rest of her family filed into the room, silently observing the standoff as they resumed their seats from the prior day. Again, Nicholas was blessedly absent.

"Because I saw how you were kissing him when you said goodbye! You're in love with him, aren't you?"

Casey's eyes narrowed. "Why are you making the sound like an unpleasant accusation? He is the father of my child and an amazing human being, and I think I'd be insane to *not* have feelings for him."

Susan shook her head at them. "Come on, now - stop fighting, the two of you. We definitely need to talk. Casey, come sit down." Both of them obeyed, Casey sitting in a chair facing the group, and Bridget perching on the arm of the sturdy chair where Patrick was lounging.

"All right, now," her mother began. "You have feelings for Neil. You just admitted it."

Casey nodded.

"Here's the difficulty: where are those feelings coming from? And how real are they?"

Casey's eyes narrowed, and she opened her mouth to defend herself, but her mother shushed her. "Hear me out. You just said yourself that Neil is the father of your child. You've only recently discovered that for certain. I think it's very natural to have feelings for him stemming from that, regardless of how suitable or real they are otherwise."

Casey opened her mouth again, but her mother kept talking, ignoring her. "The other thing we all know is this: you have been pining for that boy for ten years. Your father mentioned yesterday that you haven't really been serious about any other men, and I think we all know that Neil is why. He's been this fantasy in your head that you've never quite been able to give up, and now he's here, in the flesh, and suddenly he's got a good excuse for why he never called you. And he says he's thought of you all these years, and he was so disappointed that he couldn't find you - my God, girl, any woman in your position would feel swept away by the romance of it all." She paused, and this time Casey didn't rush to interrupt. "Add to that he's the father of your child... you need to be very careful with those feelings you're so quick to claim, my darling."

Casey sighed heavily, leaning back into her chair. She shook her head. "I love you, mother, but sometimes I hate it when you're right." Silence hung over the room for a long moment, uncharacteristic when the entire family was assembled. "Ok. So how do I figure it out? How do I know if my feelings are real, and they're coming from the right places, instead of living out some sort of fantasy of how I wanted things to go ten years ago?"

Patrick spoke up. "Have you slept with him?"

"Patrick!" Liam scolded, starting to rise.

"No, I'm serious!" Patrick replied quickly, stalling his brother with a 'wait' motion. "A lot of this could be just... well, like an itch you've been aching to scratch forever, but you can't, so it itches more and more until you think you'll tear your skin off if you can finally just itch it."

"Not the most eloquent metaphor, little brother," Liam complained. He turned to Casey. "But I think I understand what the idjit is on about. He's trying to say that if your feelings for the guy are a fantasy, or based on some sort of... pheromone thing, maybe sleeping with him will relieve the pressure and give you a little clarity."

Casey looked back and forth between the two of them, aghast. "Well, you've managed to come up with the most horrific suggestion I think I could ever hear from my family." She shook her head. "I do not want to be talking about this with you. And if I took your suggestion, I would not want to talk about it with you. So I don't know how I could possibly convey anything useful to you as a result of this suggestion."

Susan shook her head at them. "You're barking up the wrong tree, boyos. That's not at issue here."

"But mom," Patrick began.

"No. I appreciate the thought behind the suggestion, but let's move on to helping your sister in more productive ways."

Bridget rolled her eyes. "Are ye daft? She doesn't want to admit she slept with him, but that didn't change her feelings for him so it doesn't matter anyway."

Patrick's eyes widened, and Casey leaned forward, putting her face in her hands. "That's not what I said, Bridget."

"Aye, but these daft buggers won't let it rest until ye answer them, and you and mom are just too subtle for their wee brains."

She sat back in her chair again, her eyes wide and a little wild as she looked around at her family. "Can I just take a moment to remind my dear family that we are on TV, and there are lots of people judging every little thing, and I would like to maintain some level of privacy and mystery about things I may or may not have done off camera?"

Bridget shrugged. "Everyone has sex. We're made to enjoy it. I don't know why people get in such a tizzy about admitting it." She tilted her head, her gaze turning speculative. "There should be a book, 'Everyone has sex' - like that 'Everybody Poops' book."

Their mom sighed a long-suffering sigh. "And may I remind everybody that we are a good Catholic family, and that sex is intended for the purposes of procreation within the holy sacrament of marriage?"

"Ah, mom, we know you and dad are good Catholics, but the rest of us aren't so virtuous. It's hard to get behind a church that says you can't wear condoms-"

"And can't masturbate!" Patrick cut Bridget off.

"And can't love whomever you like, even if they're the same sex as you," Fiona finished.

"Alright, alright, we've gone down a tangent," Casey waved her hands in the air. "I need your help! Help me figure out how I'm supposed to know if my feelings for Neil are real, or if I'm just in love with a fantasy based on a boy I met ten years ago, who happens to be the father of my child." She leaned back in her chair. "Oh, God, it sounds so obvious when I say it out loud like that!"

"Well, why don't we start with the same questions I asked you yesterday about Richard?" Fiona suggested. "Do you see a future with Neil?"

Casey smiled a sad smile. "Yeah. I do. But I don't know what it is. We don't have some sort of master plan, like Richard and I discussed. Neil might be able to live here, or he might want to stay in Vermont. I might be able to keep my job and my life, or I might have to move out to the country. But I know he adores Niko, and wants to be a real part of his life. And I still feel that connection I felt with him all those years ago."

Hugh nodded. "These details you've skipped past aren't trivial. He admitted as much when he spoke to us. He was more honest with us than you're being with yourself right now, my girl. Neither of you seems in a hurry to turn your life upside down for the other, and maybe that speaks to not being sure about your feelings."

Susan frowned. "Let's consider this from a different angle. When we talked about Richard yesterday, you were full of positive things to say about him - how he's responsible, and a good father, and has a steady career and owns his own business. So far, you haven't had a single thing like that to say about Neil."

Casey sighed. "Well, yeah, he does well for himself at his work, from what I understand. He must, if he's talking about potentially getting a place here but keeping his places in Vermont and Manhattan. But we've never really talked much about it. When we're together, I'm usually just enjoying the moment. He's such an amazing person - so insightful, and funny, and thoughtful, and fun to be around."

Susan nodded. "My dear, I don't want to cause you pain, but the things you said about Richard were talking about how good and secure and wonderful your life would be together. The things you're saying about Neil are all about what an interesting and exciting young man he is, but nothing about your life together. It sounds like maybe you're in love with the idea of him, and not necessarily acknowledging the reality of the life you would have with him."

Casey tilted her head, staring at her mother. "Is that so bad? Would you say you love your life with dad, or that you love dad?"

Her mother smiled gently. "Both. But that's not the issue here. We're talking about you, and how to determine how realistic and real your feelings are. Don't you see that the future you've described with a man who loves you, a dependable, reliable man who knows how to be a father to your child and provide for your family - seems a little more realistic than a future with a fun guy?"

Casey frowned, frustrated. "He's more than just fun. And he's Niko's *actual* father - not just a guy who knows how to play one on TV."

Fiona broke in. "So are you saying your feelings for Richard aren't real now? The things you said in his favor yesterday are things you're arguing against today. Does this mean you've made up your mind and are going to choose Neil? Or have we made you feel defensive by the way we're talking about him?"

Casey sighed again, giving her sister a grateful glance. "Yes, my feelings for Richard *are* real. And all the positive things I said about him yesterday are good, valid reasons for considering a relationship with him. I think you're right - I'm feeling defensive about Neil because it feels like you guys are just being dismissive of the things I'm saying. I legitimately want your help in figuring out how real my feelings are, and maybe what you guys are seeing are just things I don't want to admit to myself."

She shook her head. "I don't know. Do I choose the good, realistic, solid relationship with a wonderful guy I genuinely care for? Or do I choose the slightly more uncertain relationship with someone I've been fantasizing about for a decade - knowing I might be deluding myself in my feelings for him due to all that baggage?"

Bridget answered her. "Well, if this was a romance novel, I know which one would be the right choice."

Casey frowned. "That's one of the things I hate about romance novels sometimes - so many writers have women picking the 'feel good' choice instead of the best choice. I feel like that gives women an unrealistic idea of what romance should be, or makes them feel dissatisfied with their perfectly good relationships with good men that maybe aren't as exciting as the 'feel good romance.'"

Fiona nodded. "So doesn't that mean the right choice is Richard, since this is real life and he's the perfectly good relationship with a good man?"

Casey sighed. "It does seem that way, doesn't it?"

Casey stood tall and straight in her body-skimming silver gown, the beading on the lace overlay catching the light and glittering every time she moved. Her hair was styled in a dramatic updo, and the smokey eye makeup made her light eyes even more vivid than usual. Her hands clenched and unclenched as she waited, and she finally smoothed them over her gown in a calming gesture. The beautifully lit Swann Memorial Fountain cascaded behind her, casting the scene with a romantic ambiance on the clear, starry evening.

Richard came walking toward her up the path. She smiled nervously when she saw him, and his face lit up in an answering smile. He was wearing a beautiful custom-tailored and perfectly fitted black suit; a cut above anything he'd worn so far. When he reached her, he grabbed her hand and then stepped back, looking her up and down and then twirling her in the silver dress, the fabric flaring out around her, and then draping beautifully again when she stopped. She smiled up at him, a little breathless.

"You look amazing tonight, Casey. I don't think I'll ever forget the sight of you standing here like this as long as I live."

She dipped her head. "Back at you, handsome. I haven't seen you wearing anything quite like that before. Pulling out all the stops tonight, eh?"

He grinned. "Well, it's not every day a guy has a chance to ask this kind of question of a beautiful woman."

The moment was broken by Vince's frantic voice in her earpiece. "Wait, Casey! Don't let him talk! Don't let him propose! Ask him about... Madagascar."

Furrowing her brow, Casey held her hand up to stall what Richard was about to say. "Before you begin, Richard... I have something to ask you about. Is there anything you want to tell me about... Madagascar?"

He flashed her a smile. "Is that where you'd like to go on our honeymoon?" he teased. Something in his tone was off, though; his eyes a little too bright and his smile not quite the genuine smile she'd seen so many times.

She shook her head, her expression serious. "No. I'm asking if you have anything to tell me about Madagascar."

The smile slowly faded. "You weren't supposed to know about Madagascar."

She sighed. "Well, obviously that ship has sailed. So talk to me."

His head drooped as he stared at the ground. "Well, if you know enough to ask the question, you probably know everything that's worth telling. There's not much else to talk about." He sighed.

"Is what I've heard true?" she probed. "I need to know."

He sighed. "Yeah, it's true. I imported some live plants and some soil and mulch that turned out to be infested with Madagascar beetles. The clients who got those items are now infested, and they're suing me. I really needed the money from winning the show to pay off the legal fees and try to fund a settlement. Otherwise, I'm probably going to lose my business, and maybe my house, too." He shook his head. "You weren't supposed to find out. Winning the show with you was going to be my ticket to get myself out of this mess."

In spite of herself, her eyes filled with tears. She blinked, trying to hold them back. "So it was all a lie. All made up so you could win the show. You had no plans for us afterward, you aren't madly in love with me..."

He sighed. "Well, that's not exactly how I see it, darlin'. I wasn't really expecting to fall in love with someone here - the time we spend together is so short and full of arbitrary, unrealistic activities. But then you and I kept getting thrown together in the house. You're a nice woman, and you're great with the kids, and you can't fake physical chemistry like ours. So I thought: why not give it a try and see where things go?"

She shook her head, confused and angry. "So what does that even mean?"

His expression was miserable as he took both of her hands in his. A flash of annoyance crossed her face, but she didn't pull away. "Well, it means that I do have real feelings for you. But with you knowing about Madagascar, and how I was trying to win you over so we could win the show, I assume you have no interest in seeing where things go."

She shook her head again. "Richard, I have no idea what I'm supposed to think right now. You say you do have feelings for me, but in the same breath you're admitting that you've been trying to win me over so you can get a cash payout to save your business." She sighed. "I have no idea what's real and what's not, now. Are you still trying to play me so you can get your cash? Or do you mean it?"

He opened his mouth to respond, but she cut him off by laying a finger over his lips. "It doesn't matter anymore. After all this... I could never say yes to a proposal from you right now. So I don't think there's really a point to continuing this conversation."

He sighed, stepping close and resting his forehead against hers. "What about your feelings for me? Isn't it worth taking a chance to see if we really do have a future together? We might not be ready for a proposal right this minute, but maybe we could take things a little slower and see what's real. Maybe once I work through this Madagascar business, we could have a real shot together."

She closed her eyes, leaning her forehead against his while tears leaked from under her closed eyelids. "You were the safe, secure future, Richard. You were my solid rock. Maybe that's what I was falling in love with all along - something real and dependable and reliable. But you're none of that."

She leaned back, looking up into his eyes. "I'm sorry, Richard, but I can't. You've just given me the clarity I need to know my own heart. And what's in my heart isn't you."

He smiled sadly at her. "I know. Any fool could see you've been in love with Neil all this time. I just hoped..." He gave her a hard hug, then released her and stepped back. "Don't mess up your chance, darlin'. Happiness is far too fleeting."

Casey paced back and forth in front of the fountain, agitation plain on her face. She was twisting a handkerchief between her hands, and staring down at the ground, so she didn't notice Neil's tentative approach.

He stepped closer, wearing the custom-tailored Armani suit she'd admired on him before. When she finally noticed him standing a few feet away, his face was covered with apprehension. She frowned sadly.

"I'm so sorry, Neil - this isn't how I wanted to greet you." She stepped up to him, letting the kerchief flutter to the ground as she took both his hands in hers. "You look wonderful. I love that suit. Please don't let my demeanor just now upset you; it has nothing to do with you."

She tried smiling at him, and he gave her a tremulous smile in return, clearly off-balance. "You look beautiful. That dress is amazing, and you wear it so well." His smile faded. "But your eyes are so sad, and you seem so upset." He sighed. "This isn't going to be a happy conversation, is it?"

"I just really need a hug right now," she whispered, staring at the ground.

He sighed again, but slipped his arms around her, pulling her close and leaning his head against hers. He took a deep breath, inhaling her scent. "Just give me a moment to hold you," he finally said, his lips close to her ear. "I want to remember the moment like this - you, here in my arms, before..." he trailed off.

She sniffled. He closed his eyes. They remained locked in the embrace for a long moment.

Finally, she pulled away from him, her hands on his chest as she pushed him far enough away to stare up at him. "Neil, I don't know how to say this, but it's all such a mess." His lips twitched, but he held her gaze, not interrupting. "I'm in love with you. Or I think I'm in love with you, anyway. But I'm worried it's not real - that I'm in love with some sort of ten-year-old fantasy of you, and that a real relationship between us wouldn't work."

A disbelieving smile began to creep across his face. "You're in love with me?" he asked uncertainly, his voice cracking with emotion.

She sighed. "I think I am! I believe I am. But I don't know. My family got all in my head - I was ready to pick you after our date - but they made me feel like I couldn't trust my emotions, and that my idea of you isn't real, and that I should go with the solid relationship that's built on a foundation of mutual understanding instead of basing my decision on the unexplainable connection I feel for you."

His smile grew. "You're in love with me. You were ready to pick me. You feel an unexplainable connection for me. This is how you feel?"

She nodded and sniffled loudly, her eyes brimming with unshed tears.

"Wait a minute," his smile faded again. "You said you 'were' ready to pick me. But that you 'should go with the solid relationship built on a foundation of mutual understanding.' Does this mean that you're in love with me, but you picked Richard anyway?" His face shone with hurt.

She sighed loudly. "Sort of."

"Casey," he said her name very carefully. "Are you engaged to Richard?"

She shook her head no.

"Oh, thank God!" he exploded. "I could have accepted a lot, but I don't think I could have lived with the idea that you were in love with me, but you chose Richard out of some mistaken sense of duty or responsibility or whatever."

"I tried!" she wailed, the tears finally spilling down her face unchecked. "I was all ready to accept Richard's proposal, but I asked him a question, and it all came out that he was just using me to try to win the show and get the money."

"What?" Neil said, his face a study in confusion. "I don't know whether to be angry at him, or disappointed at you, or just plain confused. Maybe you should walk me through what happened."

He shook his head. "Actually, that can wait. It's not the most important thing. Casey Marie Kelly - you are the most amazing and infuriating woman I've ever met. I haven't been able to stop thinking about you since I met you ten years ago, and I could never let you go now without asking you to be a part of my life for every single day as long as I live. I don't care if you're worried that you're in love with an illusion, or a fantasy, or whatever flattering thing you want to call me - I know that I love you deeply, and I believe the connection we both feel is real. We're meant to be together. So if I have to spend the rest of my life making you fall in love with me, it will be absolutely worth it."

He bent down in front of her, holding her hands as he knelt down on one knee. "Casey, don't worry about what you had planned for tonight.

Don't think about what your parents said, or your brothers and sisters. Instead, make your decision right here, in this moment, with me down on one knee in front of you and a heart full of love. I don't want to live my life without you. Will you please marry me, and grant me the blessing of waking up next to you every day for the rest of our lives?"

She inhaled a long, slow, deep breath as she stared down at him. Her eyes glittered. "I don't know if it's a good idea, but God, I want to, Neil. So badly."

He grinned brilliantly and stood, grabbing her in his arms and spinning her around him. "Then do it. We'll figure out the rest as we go along. For right now, it's enough to know that I love you, and you love me, and I'll do whatever I can to make sure this works, because I never want to be without you again."

She buried her face in his neck, hanging on for dear life as he spun her. When he set her down again, she finally looked up at him, radiant joy shining from her face as she smiled brightly. "Yes, then. I'd be a fool to say no with a promise like that."

Nathan stood in front of the two of them, smiling broadly as they beamed at each other and clung tightly to each other's arms. "I couldn't be happier for the two of you. Congratulations on your engagement. It's been such an amazing experience watching you fall in love, and I'm so glad we were able to help you find each other."

He held up a sealed envelope, waving it back and forth a few times. "Now that we've reached this point, it's time to find out if you're America's Favorite Couple." He let his hand drop down to his side, still holding the card. "As you know, we air the show each week, and the audience gets to vote on who should go forward to the next week, and whose journey should end. Most weeks, some of our contestants are safe from being eliminated; if they get enough votes from their fellow contestants who want to pursue a relationship with them, they automatically get to go forward and see what happens the next week - regardless of audience voting. Here, in the final week, things work a little differently."

"Casey, because you're the last woman standing, you're automatically a part of America's Favorite Couple. But this week, we're down to two men, and neither of them is safe from elimination. You've chosen Neil, and we wish you the best as you move forward with your relationship together. But voting ended before your final meeting with each of the men, so the audience didn't know what the outcome would be when they cast their votes. Instead, they voted based on who they thought was the best match based on everything leading up to today."

"Now, we're going to take a look at those results. If the man you've chosen is also the man that America chose for you, you two will become America's Favorite Couple. If that happens, you'll win a quarter of a million dollars to start your lives together. Wouldn't that be exciting! You could buy a house, or save it to invest in Nicholas's education - anything you can imagine. Let's take a look at the envelope and see what happens."

Nathan lifted the sealed flap of the envelope and pulled out the card, holding it up in front of him to read. After a moment, he looked over the top of the card at them, his gaze moving from Casey to Neil and back again.

"Well, it's time to find out what we've all been waiting for all season: who will be America's Favorite Couple. Are you ready?" Casey nodded, and Neil squeezed her arm. "Ok. This year, America's Favorite Couple is... Casey and..." he paused, the pause stretching as he gazed at the two of them. His face was expressionless, giving nothing away. The silence dragged out one beat, then another. Finally, he finished: "Neil!" His face lit up in a big grin as he held his arms out to the two of them. "Congratulations! The two of you are America's Favorite Couple!"

"Big reaction now, Casey. Make it good," Vince said in her ear.

Casey grinned hugely, turning to Neil and leaning into his embrace. He picked her up and spun her around, smiling at her. They kissed, closing their eyes and letting the moment stretch. Eventually, they turned to Nathan, stepping close to enfold him in a hug, one of them at each arm.

"So how does it feel to be America's Favorite Couple?" he asked them, leaning back to grace them with another broad smile.

"It hardly feels real," Casey replied, gazing into Neil's eyes. "To go from thinking I'd never see him again to being engaged to him in just a few months... to know that we're going to have our happy ending after ten years of wondering about him... I feel so blessed."

Neil nodded, smiling, and gazed into her eyes.

CHAPTER EIGHT

Epilogue

Casey and Neil sat together at a small outdoor cafe, smiling and holding hands as they sipped their iced coffees, when Vince walked up.

"Hey, man!" Neil jumped up to greet him, stepping forward and shaking his hand enthusiastically.

Casey rose a little more slowly, her grin shy as she stepped close. She surprised all three of them by hugging Vince tightly, tears welling up in her eyes as she laughed and smiled at the same time.

"I really don't know how we can thank you enough," she said to him as the three of them sat down at the table. Neil nodded.

"She told me all about your help," he added, waving the waiter over to get a drink for Vince. "I don't know what would have happened if you hadn't told her to ask about Madagascar."

Vince grinned as he smiled at Casey, and she grinned back. "Buddy, I did a lot more than that."

"What do you mean?" Neil asked after the waiter had gone to fetch Vince's latte.

"Oh boy. Well, if you ever watch the show back, you may notice some things you didn't see while you were in the house. I tried to keep you from seeing too much that would make you upset."

Casey nodded. "But more importantly: Vince told me how you got on the show on the first place."

Neil tilted his head as he looked back and forth between the two of them. "Well, yeah, it wasn't exactly the usual route. My editor pitched it to me. I think he thought we'd do more of a 'thinking man's piece' - something about the lack of reality in reality tv, or something exposing the ridiculousness of thinking a love match could ever come out of such a contrived setting. I guess we weren't quite prepared for how much the NDA would cover, or how aggressive the studio would be about enforcing it, because what I got to write was a far cry from what we'd envisioned."

Vince shook his head as Casey bit her lip. "I hate to break it to you, buddy, but we're the ones who put that idea in your editor's head. Me, specifically. I was one of the senior producers on the show. I pulled your name right from Nicholas's birth certificate. I thought having the baby daddy on the show - surprise - would give us a little extra drama. I also orchestrated Niko's whole 'running away to go to the circus' trip. We always had our people on him - we weren't going to let anything happen to him. And I'm the one who suggested you be the guy to go 'rescue' him. Some of the staff wanted it to be Richard, because they were pushing for the Casey-Richard storyline, but I thought it'd stir up more action if it was the baby daddy. Although I didn't quite anticipate him spilling the beans - that was pure luck."

Neil leaned forward, his brows drawing together. "Are you saying you orchestrated the entire thing? My entire relationship with Casey?"

Vince held out a placating hand at Neil's aggressive tone. "Not exactly that. I got you on the show because I thought it would make the show more interesting to watch. But in your entrance interview, you talked briefly about how you hadn't had a serious relationship... I smelled something there. I knew you were the father of Casey's child - or at least she thought you were - so I thought maybe there was something about dating her that you just weren't telling us. Once I figured out the truth - that both of you have been pining for each other all these years and really, genuinely had feelings for each other - I was there, behind the scenes, pushing for your relationship the entire time. I tried to be subtle. I wasn't sure they'd let it go down - I thought they might find the "single parents find love together" storyline more compelling. But you guys were genuinely falling in love, so I did some digging on Richard and found out about Madagascar." He shrugged. "The rest is history."

Casey wrinkled her eyebrows. "Are you saying the show didn't know about Madagascar?"

Vince shook his head. "No, apparently they knew. I just didn't know. I didn't pay too much attention to Richard, to be honest - not until it looked like we were going to have a love triangle situation. But Madagascar was in the production notes - someone on the show knew all about it. Probably several someones. Richard probably shouldn't have gone through to become a contestant - we don't like to involve ourselves with people who have pending litigation against them - but it's not unheard of for people to offer a cut of the final pot to someone in production to get on the show. I think that's probably how he got past screening."

Casey sighed. "Well, it doesn't matter now, anyway. I just hope he's able to save his business and give poor little Cassidy the life she deserves."

Vince shook his head. "I don't see how he could do that, Casey. His legal fees and funding a settlement would eat up most of the winning pot. Without that money, I think he's sunk."

Casey and Neil shared a glance. "We gave him the money," Neil said to Vince.

The blonde man's jaw dropped. "What?"

Neil nodded. "We actually don't need it. Apparently the show didn't vet my finances too closely. Or realize exactly how successful Casey has been. Richard needed the money a lot more than we did; we were happy just to have found each other out of the experience."

Vince shook his head in disbelief. "Wow. I never saw that coming. Well, that's more than that poor bastard deserves, if you ask me. But it's really generous of you guys. I hope you're blessed with a long and happy life together," he smiled at them.

Neil grinned back. "Actually, there's one more reason we called you here." The other man tilted his head and raised an eyebrow in response. "I hear you've lost your job after all the brouhaha."

Vince nodded. "I did, but honestly, I kind of lost my stomach for it after you two. I don't think I'd be happy with all the contrived storylines again after seeing the real deal in you. I think they did me a favor."

"Well, how would you like a new job?" Neil asked. "You've clearly got a knack for sniffing out details, following the story, and figuring out what the American public is going to want to consume. I got you an offer from my magazine."

Vince's jaw dropped open. "Seriously? A legit publication like that would hire some slimy creep from reality tv like me?"

"Way to sell yourself," Neil winked. "But yeah. The skills you've demonstrated aren't unlike the skills required to be a good reporter, these days. And sometimes a little slime helps - some of the sources don't want to deal with a squeaky clean kinda guy. I get the impression that won't be a problem for you."

Vince didn't respond right away; he seemed lost for words as he looked back and forth between the two of them. Eventually, Neil continued. "The pay might not be what you're used to. I have no idea how much you make in reality tv, but rich writers are the exception, not the rule. Most of my money came from my books. But the magazine paid me well enough to travel and enjoy life, and I could expense most of what I did because I'd find a way to tie it to an article."

Finally, the other man nodded. "I don't have a family. My needs are pretty modest, to be honest. What you're describing sounds just about perfect for me. Especially when compared to unemployment." He grinned ruefully.

Casey smirked, unable to hold back any longer. "But wait, there's more!" she exclaimed, doing her best cheesy game host imitation.

Neil chuckled as Vince looked back and forth between them again. "What my darling fiancé is trying to say is that I've also prepared the documents to hand over ownership of my Manhattan loft to you." The blonde man's jaw dropped open again. "I don't spend much time there anyway, and when I do go to New York, it's usually for work. I can just have them put me up in a hotel if I need to spend the night." He sighed and looked at Casey. "It's paid in full, and it's worth... a lot. A sizable loft in Manhattan. You can sell it, if you want. Or you can stay there while you're working in New York, and you'll only have to worry about condo fees and taxes. The building is good. It even comes with a parking spot."

Casey leaned forward, placing her hand over Vince's and looking earnestly into his eyes. "We owe you everything, Vince. I might have never seen Neil again if you hadn't gone digging and brought him onto the show. And then you were working, behind the scenes, to help us out... and you lost your job because you told me about Madagascar..." she shook her head. "We only got our happy ending because of you. We had to make some kind of gesture to thank you."

Vince shook his head again. "Wow. You guys are unbelievable." He sighed, coughing into his fist and blinking his eyes a few times before continuing. "I've worked in this business a long time, and I didn't think people like you really existed. I certainly never expected to encounter a real love story on the show. You really do deserve to be America's Favorite Couple."

Sneak Peek

Have you enjoyed reading about Casey's quest to find love on America's Favorite Couple? Then join her friends on their own journeys through the twists and turns of reality TV.

In the next Reality TV Romance, we'll follow Violet as she arrives at the mansion and begins her own quest to find love. Enjoy this sneak peek at Violet's story in the next Reality TV Romance novel.

Coming Summer 2017

EXCERPT

When Violet stepped out of the van, the bright L.A. sunshine was practically blinding. The heat coming off the sidewalk felt warm through her thin flip-flops. She took a moment for her eyes to adjust and get her bearings, as people bustled past her on the sidewalk.

A woman paused to look at the camera filming Violet's arrival, but most people ignored it - a commonplace enough sight in L.A. When the woman decided that Violet wasn't anyone famous, she sniffed and walked on, apparently feeling put-upon that she hadn't just encountered a starlet. Violet's travel-rumpled denim shorts and her comfortable, worn t-shirt certainly didn't mark her as anyone worth noticing.

The driver handed out her two large suitcases, and she grabbed her duffle bag from the floor of the van where she'd scooted it out of the way. When she lifted it toward her, the strap ripped out the side of the bag, tearing a large hole and spilling her cosmetics and personal belongings across the sidewalk. Giving the camera a shrug and a rueful grin, she bent down and started grabbing her scattered belongings, quickly grabbing her pocketbook and biting back a curse as passing pedestrians kicked her favorite lipstick down the sidewalk.

A man in oversized business shoes stepped on her purple nail polish, and the glass bottle shattered under his weight. He jumped back with a snarl, giving her a filthy look, but he didn't dare open his mouth under the ruthless gaze of the rolling camera. Instead, he turned his ponderous bulk with a huff and continued on down the sidewalk, leaving a large purple splotch in his wake every time his shoe hit the pavement.

Annoyed, Violet called after him. "That's a good color on you. You should wear it more often!"

A competent-looking redhead snickered as she hurried up, bending to help Violet quickly retrieve the rest of her spilled belongings. "Sorry about your poor nail polish, but we'll have you all fixed up before you know it," she offered, as she took the remnants of the busted duffle from Violet and stood up. "I'm Tiffany," she added, glancing down at the bag in her hands and then shrugging. "I'd shake your hand, but..."

Violet laughed. "Yeah, off to a great start. Here I am, ready to be a big TV star!"

Tiffany threw a smile over her shoulder as she turned to lead the way into the hotel, holding the bag carefully to keep all of its contents inside. Violet grabbed the handles on her two large pieces of rolling luggage and followed in her wake, narrowly missing running over a small blonde woman with a dog in her purse.

"Watch where you're going!" the woman complained, in a thick Valley-girl accent. She quickly sidestepped around the suitcase like she was avoiding stepping in something her dog had just produced.

"Toto, we're not in Kansas anymore," Violet muttered under her breath, as she moved again to follow Tiffany, who stood in the doorway holding the tattered remnants of her bag.

When Tiffany showed her into the living room of a large suite, Violet paused and took a deep breath. Nearly two dozen people were milling about, and there were at least four cameras in the suite, their operators pointing at various things and looking serious. Tiffany shoved aside some electronics on a folding table, and deposited the ripped bag, then waved Violet into the room.

"I'll be your personal production assistant," Tiffany offered, picking up a camera mic and power pack. "Let's get you miked up, and then I'll introduce you around."

Violet held up a hand to ward her off. "Wait, I'm not going to wear this to the mansion! Shouldn't I change before you put a mike on me?"

Tiffany shook her head, and dodged around behind Violet, tucking the power pack into the waistband of her shorts and applying a piece of tape to keep it in place. Violet started to turn and object, but Tiffany grabbed her shoulder and held her stationary, the smaller woman's grip surprisingly strong. "From the moment you wake up in the morning, you'll be miked. We film everything except the bathroom and the showers - but the vanity is fair game. When you change clothes later, we'll re-mike you." She finished tucking the mike into the neck of Violet's t-shirt, and then stepped back to the table. When she turned back again, she was holding out an earpiece.

"This is your lifeline. Someone will be watching the live footage and listening to the mic feeds pretty much all the time. Most of the time, it will be me, since I'm assigned to you." As Violet tucked the earpiece in her ear, Tiffany fiddled with something in her pocket. When she spoke again, Violet heard the producer standing in front of her - and also in her ear.

"This way, I can give you instructions and set up shots without actually being in frame. I could be on the other side of a wall, or in our production room back at the mansion, and I can tell you to move two feet to your left, or go talk to so-and-so, or do whatever we need you to do for the next shot. And if you have questions, you can just say them out loud; I'll be listening to your mike feed and I can answer in your earpiece."

Her voice dropped. "But keep in mind that any questions you ask will also be filmed, and we could potentially use that during the show. From now until you get on a plane to go home again, everything you say and do is fair game. Consider this your one and only warning. The big guys don't like it if we remind you too often that you're behaving like an ass on national television - it makes for better ratings if we just let you go ahead and do it." Tiffany gave her a crooked grin, but her green eyes were flat and steely.

While Violet absently pondered what Tiffany had just said, the production assistant grabbed her wrist and led her over to a group of women clustered in front of one of the cameras. "These are some of your fellow contestants - Casey, Olivia, Anastasia, Lily, Louisa and Sandy." She pointed vaguely as she rattled off names, but Violet was lost as she looked around the group. "This is half of the women. The other half are in the suite next door. We couldn't fit you all in one room," she quipped with another grin, but this one seemed even less full of actual humor.

The friendly-looking chestnut-haired woman stepped forward and shook her hand. "Hi, I'm Casey," she introduced herself with a smile, noting Violet's overwhelmed expression. "Olivia and I are actually down the hall - we're two of the single moms." She gestured to a small Latina woman at her side, with beautiful wavy black hair and striking olive eyes that sparkled in her quick smile.

"Hola chica," she offered, extending her own hand in greeting. "Our kids are down at the pool with a PA, but I cannot wait for you all to meet them." She cast a glare over her shoulder at the group of PAs clustered across the room. "Apparently they thought it would be better for us to 'get pretty for the mansion' without the kids underfoot to interfere with the montage of women getting all 'dolled up.'" She rolled her eyes.

Casey's smile grew wider. "Well, they might actually have a point about that... it always takes me twice as long to get ready for a formal event with Niko around. And there's a better than average chance that whatever I'm wearing will have some evidence of his presence by the time I leave the house." She winked at Olivia, and the smaller woman laughed.

"Ok, chica, I surrender. Natalie is very easy - the most I would have to endure is letting her put on makeup alongside me. Boys must be very different."

Casey nodded with a broad smile. "Yup! But let me tell you, Olivia - you might think girls are easier now, but I wouldn't want to be you in a few more years when you have to start worrying about boys. And those hormones... ay caramba!"

Violet laughed with the two women, remembering her own, rather trying, teenage years. With no mom, and only brothers in the house, dealing with her changing body - and all the emotions that went along with it - had felt kind of like being invaded by aliens.

"Don't you worry about that," Olivia winked. "I have prayed every day for Natalie to be a lesbian. My traditional grandparents might be horrified, but I would be so relieved to not have to deal with horny chicos, followed by little baby niños." She shook her head. "Dios mio! Let it be so."

Violet laughed again at the Latina woman's earnestness. Before anyone could respond, though, a harried-looking production assistant interrupted the small group. "Alright, ladies, time to start getting ready. We need to leave with the first group in one hour."

Another man stepped up beside him, this one holding a small whiteboard. The whiteboard held groups of names - a cluster of women's names, followed by a cluster of men's names. He cleared his throat, and then held the whiteboard up high. "Here's how tonight is going to work: we'll be taking you into the mansion with four people per limo. There will be a one-hour pause between each group of arrivals to let everyone who is already there start to get acquainted. Then, the next group will come in and mingle with the prior groups, et cetera. The parents with kids will go in at seven and eight o'clock, since the kids will have to go down early. The rest of you will go before and after. That means we're going to have a long night."

He looked around, catching everyone's eyes. "We'll bringing in the last group at three in the morning. We're requiring that group get at least two hours to mingle with everyone else. That means you can go to bed at five."

Casey and Olivia traded glances. "Our kids will be waking up like two hours after that. Surely you don't expect the single parents to stay up until dawn with everyone else, do you?"

He shrugged. "You signed up for this. You went through the audition process, and beat out tens of thousands of other people to be here. Are you really going to complain about a little lost sleep, when we've given you the chance of a lifetime?"

One of the female PAs stepped in. "We're aware of the differences in your lifestyles, of course. Most of the time, we'll try to make allowances to give the single parents a chance to get enough sleep, and spend quality time with the kids. But since this is the initial meet-and-greet, we can't afford for any of you to be absent early. Otherwise, the relationships you begin forming will be lopsided from the start."

"This is mierda," Olivia spat. "I do not accept this. Who can I talk to about this?" One of the production assistants peeled off from the group and motioned to Olivia, leading her outside.

Violet started as she heard an unexpected voice in her ear. "Word to the wise," Tiffany said quietly. Violet had nearly forgotten that the other woman was there. Hearing the voice in her ear was almost like having someone inside her head.

"Don't complain about the production requirements. It makes the PAs cranky. If they get unhappy with you, they can change the storylines around and make sure you get an unfavorable edit. You want to get on their good side - or barring that, just don't be noticed at all. Make waves in a bad way, and you'll regret it. But do me a favor and don't mention I told you this - it's another one of those things they don't like us to remind people about, because everything is supposed to appear to be as natural and uncontrived as possible."

"So you're saying that if we piss off the wrong people, they'll get their revenge by making sure we look like horrible people on national TV?" Violet asked quietly, turning away slightly so as to not be overheard in the general buzz of activity.

"Your words - not mine," Tiffany returned. "But remember - you're here to find love, so why not start getting dressed and prepare to meet Mr. Right?"

What have I gotten myself into? Violet wondered, as she obediently stood and moved toward her suitcases to pick out her outfit for the evening.